B.H. FINGERMAN
BOTTOMFEEDER

A NOVEL

PRESS™
Milwaukie

Book design by Debra Bailey and Heidi Fainza
Cover design by David Nestelle
Cover photograph by B.H. Fingerman

M Press
10956 SE Main Street
Milwaukie, OR 97222

mpressbooks.com

Library of Congress Cataloguing-in-Publication Data

Fingerman, B. H., 1964-
  Bottomfeeder / B.H. Fingerman. -- 1st M Press ed.
    p. cm.
  ISBN-13: 978-1-59582-097-6
  ISBN-10: 1-59582-097-3
  1. Vampires--Fiction. I. Title.
PS3606.I383B68 2006
813'.6--dc22

                            2006021085

ISBN-10: 1-59582-097-3
ISBN-13: 978-1-59582-097-6

First M Press Edition: December 2006

10 9 8 7 6 5 4 3 2 1

Printed in U.S.A.
Distributed by Publishers Group West

DEDICATIONS:

For Michele, the love of my life, the center of my universe, the brightest spot in any circumstance. I love you more than words can express.

Also for my mom, Helene, and my dad, Saul, who instilled in me a love for the written word. Thanks for being great parents.

Though any order implies favoritism, if possible I'd place all of them on the same line. I love you all.

BOTTOMFEEDER

"Living is abnormal."

—Eugene Ionesco

1

Maybe this whole immortality thing isn't all it's cracked up to be. Oh, sure, they pump it up like it's going to be some nonstop party, but let me tell you something: *don't believe the hype.*

A Little Background, but Only a Little . . .

In my folks' declining years their tunes about my perpetually youthful—if a bit pallid—good looks changed from pride and admiration to scorn and resentment, and then finally fear and distrust.

"You've got some great genes, let me tell you," my dad said many a time. He said it again that day, complimenting me on my forty-fifth birthday. "You don't look a day over thirty."

The fact was I didn't look a day over twenty-seven, but why split hairs? I still don't today, and guess what? That's right, I won't tomorrow or the day after that or the day after that. No Dorian Gray portrait tucked away in a dormer, attic, or closet either. Not even under the kitchen sink. Lucky me.

By the time he'd been consigned to his deathbed—mercifully in his own home instead of some grim hospice—my dad's tune had done a one-eighty; apropos in a dyslexic way, considering he was eighty-one. No longer was I getting the flattery, the "I'll have what you're having" type of good-natured ribbing. Beyond his abiding antipathy for my inconstant visits—and those taking place only after dusk—he looked on me as an abomination, his rheumy, cataract-glazed eyes focusing as well as they could on my smooth pale face. He'd never been a religious man, but I felt him yearning to characterize me as unholy—unclean.

"*You*," he'd rasp, the tubes up his nose and the coating of phlegm in his throat somewhat garbling his speech, which was gristly and punctuated by thick, emphysematous wheezing. "You never amounted to anything (*wheeze*). All you've got are your looks (*wheeze*), which count for nothing. *Nuh*-thing. Is that (*wheeze*) what you've devoted your pointless (*wheeze*) existence to? Maintaining your looks? Is that (*wheeze*) what you spend your (*wheeze*) money on? You're not a man. Not as *I'd* define one. You're pathetic."

What was I going to do, argue with him? You don't argue with a man who's counting down the final minutes. I just sat there, or paced, or whatever. I paged through magazines and listened to his litany of condemnations because that's what any dutiful son would do for his old man. Let him rail, I thought. Let him get it out of his system. It's not like I had any siblings to share the burden with, so let him do as he pleased.

"The roles have really reversed. As the sexes draw closer (*wheeze*) together, the lines separating he from she (*wheeze*), vanity has shifted from female to (*wheeze*) male. Used to be vanity was a strictly (*wheeze*) feminine failing. But my son, my (*wheeze*) modern son."

His eyes would often narrow during those last days, squinting, trying to focus through the tacky glaze of semi-blindness, the layer of clouds between he and I.

"You can't even come visit (*wheeze*) during the day, like a normal (*wheeze*) person? I need my rest and you can't even accommodate that like a decent (*wheeze*) human being?"

Normal? Decent? *Human?* Who was he talking about? Not me. It sometimes took me a while to recognize myself in his tirades. Human? Not hardly.

Sometimes he'd get loud and his caregiver would poke her dark head in the room to make sure none of his tubes slipped out—his catheters, his drips, his I-don't-even-know-what-they-weres. He had many fluids coming and going through clear vinyl tubes, but none of them were my cup of tea. Sometimes it would get really quiet, and that's when her appearances at his bedside became more frequent. I figure she was checking to see if my patience finally evaporated and I snuffed the old bastard. It was probably wishful thinking on her part. He wasn't exactly copacetic with her either.

"I can't come during the day, Pop. I've got work." A lie. I work at night.

"What about weekends? How much (*wheeze*) time you think I've got, you can't come around some Saturday? Like it would (*wheeze*) kill you."

Well, as a matter of fact . . .

"It *is* Saturday," the response would come—when apropos—and I'd get a scornful look.

"Night. Saturday *night*. N-I-G-H-T." Then the derision: "Mr. Goodlooks doesn't (*wheeze*) have a date on a Saturday night? All those (*wheeze*) good looks and you spend your Saturday night with (*wheeze*) your dying dad. I guess I should be (*wheeze*) flattered, huh?"

"I guess." I'd run out of guesses.

We'd sit in wheeze-punctuated laconism disturbed by short cameos of his fat Jamaican nurse's stern puss, each accompanied by a clucking failed attempt at jocularity. "You two boys behavin' yahrselves, arighty? I don' wanna be separatin' de two of yar." That's what came out, but it always sounded more like, "When's dot cranky ol' bahstard gwan t' c'lect his final reward so's I kin get on wit' m'life?"

He finally did and I got to witness it firsthand. His final words were, "Well, I hope you're happy." He didn't mean it the way one would hope. It wasn't a benediction. I made some arrangements for a quick and easy interment. No funeral. Who'd come? No mourners. Not me. It was cold and impersonal. I think he'd have appreciated the sentiment, so to speak.

My mom was harder. Much. I'd been her golden boy, the apple of her eye, the whatever cliché you like best to describe the son who can do no wrong. Losing her approval was a slow death for me, which was ironic considering she was doing the actual dying. She'd been a tough lady all along and with death on the near horizon she remained so. But she'd allow me to offer no comfort.

"How do you look so good and yet so bad?" she'd ask. "You can tell me. Is it vitamins or exercise or what? What is it? It's not normal to look the way you look. You're too smooth. Not even a crow's foot. But so pale. That pallor. When you were a boy you were always tan and healthy-looking. I've never seen such a well-preserved man look so unhealthy. How is that? You live like a walking oxymoron." She'd laugh a smoky laugh between drags at her cigarette. "Not like a moron moron, you understand." In case I didn't get the joke. She'd touch my face and shudder. She no longer kissed me. Not much, anyway, and when she did it was an obligatory peck. A golden boy misses his mother's kisses and unconditional love.

She didn't bust my hump about the after-dark visits, but I always looked ashamed around her. I couldn't hide it and it tainted every call I paid her.

When she died I cried plenty, believe me.

But enough nostalgia. I'm getting all misty over here.

2

Tuesday, January 9th, 2001

The pickings are slim and unappetizing, but then again they usually are. I shouldn't be thinking of food right now, anyway. Especially this time of night. Hey, remember how great New York City was back in the seventies and early eighties? Oh wait, I'm sorry. It was a complete shithole. Yeah, that's right. It was a bottomless cesspool just oozing with filth, depravity, and depredation. The gutters were choked with litter, the subways were covered in graffiti and garbage and everything smelled like piss or worse.

Well, the patina of those departed glory days seems to have made a comeback. Maybe I'm just being oversensitive, but then again that's what I am. In general, heightened senses are no bargain. Sure they come in useful from time to time; maybe if I was stuck in some wooded area with no artificial light I'd be thankful for seeing well in the pitch dark. But I'm on the subway and it's too bright, so I'm not. Call me an ingrate. I'm used to it. Besides, what the hell would I be doing in the middle of the woods? I'm not the outdoorsy type.

Witness this: I'm on my way to work, taking the R train from Elmhurst, Queens to Times Square. I'm reading my magazine peacefully when one of my top ten worst sounds assails my ear-drums: nail clipping. To you maybe it's an unpleasant sound, but to me? Amplify it through a Marshall stack turned up to eleven. I look around but don't see the culprit. I resume reading. The sound begins again. I turn around. Calmness. I return to my magazine.

Clip! Clip!

This time I spot the bastard: a sallow-complected Asian with scrotum-like pouches under his eyes. After giving him the requi-site dirty look—like shooting a dog or not very intelligent squirrel such a glare, it's completely ineffectual—I get up and move to the other end of the car. That's okay; I'm not in the mood for Chinese. Bad joke, I know.

This is to be the pleasantest part of my trip to work.

At Times Square I change for the southbound local but an ex-press pulls in, so I hop on, opting for forward motion. As I take my seat, a youngish black dude with filthy oversized jeans worn so low that the waistband has got to be several inches below his taint steps on, hollering at someone—or not—on the platform, "Shoulda heard what da judge said!" He does the back and forth, on-and-off dance with the doors before fully boarding the train. Then he shouts it again, "Shoulda heard what da judge said!"

Okay. Once aboard he struts back and forth, nearly jams his flaky-caked ass in my face, whips his turd-like links of dreadlock, and then struts around again, blathering semi-coherently. The waves of stink are coming off this guy so strong I can practically see them like in a cartoon.

The white trash chucklehead sporting the classic undercoat-beige blond molester-mustache to my left sniggers to himself, amused at this guy's antics. It's funny to him because he's swig-ging low-octane domestic suds from a sweating tallboy. Did I mention it's January? Just thought I'd point that out. Then the black dude with the super-lowrider pants bellows, "I been to a *crackhouse*! Oh *yeeeaaah*! Tha' shit was cray-*zeee*!"

You could knock me over with a feather.

This guy is the living embodiment of crackhead. If you were to go to the hobby shop and say, "Hey, lemme get the crackhead model kit," guess who it would look like? Central casting, we need an archetypal crackhead. Perfect. And on he goes, Stereotype Q. McCrackhead, about his crackhouse encounter, his eyes bugging like some thyroidal mixture of a Basil Wolverton cartoon and Mantan Moreland.

"Tha' shit was *na-steeeeeee*, yo, but sheeeit, da shit was da *bomb*, kid! *Cray-zeeeee*!"

The train pulls into 34th Street and he gets off. Wonderful. I'm thinking, *missed opportunity*? Christ, it really comes down to basic needs. But it's too crowded. I have to wait until my shift is over. It's always this way. I run on empty at work then a good feed is my reward. It's all about the reward system, like a doggie and his little treats. "Do your work, Philip, and you'll get a lovely treat!"

Sit up.

Roll over.

Play dead.

Well, play *alive*, actually.

The two teenage black girls beside me start talking loudly— both understandably mute during Cracko the Clown's command performance.

"That shit ain't funny," one says. She's full-bottomed and cute, but her fondness for twinkly gold-plated costume jewelry is murder on my eyes. And those talons. Why always with the gaudily airbrushed two-inch fingernails?

"Hells yeah," her plain-featured companion agrees. "Nigga like that could do any shit. There been those slashings lately. Shit, nigga could do any crazy shit."

Word. We're back to the days of box-cutter slashings. Several this week alone. Kinda takes you back, huh? What's next, those wacky mystery-disease syringes in the tuchis? Silly mortals.

At 14th Street I get off to wait for the local train. Cue next fucked-up scenario. A hefty black girl is conducting a loud conversation on her cell phone. In the subway. On the platform. Wearing the earbud. So she looks crazy. Used to be you'd see someone chatting away and no one was with them you'd chalk it up to Multiple Personality Disorder (or Dissociative Identity Disorder or whatever you want to call it). These days it's a cell phone conversation. What I want to know is how is she getting a signal down here? Maybe she is crazy. Maybe it's all a sham. She's not getting a signal down here. Hell, she doesn't even have a phone; it's just a prop. No, I'm just caricaturing the situation. It passes the time.

She hangs up—or loses the signal—and in steps scary, crazy black dude number two. This guy, same basic age and description as Crackhead McLoudmouth only less unhygienic, starts right in on the girl.

"Yo, girl, I seen you fum acrossa street outside yo project." Smiling. Leering, actually.

"You said what?" Her hands are on her hips. She ain't havin' it. Highly glossed ruby lower lip jutted in pugnacious dissent.

"Yo, I seen you. You live acrossa street fum me. I seen you. Yeah. Standin' in fronna th' project. Yeah."

"Nigger, I don't live in no project." She's nonplused. Even if she did live in the project—and I'm not saying she does—she wouldn't own up to this potential stalker. But he's on her like white on rice. Wrong metaphor? Fuck it.

"Yeah. Yeah, you do. I seen you. Fum acrossa street."

And on it goes. She denies it; he avows it.

Another express train pulls in.

Then, moments later, the local. Finally. And who should shove past me on my way in? Everyone's favorite crackhead from the express train. Hooray for continuity. His scent precedes him as he shoulders past me and plunks his now nearly pantsless ass into an empty seat, still blathering. The scent of his dorsal crevasse wafts and I nearly swoon. Is this din-din I'm smelling? Oh, momma, I miss "real" food.

I move away to a less populated part of the car to join the next enchanting tableau. Here I find the charm couple. Two heavily burdened vagrant-types, a gray-bearded old black fellow, thin, wool cap, thick army surplus coat. His companion is an old white lady with unearthly purple-dyed poodle hair (probably a wig) and crazed eyes. She's speaking to him in muted coos and chirrups. "You okay, Pooki? You okay? It's okay. You're okay. It's okay. Yes it is." She's prodding him. He ignores her. Around his mouth is caked, calcified saliva. It's chalky and the whiteness of it is terrible against the ashy blackness of his face. His lips are cracked and I can see rust-like dried blood in the fissures. So unappetizing, but still . . .

The train pulls into Christopher Street and he staggers toward the door, listing heavily to his right as he gathers up his rucksack. It turns out the old woman's little noises were not for him; she has a small, quivering black-and-white Chihuahua, which drops to the floor, its nails clattering, its eyes twitching. It shivers uncontrollably and I'm thinking, where's its little sweater? What kind of nutty Chihuahua owner doesn't give her weensy south-of-the-border poochie a damned sweater? She tries to collect its leash with her gnarly claw-like hands, and then off she gets, joining her mate on the platform. I look around. No one's even noticed this scene because they're all zombies.

I look at my fellow travelers' faces and it stuns me how hideous most of these people are. Not run of the mill homely, but truly, brutally, bestially ugly. They're Bruegel ugly by way of Dr. Moreau, their pallid flesh loose, translucent and grotesque, as if rendered by Lucien Freud channeling Ivan Albright. One strap-hanger's features are so haglike they defy caricature: nose drooping like a putrefied bratwurst; melanoid eyes swimming above and below lids too heavy to keep open; slackened jaw hanging, revealing the lusterless strip of roseate gum devoid of teeth. Daumier would have gotten an eyeful of her and tossed away his litho crayons in futility.

When, I wonder, did everything become so goddamned medi-eval? I'm not sure how, but for now I'll blame the Republicans.

From the north end of the car I hear a yelp and look over. Crackhead has a forty-ish Hispanic woman's nipple clenched between his fingers. I should clarify: the nipple is still attached to the breast of the woman who has let out the yelp. The breast is still attached to her. She stares in amazement. How has this happened? You turn away for a minute and boom. Her blouse is torn, buttons scattered on the floor like the work of some garmento Johnny Appleseed, her brassiere ripped in the middle. Maybe it's a front clasp. I can't see that from my vantage point. Her right breast is still tucked away in the compromised safety of her lacy undergarment, but for all the world—especially her crack-crazed assailant—her left breast is exposed, violated, and stretched up, the tormented nipple caught in his unwelcome nipper. But does anyone help her? This is theater of the most absurd stripe—Ionesco on crystal meth.

"Yeah, girl, you're feelin' it, yo!" Equine, he brays with crack-fueled glee.

It's a classic New York moment. What do you do? Do you cower in fear and do nothing? Do you sit back and watch the show (and do nothing)? Do you press back into the closed door praying for it to open so you can make your escape (ibid.)? *Please, God*, you implore silently, *don't let this—or something similar—happen to me.*

Me, I don't like to draw attention to myself but I also don't like seeing women assaulted by stank-ass nutcases. Or anyone. It's so early, too. It's only seven at night. It's too early for this kind of freak show ambience. I've only been up for an hour or so.

"Tha's some good-ass tittyball!"

The woman has the look of a trapped animal. Should she chew off her own tit to make her escape? I take one step in that direction and then wouldn't you know it? A cop actually shows up on time. Well, *almost*, but "A" for effort.

"I ain't had no titty in a long . . . " *Clonk.* "Guh."

Nightstick plus head equals naptime.

The train pulls into Franklin Street, the breast pulls back into torn blouse, and I make my exit, grateful for not having had to intercede.

Hungry as I am, I'm glad to put off breakfast for a while.

3

At least I don't work in a cubicle. That would be the worst. Modular compartments with shiftable gray or beige cloth-covered partial walls that afford no privacy. Awful. Cute posters with twee aphorisms and pastel hues. Unfunny daily strips wretchedly mirroring the lives of their readers. Holiday snaps and studio portraits of the wife, the husband, the kids. Colorful novelty pushpins.

At eight I arrive at the offices of Güdegast Photo Archives (formerly independent, now absorbed by a large news and stock photography conglomerate, itself part of a corporation even more byzantine, and so on; we expect a name change to something more bland imminently). I show my ID and make my way to the elevator bank that serves my floor. There are two such banks: one through twelve, and fourteen through twenty-four. There is no thirteenth floor. As if. In the elevator soft music plays, competing for attention with the LCD screen that displays news headlines, fun factoids, and stock quotations. I do my best to ignore both; the news is always bad, and that flurry of numbers has never meant a thing to me. I share the ride to seventeen with one of the other anonymous drones. I see him several times a week and have never bothered to introduce myself. I'd feel bad, but he's never made any cordial overtures either, so we ride upward in silence, staring at our feet or expectantly up at the advancing floor numbers. Silence—apart from the soft, meandering cover of "Afternoon Delight," which seems wrong when played after sunset—is golden. The elevator dings and we get off, going our separate ways.

So, my office. It's not technically *my* office, per se. But during my shift I'm alone in the large room, so it feels like mine. The best thing about not having to toil in a common area cubicle is that I can choose the level of illumination in my workspace. The first thing I do, even before taking off my coat, is switch off the bank of glaring fluorescent ceiling lights. Even when I was a "regular guy" I hated fluorescent light. Awful, odious, unhealthy looking; light that makes the living look dead. Imagine what it does to someone like me. My complexion, smooth and porcelain, attractive and even enviable under some circumstances, takes on a gauzy varicose translucency under the deadening glow of fluorescence. With the low-wattage gooseneck incandescent table lamp clicked on, I can toil in comfort.

Before I situate myself at my work table I settle for a few minutes, taking off my coat and hanging it up on the rack by the door, looking through the in box, shuffling through some papers and mail. I take a seat and check my e-mail, most of it intra-office communication, the rest external spam.

From: A Friend

To: Philip A. Merman

Subject: WOULDN'T YOU LIKE A BIGGER, FIRMER TOOL?

Subject: Aren't you tired of BEING SINGLE???

Subject: Would you like a THINNER WAIST?

Subject: You don't have to be a HOMO to like CHICKS WITH DICKS!!!

They're not chicks with dicks, they're guys with tits. Big difference.

How do these solicitors get my corporate e-mail address? Why do they think I'm a likely target for dating services, penis enlargement, lower mortgage rates, and tapes of Aryan girls making it with farm animals? No matter how many times I hit "block sender" they keep getting through. I'm not offended, just baffled.

Once acclimated, I reach into the in box and retrieve the night's work. There are ten plastic boxes of slides, some black and white, some color. All are of accidental and/or violent death scenes. And this is my job. I transfer and archive photographic images from film positives, negatives, or prints to digital media. Some nights it's presidential inaugurations, others it's whimsical sequences of children and exotic animals interacting in a manner entirely more suitable than the offerings from those Teutonic bestiality spammers. It used to be I'd do just one kind of thing, but that's before all the corporate mergers, hostile takeovers, and absorptions. Anyway, tonight it's accidental and/or violent deaths. That's what I mostly do. It's my "specialty." There is a typically apologetic Post-it note stuck to the top box from my boss, Kate Abernathy.

Phillip,

I apologize for the graphic and unpleasant nature of the images you'll be subjected to tonight. I wish it could always be more pleasant or uplifting subject matter, but we both know that this job doesn't always afford that kindness. You know you're our "go-to guy" when it comes to this kind of thing. No one else seems to have your constitution and cast-iron stomach. Please accept my apology. As always, I feel really bad.

Kate

I don't feel bad looking at this stuff, but she doesn't have to know that. I've always maintained that a little guilt is good for the soul, so her soul has been enriched tonight. If I confessed that looking at these images has the same impact on me as the cute baby orangutans she'd just feel worse. See, I'm doing my bit. The only part of her note that bugs me is the extra "l" in my name. You'd think after all these years she'd learn to spell it correctly.

Before I get to work I have to move the trash can out into the hall. The guy who works the day shift drinks these exceptionally aromatic herbal teas and the scent really nauseates me. That heightened senses stuff again. I won't harp on it, but out the can goes, full of his tall cardboard empties. Why doesn't he just use a ceramic mug and wash it out? I'll have to ask him sometime, when our paths cross. But I won't complain. That would be so lame. "Uh, your fruity, flowery tea bags really kind of turn my stomach. Do you think maybe you could . . . ?"

Yeah, and you thought non-smokers were annoying. No, I'll just ask him. In fact, no, I won't. Never mind.

I switch on the transparency scanner and it hums and whirs into vitality, its internal lamp casting a faint cool light onto the Formica surface of the workstation. While it cycles through its startup sequence I open the first box and check the label on the lid's interior for the pertinent info: photographer, location, date and time, who controls the copyright. This is often tedious work, fairly mindless but requiring precision nonetheless. I'm not merely scanning by rote. I do color and contrast correction, limited image enhancement, and save each image in four different degrees of resolution: low, medium, high, and ultra. Slipping on a pair of fresh white cotton gloves, I settle down to the night's work, mindful of the hours that pass. This is only part-time work, without benefits, but that's fine. I never get sick. I never need hospitalization. In at seven out at one, though the hours are somewhat flexible, usually leaving me sufficient time to do what I've got to do.

I give the first slide a couple of blasts from the can of Dust-Off, tap in some settings—film type, image type, output resolution—

then slip it into the scanner. The machine does its preview pass and in incremental vertical strips the image of a seventies vintage car with a severely crumpled front section reveals itself on my monitor. It's a grayish daytime shot, the street slick with rain though it's no longer raining, fluids leaking from under the buckled hood, mingling together on the asphalt: oil, windshield wiper fluid, antifreeze, and a darker, tastier looking substance. There are no gawkers or rubberneckers in the background, which is rural, bucolic. The handwritten label on the box says, "Bert Larsen. Rye, New York. May 18, 1982. Early morning. ©1982 Associated Image Bank Syndicate." There are no people at all, just this tan, boxy, mortally wounded automobile. I think it's a Dodge Dart, but I'm not certain. Maybe in one of the other shots the emblem will be visible. I was never very good with cars.

Over fifty years old and I still don't know how to drive.

I work through the first box, each image more lurid than the last. More intimate, prying. Interior shots with the doors pulled open or completely removed. The inside of the car looks like X-ray shots of the core of a strawberry jelly donut, the roof, seats, dashboard liberally coated with fresh blood and viscera, bits of bone and soft tissue. The photos are very professional, as per, so the detail is fine. Fragments of teeth, a clump of hair attached to scalp that is no longer attached to the person it belonged to. In some shots are portions of the emergency workers—a gloved hand, a smeared boot, shoulders in a raincoat—though clearly the emergency is over. The only work to be done here is cleanup. When human beings finally begin to show up in the images in most shots the faces are serious, grim even. But in some of the backgrounds the truer nature of the players shines through.

A local law enforcer in a plastic rain poncho laughing over his coffee.

An EMS worker shrugging with a look of benign indifference.

An irked deputy rubbing a tired eye.

No one looks sad. It's just business.

The final slide is an incongruously cheery shot of the sun break-ing through the clouds, the sky cobalt and vibrant. Was this the photographer's way of dealing with such unpleasant subject mat-ter, to put a sunnier spin on death? Life goes on. Like that. I jot down the lens jockey's name, Bert Larsen, and make a mental note to see if this is his usual coda.

I more or less remember the sun, but again, I don't want to get all wistful.

I put away the final slide and close the box of Larsen's early morning auto wreck.

Next.

Label: "Maureen Dooley. 126th St./Lennox Ave., Upper West Side. 6/27/93. Midmorning. ©1993 Metropolitan News Media, Inc."

No wasting time for Ms. Dooley. No fucking around with atmo-spherics, she goes straight for the carnage. This has got to be the scene of some drug thing that went down badly. There are glass-ine envelopes on the floor, streaks of white powder and blood, blood, and more blood. What a waste. Three lifeless figures assume less than decorous poses as the boys in blue and their plainclothes counterparts go through the motions. No one looks particularly concerned about the victims, the grins caught here and there look comfortable, familiar. The cadavers are all young and black, some with their eyes wide open, paralyzed in permasurprise, clothes darkened with blood, crotches darkened with something else. Death really isn't all that dignified. One is seated on a stool, slumped to the side, the weight of his deadness keeping him in place against the kitchen counter. Small packets gummed down to the counter in spilt gore.

Work tonight takes on the sensation of flipping through one of those colorful menus from Denny's, or IHOP, with the enticing idealized photos of the various meals they serve. You know, the ones that never look in real life like they do on the menu. The eggs always so fluffy and yellow, the sunny-side-up yolks gleaming and unbroken, perfect orbs staring up from the plate, bacon strips crisp and greaseless, pancakes perfectly round and unblemished. Lovely garnish of fresh-from-the-orchard orange wedge and verdant sprig of parsley. Pure fantasy.

Who knew I'd be taunted by the illustrated menu?

The cops in these pictures seem like kids on a field trip to someplace familiar yet still fun. Thirty-six exposures of dead drug dealers and bemused peacekeepers.

Label: "Sven Lindquist-Gonzalez. BMT uptown tunnel, 23rd St. August 29, 1974. Noonish. ©1974 Lindquist-Gonzalez Trust."

As the first image takes shape I feel a gentle ripple of déjà vu. It's the interior of a subway tunnel, the walls blackened, moist, and cracked. Illegible hieroglyphic graffiti sprayed, scrawled, carved, and buried under the ever-thickening topcoat of grime. Stalactites of solidified drip hang down from the cement and iron crossbeams, pitted and rusted. How they don't buckle under their own decrepitude is a true mystery, the weight of the entire city pushing down on them. I've been to this place. The raised catwalk is strewn with garbage: fast food wrappers, soda and beer cans, empty forties. Same goes for the tracks below, the spaces between the ties choked with detritus, puddles, rats.

This time the figures are present from the get-go: cops, EMS, plainclothes detectives, other photographers. A young uniformed transit cop beckoning, waving the group forward with one hand, gesturing with his flashlight with the other. Slide by slide the sequence unfolds, the soft whir of the scanner bringing each image into clarity before my eyes. As I fix the contrast and boost the sharpness in small increments I take in the unfolding tableau. More pointing figures, they motion toward a chink in the wall alongside the catwalk.

Next image: a man's feet sticking out, one with a shoe, one just a dingy threadbare sock exposing a sad, pale big toe.

Next image: the body, face down in a fetal position.

Next image: the EMS guys trying to wedge themselves into the small space.

Next image: the EMS guys pulling someone—a guy—out onto the catwalk.

Next image: turning him over.

Next image: I know that face.

I know that face.

It's always a jolt seeing your own handiwork.

4

Monday, August 26th, 1974

It's just after two in the morning and I'm beginning to feel pretty rundown. Scratch that. I'm not beginning to; I *am* rundown. I can't do what I've got to do. I can't wrap my head around the concept. It's too weird. It's too unreal. I mean, how did it come to this? I've lost eighteen pounds in two weeks and I'm not wearing it well. No one is complimenting me on my trim figure. I'm getting stuff like, "Holy shit, are you dying?" I don't even know what to think because I have no frame of reference. I've learned that I have what could be described as a rather strong aversion to the sun these days. The last time I allowed myself to get up before sundown was two weeks ago. I made the mistake of drawing the drapes and it wasn't pretty.

The burns on my hands are still raw and tender, even after a nighttime visit to the local emergency room. Two weeks ago. Not being able to come in during normal business hours has cost me my job. Monica's freaking out, as any good little wife would. Plus I don't have a whole lot saved up for a *sunny* day, if you get my meaning.

I'm sickened by conventional food. The smell, the taste, the texture. I can't even get it in my mouth before I start gagging. I'm going to have to do it. Tonight. I can feel I'm going to die, and I mean *die* die, like for real no coming back from it dead. The big sleep. I am twenty-seven years old and I'm not ready for that kind of letdown.

The sun set at about seven-forty-something, so I've been riding back and forth from Forest Hills to Coney Island since eight o'clock. That's nearly two hours each way of me sitting, pacing, fretting, biding my time, and procrastinating. I keep my prop paperback open and watch people come and go, but as sustenance they look as unappealing as they did as plain old fellow travelers. Did they always have such greasy hair, such pasty skin, so many pimples and bad odors? That it's summer doesn't help. The profusion of b.o. is overwhelming. I've become so aware of the myriad secretions humans pump through their pores and orifices. So sweaty; so oily. Walking sebaceous glands. Christ, humans really are disgusting. Bad breath, flatulence, nose breath. Why hasn't anyone come up with a minty freshener for nose breath? Like mucus-tinged exha-lations of lung stink are any bargain. Burps. Waxy ears. Waxy complexions. And I'm supposed to chow down on one of these fuckers? *Oy.*

To avoid obsessive hair washing I've cut my hair real short so I'm getting distrustful stares from the younger passengers. They see a young guy like me, thin, wired-looking, both hands wrapped in gauze, they think I'm some baby killer freshly back from 'Nam. I never went to 'Nam. I have a heart condition. I'm a delicate flower, if not flower child. All the same I'm thinking, *I might have to kill one of you tonight.* Peace.

The train is just pulling out of the Kings Highway station. Three stops to go until the last one, Coney Island. I'm getting tired of this indecision, not to mention the gnawing in my gut, the scrubbed feeling in my veins, the throbbing of my singed mitts. I'm down to the six remaining candidates in this car: a teen peacenik couple, an older Puerto Rican who looks like he's coming home from a soul-killingly shitty job, a middle-aged black wino, a couple of young toughs, and an unconscious junkie.

Let's break it down into the real particulars. The couple keeps giving me the aforementioned dirty, distrustful looks; the "baby killer" furtive glances I could do without. I don't have to explain myself to you sanctimonious wrongheaded pimply motherfuckers. I'm just a guy, a simple ordinary guy. Okay, maybe that's not entirely accurate, but I'm no baby killer. I've never killed anyone. I can't say any*thing*, because that's not true. Roaches, sure. Silverfish. Mice. What could be classified in general as household vermin. But people? Never. Babies or otherwise. Maybe it's the hunger I can't hide that's putting them off. Maybe they're thinking I'm a junkie in need of a fix. That's sort of true, although I've never done this drug before—I only supplied it. Once. But once was enough to get me in this bind.

Once was definitely enough.

So the hippie couple doesn't dig my creepy, strung out, crazy 'Nam vet who never really went to 'Nam vibe. They're peaceniks. I see their "Impeach Nixon" buttons and think, like, time to update your buttons, *maaaan*. As if Ford's going to be any improvement. Nope, they're not on the menu. I refuse to validate their mistrust.

The Hispanic guy in the sooty overalls? Can't do it. He's a hardworking family man. I can tell. His eyes, set at half-mast, are weary with the weight of pure drudgery and a lack of balance in his life. Not enough pleasure, too much responsibility.

The leather-jacketed young toughs? I've been watching them since they got on at DeKalb, and their antics have gone from somewhat menacing to drearily amusing. They talk too loud, gesture too broadly—I'm sure if I said to them that they were a tad theatrical they'd interpret that as my outright dubbing them fags, a capital offense in the court of goombas. Even in August they're sporting their leathers, their hair slicked back into well-pomaded DAs. I'm thinking, *they still make you guys?* I thought they closed production on your model ages ago. It's almost touching to see this kind of thing. White T-shirts, black motorcycle jackets, pegged jeans tucked into engineer boots.

"Fuckin' I'm not even gonna fuckin' *talk* to dat bitch no maw, fuh Chrissakes, Tony," sputters the one on his feet, his arms slung at the elbows through the swinging metal straps. He looks like an escapee from the primate house at the zoo, only not as intelligent. Any minute I expect a dazzling display of champion turd flinging and jacking off. "Dat fuckin' *hoo-ah*. She t'inks I'm gonna admit dat fuckin' kid is *mines*? I says ta her, 'Gina, you show me da fuckin' *blood test*, you money-grubbin' *hoo-ah*,' an' youse know what? Her fuckin' ol' man is all ovah my shit like *I'm* da bad guy! Dat whole fuckin' family can go fuckin' fuck itself right in da fuckin' *asshole*!"

Tony's laugh is a nasal series of staccato bleats. I can smell the tang of snot, as well as sausages and peppers and onions being digested with each burst of second-hand air. Tony I don't love so much, actually. But they're both kind of amusing in a Neanderthal way.

"But Terry, dincha say dat Gina gives da most mind-bendin' head? I means, how can youse walk away fum dat? An' she swallows? Hoo-*hoooo*!"

Terry? This guy's name is *Terry*? What the hell kind of *paisan* name is Terry?

"Yeah, well I ain't goin' in fuh no blood test. Fuck *dat*. Dere's plenny udda girls who'll swallow the goo fum *my* trousah snake. I guess I'll just hold off onna pussy till I'm married."

"Yeah, jus' fuck 'em inna *ass*, I say. Then they're still a *virgin*."

They both laugh and slap each other five. I'm not afraid of them, but that's not why I've decided in their favor. They're somebody's sons, and I can tell they both still live at home. Misogynistic. Stupid. Loud. Boorish. Obnoxious. Classic momma's boys. Somewhere here in Brooklyn, in some row house with a statue by the stoop of the Blessed Virgin—who I very much doubt took it up the ass to preserve that status—somebody loves these two knuckleheads.

The wino? A distinct possibility. He's well marinated—ha ha—and completely grubby. Probably a vagrant. He stinks like a low-rent distillery located in a sewer, but he fits the bill. I doubt whether he's got anyone waiting for him at home, or whether he even has a home. Still, am I going to let one's stake in real estate govern my decision-making? This guy has probably had a real hard life. Maybe he came up north to get away from segregation and found out the hard way that life is no cakewalk up here either. Let him marinate a little longer, I say.

The junkie? Good lord, what a heinous specimen. A living—if you can call it that—billboard from the anti-drug lobby. I can see and smell the open sores on his emaciated arms and ankles from where I'm seated. He's a tall stringy ulcer of a man, junk sick and trembling. His hair is a tangle of clotted, greasy, dirty blond, plastered down to his face. Occasionally his eyes pop open and look heavenward, his cracked lips mouthing a silent prayer. He looks like every portrait of Jesus on the cross you've ever seen, except he's wearing more clothes, less thorns. I've made my choice.

Junkie Jesus is going to die for my sins.

The train stops at Avenue U and then 86th Street. One more stop and then I take the plunge. The conductor's garbled announcement, "Coney Island, Stillwell Avenue, Surf Avenue. Last stop, all passengers off!" blasts out of the tinny speakers, muddied further by feedback and static.

The train shudders to a halt, the doors clatter open, and the hippies and toughs disembark. I remain in my seat, sweat collecting on my forehead and upper lip, unsure as to how to proceed. The wino is still asleep, but the junkie fans the air before him, his long fingers playing phantom chords. He cranes his neck and I can hear a few internal cracks and pops, the percussion to accompany his spastic air guitar. A cop boards the car and taps the doorframe with his billy club.

"A'right, now, last stop. This ain't a flophouse, fellas. Take it on the road."

The flatfoot eyes me suspiciously. Though ashy and unhealthy looking, I don't come across as impaired. I guess I don't look like I should be lingering. The junkie takes a faltering step toward the last doors of the car, avoiding the fuzz on his way out. Mr. Lawman steps in and raps his nightstick on the wall behind the wino's head, attempting to revive him. I get up and stretch, pantomiming newly achieved wakefulness, and make for the exit. The cop, now fully invested in rousing the rummy, doesn't give me a second glance. Good.

Yellowed bare light bulbs illuminate the exit ramp, saturating everything with a patina of purest urine bisque. See it, smell it, so strong you can even taste it. Mix in the piss with the stench of rotting garbage, sickly sweet cotton candy, and frying medium that predates the last czar and that's Coney Island in the predawn hours. During the day it's worse.

At a discreet distance I follow the junkie out the exit, past the closed newsstands and lunch counters onto Coney Island Avenue, which simmers even at this late hour. There are few places on earth as rank as Coney Island at night in the dead of summer. Maybe someplace in Calcutta could compete, but the Coney would hold its own. Aside from a few shell-shocked skells and malingerers, the street is pretty much deserted. A few silhouetted heads bob in the fogged up windows of parked cars, the only vital activity to be seen. Hookers plying their trade or teenagers, more likely, who can't blow their beaus at home. How romantic.

Pretty soon the workweek will begin, it being the transitional hours between Sunday night and Monday morning. When dawn arrives the street will be filled with working class folk making their way to various jobs, some heading into the city, others to operate the rides and concession stands of Coney Island's charmingly charmless Astroland, the most dangerous place you'd ever wittingly take the kids. I'd better be long gone by then.

The junkie teeters toward the boardwalk and I'm beyond pins and needles. I've got medieval lances and crossbow bolts and razorblades and sticky, pointy, sharp poky things jabbing me inside and out. My bandaged hands feel purulent and pan-seared. I'm doing all I can to remain upright, fighting my desire to just buckle at the waist, knees, wherever and hit the dirt. And we're talking Coney Island dirt, so that's a bad option.

Why is it whenever relief is in sight the symptoms grow worse? Like if you have to take a dump but you're still on the subway you manage, even if it's somewhat uncomfortable, to contain the sensations. But once you're on your block and release is almost at hand, the peristalsis really kicks in. You can almost feel it crowning, the discomfort level spikes through the roof, and you find yourself thinking, "Please don't let me shit my pants. That would be so unfair. I'm a grownup. Grownups do not shit their pants. Stay together cheeks, stay together."

Now magnify that by a hundred thousand million. Am I overstating my case? A little, but not much.

We pass the Hell House, an Astroland "attraction" that boldly declares what it isn't but not what it is. A sign hung from the chain link says, "THIS IS NOT A SPOOK HOUSE!" The enormous mural on the façade is a garish panorama of Hades, presided over by a wall-mounted sculpture of a muscle-bound, pitchfork-wielding, naked—yet genitalia-free—Satan. Sort of Hieronymous Bosch by way of a carnie, full of tormented souls, bizarre creatures, and licking flames. A few summers back, a couple friends and I went out to the Coney for a day of fun and sun and ogling chicks. My friend Doug and I decided to find out just what the heck the Hell House was, so we paid our admission and walked down the enclosed open-air passageway toward a closed door.

So what was it?

A centrifuge. I turned on my heel and bolted, but Doug had paid and dammit he was going to get his money's worth. Fifteen minutes later he was on the curb dry heaving and my buddy John and I were laughing at Doug's parsimony-induced misery. What are friends for? But enough strolling down Memory Lane. I've got to focus on my game.

The junkie looks as bad off as I feel, rubbing his arms and shivering, but unlike me he's losing the battle to fold up in the middle, his upper story dipping like a dowser's rod. His knees give for a moment but then he's up on his feet again, with renewed focus. Great, he's going to score. I'd really like to catch him before he makes the buy.

This is so ugly.

I'm a nice boy.

I have good parents.

I was raised right.

What am I doing in Coney Island at three in the morning playing follow-the-junkie? This is so unfair. Even more unfair than shitting one's pants. The junkie makes his way up the ramp to the boardwalk and I hang back a little. He hikes up his slacks, smoothes his shirtfront, and rakes his fingers through his long, greasy hair, arranging it into a makeshift ponytail. He's prettying himself up for his connection. Oh, this is too pathetic. But I don't know who to feel sorrier for, him or me.

Okay, me. Definitely me.

I'm starving to death; he's jonesing for a fix.

I'm an upstanding citizen; he's just some junkie scumbag.

He goes over the top and I lose sight of him for a second. The pain is so extreme I nearly black out. I have spots before my eyes. Seriously, spots. I see the junkie go down the steps on the beachside of the boardwalk and I get there in time to glimpse him duck under the boardwalk. I slow down and follow his movements in the shadows under the rotting wooden gangway. Though I'm still seeing spots, I'm also seeing much better than I should be considering the poor illumination. The air is thick with the funk of low tide, the sand dank and humid, peppered with discarded condoms and other foul litter.

And then, out of nowhere, I feel a flurry of intensely painful stabbing sensations in my lower abdomen.

"Motherfucker, you were tailed."

"But I . . . " the junkie stammers and I hit the soggy sand, adding to its wetness.

Hey, those stabbing sensations were *actual* stabbing. *I've been stabbed*!

The junkie's connection steps around from behind a splintered pilaster holding a large hunting knife coated in my thick gummy blood, which I can ill afford to spare.

"You are one stupid motherfucker, man. Didn't I tell you to shake any tail if you were followed? Who is this lame Jones?"

He gives me a violent kick in the side and I swoon. Next stop, oblivion.

"But I didn't know I . . . "

"Just shut up. You got the bread?"

"Yeah, I . . . "

"Check his pockets. Might as well see if he's got any . . . "
Oblivion.

• • •

Ever stir from a deep nightmarish sleep completely covered by a heavy comforter and for a moment panic, thinking you've been buried alive? Maybe your arm stays asleep and feels dead and you think it won't revive? I wake up feeling a heaviness like I've never felt before. I try to lift my head and it feels like I'm being held down by a lot more than a bulky blanket. What's worse is I can't breathe. I've been congested before, sure, but not like this. My arms feel pinned. I try to part my eyelids but when I manage to I wish I hadn't and it hits me. Sand in my mouth, up my nose, clogging and scratching my eyes. And the fucked part is that this is a good thing. What those two accidental Samaritans—the junkie and his connection—don't realize is that by burying me they've inadvertently saved my life.

By now I'm getting used to constant pain. Hell, I've got so much I can't differentiate where it's coming from. I've got this pervasive sickness and hunger, I've got the multiple stab wounds in my gut, I've got the singed meat hooks. The quality assortment. Wriggling like a worm I manage to poke my head up through the sand and push a pile of piss-sodden newspapers off me.

Thanks, junkie!

Thanks, pusher!

It's either dusk or daybreak, but I'm betting dusk because I can see a fair amount of people on the beach, packing their crap up and making for the boardwalk. I rock back and forth as best I can to loosen up the sand and with some difficulty I free myself from my shallow grave, blowing sandy snot out of each nostril.

I don't appear to be bleeding any more, but the wounds are still open and angry looking. I take a leak—add urethral burn to my list of maladies—contributing my unique bouquet to the Coney Island Collection, then hunker down in the shadows and wait for the stragglers to depart. Once it's down to the diehards, I get up and make for the showers by the bathhouse. Fully dressed, I turn on the faucet and wash as much of the grit off me as possible. No one notices. No one cares.

I don't know what time it is; they pinched my watch. Wallet, too. Surprise, surprise.

I pass a mirror and barely recognize myself. Who is that dissipated drowned cat of a man? I take a seat on a bench and attempt to air dry before getting back on the subway and heading home. I've got to feed. It's as simple as that. A few hours pass and my clothes begin to feel less wet. Not dry, exactly, but moist in a gross, sweaty, summery way.

The boardwalk, liberally strewn with scuz, is packed for a Monday night. Families come and go, kids crawling all over each other and everything else. Lots of distrustful faces, but they're not eyeballing me. Black guys give poisonous looks to the *cugines* who return the favor but also spread the love to the Ricans who do likewise. A circle jerk of racial unrest. They mill about, jostle each other, jockey for position at the food stands. There's limited seating so they watch the tables with feral acuity, checking for nice posteriors all the while. Checking out each other's women is part of the covenant. Italian guys looking at Latinas and sisters; Puerto Rican dudes fingering their mustaches, surreptitiously scrutinizing the black girls and Guidettes, comparing asses; the brothers checking out every girl in sight, not in the least furtive. They just look and smile and make catcalls. The girls pretend to get mad but their egos draw sustenance from the allegedly loutish remarks.

I count *cornutos* dangling around thick Italian necks—those red pepper-looking pendants that evoke a devil or animal horn—many worn in tandem with shiny gold crosses. How do these God-fearing Catholics make peace with this conflicting symbolism? The horns are to ward off the evil eye, I think, but shouldn't Christ in his torment be the plenary phylactery, the Swiss Army knife of good luck charms? Maybe the horn's got nothing to do with the devil at all. What do I know about Italo-Catholic symbology? I'm just a waterlogged atheist dying of multiple stab wounds and malnutrition. Some of the horns have a little man in a tuxedo and top hat from the waist up, looking like a diabolical combination of the Monopoly man and a mermaid.

Merman.

What's that all about?

A little girl climbs up onto the bench and gives me the *malocchio.* Where's my horn when I need it?

"Wha' happen a you?" she asks, brow furrowed but stifling a smile.

"Somebody thought I was a bag of kittens, so they tried to drown me."

"Really?"

"No. Worse. I don't want to talk about it."

"I wanna know why you're all wet."

"I've wanted to know that myself for years."

"You been all wet for years?"

"That's what they tell me."

"The same ones who tried to drowned you?"

In spite of myself I let out a choky laugh. It sounds more like a drain unclogging.

The little girl's mother comes along and yanks her pigtail, eliciting a pained squeak.

"Whudja do that for?" the girl whines, justifiably I think.

"Don't talk to perverts," mom says, and snatches the girl off the bench, hustling her toward Gregory & Paul's mondo concession stand for a greasy, fattening repast, the kid's high-pitched klaxon parting the crowd like Moses. Boy, I wish I could chow down on a hero and some corn on the cob. People food instead of people = food.

They say you can't smell yourself, like when you're checking yourself for body odor, but that's bullshit. Even though I've showered—sort of—I reek. I smell like stagnant blood, sweat, salt, urine, failure. Weak as I am I've got to motivate soon. The Paul Cadmus procession of uglies (interspersed with a few beauties I'm too depleted to appreciate) deliquesces into a blur of color and texture. Weegee captured Coney Island in all its elemental glory. That charming father of American independent cinema, *The Little Fugitive*, paraded the chaos and caprice and plebeian splendor of this locale, but my dimming vision and singular need reduces it all to a moving buffet, the candy conveyor belt in that *Lucy* episode that everyone thinks is so goddamned hilarious. I never thought Lucy was funny but all I feel like saying right now is, "*Waaaaaah!*"

The crowd is thinning so the hour must be late. It is a work night, after all, so only the teens and dregs remain. They look too formidable for me in my present shape. After the knifing last night I don't feel up to the Coney Island challenge. I pry myself from the bench and hobble back toward the subway station, although in Coney it starts as an El.

On the way I spy a clock.

It's one forty-five.

If I don't chow down tonight I'm a goner.

Heading back toward the city on the last car of the train I once again scan for palatable nominees. This time it's four toughs—

thanks but no thanks—a couple of junkies—after my recent debacle, also no thanks—and a family. With kids. How irresponsible do you have to be as a parent to be out with your preschoolers at two in the morning? I don't care. I'm not with child protection services. But there's nothing.

At Bay Parkway the family gets off so now I'm stuck with the dope fiends and the hooligans. I look like death warmed over. Scratch that, I just look like death. Period. The toughs keep looking at me like they're not sure whether to throw some misery my way or not. Deep in discussion, hissing in hushed menacing tones and throwing sneaky glances my way. Ones *tsks* loudly and lets out a barking guffaw. They lose interest in me. I clearly have nothing to steal and maybe I look so bad they don't want to sully their hands by roughing me up. At New Utrecht they clomp off the car and I'm left with the junkies. I've never had one but I've unquestionably lost my taste for them.

I nod out, and to anyone who'd care to notice the car now boasts three of a kind. I hate to admit it, but I look less savory than the others.

At Pacific Street I'm awakened by the conductor's voice crackling over the PA system announcing that this is the last stop in Brooklyn. The next stop will be Canal Street. I slap my face with my wrapped hand, giving me a twofer in the pain department. I need to be sharp. I want to feed before I return to my own borough, Queens. I've got Manhattan ahead and I want to make this a one-way trip. I did the back and forth thing ad nauseam last night. Enough is enough, already.

I run my tongue over my teeth, lingering on my upper cuspids, which are now ludicrously sharp and have grown about a quarter of an inch over the course of the last week. Adjusting to my revamped teeth has been the easiest part of this whole transmogrification, but

I've still managed to cut my tongue on them several times, each time savoring the taste of my own blood. I can feel the pulp chamber of my canines—the soft inner structure of the tooth, the part full of nerve endings and blood vessels—throb with potential for mayhem. I bite down on my tongue now, and whet my appetite with the snappy metallic tang. My blood is thick, coagulated and unhealthy but I keep sucking it out and swallowing it anyway.

When I think about it I can't help but be revolted. What the fuck have I become? I mean, I *know* what I've become but people don't become that. But I guess they do. I do. I got bit and sucked half dry and now I'm looking to do the same to some other poor schmuck, only I plan on sucking him all the way dry. No half measures. Maybe that's why I'm still up and about. Maybe if I drain him he'll just be dead, the lucky prick.

At 14th Street my quarry steps on, beady eyed and radiantly unwholesome. After surveying the car he situates himself at the southern tip, the full span of the car away from me, right near the rear doors. It's just the two of us. As the train rumbles out of the station he cautiously pulls something out of his pocket and begins to riffle through it: a wallet. He's examining it like he's never seen it before, which he probably hasn't. Oh, this guy is too perfect. He's either a pickpocket or a mugger. Something unsavory.

Then the guy looks straight at me, piqued. I don't want to stare at him, scare him off, so I let my head loll; drool a little. If I look like a drug addict I might as well act like one. When he sees how out of it I look he relaxes and grows more bold in his actions, pulling cash from the billfold and dipping into the pockets, palming credit cards. I can't help myself; the pain in my guts, the knife wounds, the hunger. I still look at him, even if I'm doing this dinner theater pantomime of the zonked-out lowlife. Before the next major station, which would be 34th Street, I want to get this done. Even this time of night the express stops can be busy, especially Times Square. I got lucky at 14th.

"What the fuck are you lookin' at, *freak*?"

Shit, I was staring. I shake my head and rub my eyes, feigning lassitude.

"Huh? What's your *problem, maaaan*?" I let the word slime off my tongue in my best simulation of a drug addict, hoping I don't sound like some cut-rate Cheech and Chong impersonator.

"Just don't look at me," he snarls, attempting menace. He's no mugger. He's about as menacing as a toothless dachshund.

"I don' need this kinda 'buse, *maaaaaan*," I sputter, rising shakily from my seat. "Fuggin' square mutha*jfkjg* . . . " I trail off in some inarticulate approximation of language and push open the door to move to the next car, looking over my shoulder with bleary hauteur. The pickpocket, master of his domain, smiles in triumph and as the door slams shut behind me I crouch down between cars and wait, holding on to the doorframe, the train rocking violently as it plunges through the tunnel, he and I the sole passengers within eyeshot.

As the train nears 23rd Street, slowing, I risk a peek through the window and see my new traveling companion rise and stand near the doors, rocking back and forth on his toes, readying to make a quick departure. He looks my way and I duck and ride the rest of the way into the station in shadow. The train pulls into 23rd and he gets out. This is dicey. I want him to feel safe, let his defenses down. The doors close and the train shudders, about to pull out. Gripping the handholds on either car I launch myself over the safety chains and land on the platform, both hands sending angry messages up my arms. Fortunately the roar of the departing train covers the sound of me dropping onto the platform.

My turn to scope out the venue: desolate. *Parfait*.

The pickpocket is at the mouth of the tunnel, near the half gate with the sign that warns not to go any further. He tosses the purloined wallet into the tunnel and while his back is turned I sprint toward him, head down. He turns to leave and my noggin catches him right in the breadbasket, knocking the wind out of him.

"Fuh . . . " he manages, and I get him in a headlock and drag him past the warning sign, deeper into the tunnel. The catwalk is narrow and slippery and his struggling doesn't help my footing. He bites my wrist and even though it hurts like a motherfucker I let loose a laugh that scares us both a little. Him biting me. Now if that isn't reverse foreshadowing. He bites me again and this time I don't laugh. I rear back and bat my forehead into the back of his head, hoping his fontanel never fully hardened. No such luck.

"Stop biting me, asshole," I hiss in his ear. "You're only making this harder than it has to be."

"You a cop?" he croaks and I laugh again. Do cops have that bad a rep that this scumbag thinks one would shanghai his worthless ass into a tunnel to do God knows what to him? "What? *What*? You want what I took? I seen you checkin' me out back there." He's put two and two together. His speech is choked, the crook of my elbow crushing his Adam's apple. "Fine. Take it. It's only like thirty bucks. It's yours."

Once we're about fifty feet into the tunnel I feel an opening in the wall with my back and duck in, pulling along my twitchy prey. His struggling grows more agitated. The writing's on the wall, and I'm not talking about the chicken scratch graffiti. I'm talking about the five-foot neon lettering that says to my companion, "PREPARE TO MEET THY DOOM!" With my free hand I rabbit punch him in the midsection and, surprised at my surge of new-found vigor, he drops to his knees, taking me down on top of him.

That's fine; save me a trip. With my mouth open wide near his jugular I hesitate for a split second.

This is so incredibly fucked up.

Seriously, this is not what anyone civilized should be doing.

But I smell the blood under the surface and grossed out as I am, morally conflicted as I am, freaked out and astonished as I am, I sink those shiny new fangs into the meat of his throat and suck like Linda Lovelace. He thrashes for a second or two but then placidity comes and he goes quiet, like a sleeping baby in my arms.

I let the blood flow down my throat, trying not to taste it. But then I do. There's too much to avoid tasting.

The blood tastes . . . good.

No, better than good. It's ambrosia, the sweetest delicacy I've ever had. I guzzle until the emptied artery collapses and I'm just sucking air, then I let him drop away. Feeling like a gorged tick I plop my keister onto the filthy ground amid the Krylon, Red Devil, and Rust-Oleum empties. I feel euphoric. All my pain is gone. It's like I just came and came and came again. I feel energized and spent simultaneously, shimmering waves of transcendent serenity washing over me. Maybe I did come. I don't know. I hope not. It would cheapen the purity of this moment.

For two weeks I've put this off and felt like hell.

I remove my bandages and rub my hands together, the burnt dermis flaking off, revealing skin good as new.

My knife wounds are healed.

What an elixir.

I've learned my lesson.

Give in to the hunger.

Go out on the prowl.

Live a little.

5

Tuesday, January 9th, 2001

On the chit that's in with Sven Lindquist-Gonzalez's slides, my first quarry is described only as "Unidentified Caucasian male, late 20s/early 30s." I could add "pickpocket" and "blowhard" to that description. Oh, and "delicious," but that's just my opinion. Maybe I'm looking back through rose-colored taste buds, but I do remember that under that gruff exterior and tough, stubbly neck was a real sweet cache of the good stuff.

Before calling it a night I do another box of nondescript miscellaneous accident shots.

A head through the windshield.

A subway jumper's dismembered corpse, each scattered part documented on a separate slide.

A hit and run victim.

A fork-in-the-toaster home electrocution.

When did I stop seeing these slabs of meat as people?

I'm not sure if that's a recent development or not. I mean, I was never part of the rah-rah, up with people pep squad, but I used to have some empathy. The late great Bill Hicks once described humanity as, "a virus with shoes." Maybe so. But to paraphrase the Beef Council, "[*Human*]. It's what's for dinner."

On to the buffet.

I skulk past the napping security guard and leave the building at one fifteen in the morning allowing plenty of time to get my feed on, maybe even enjoy some of the night. Sun doesn't rise until about 7:20, so I'm pretty relaxed. What was once a stressful ordeal is now just routine. I step out onto the pavement with my coat open at the collar, the air crisp, the street deserted. The sky is clear and around the moon is a crystalline halo. I look up at the stars and think, who needs the sun? If every star is a sun, I see an infinite number of them on cloudless nights like this. Winter used to be my worst season, but I've come to love it. The cold doesn't bother me and the nights are luxuriously long. Summer nights are brief, hot, humid, and there's too much to do in too little time; work, some mixing when I can manage it, feeding. All crammed into nine hours.

Winter, at its best, generously gives me about fifteen hours to play with outdoors, just like regular people. I should move to one of those places where it's dark for months at a time. I really should. But what would I do for a living? And those places are too sparsely populated; too intimate. I'd tip my hand too soon. Deplete the livestock. Get caught. New York might suck, but its anonymity and escalating population make it hard to abandon.

I'm in the mood to mingle.

Or at least observe.

"Philip!"

Fuck.

"Hey, Phil, glad I c-c-caught you."

Shelley Poole, the one human being on the planet who exudes no heat, no sound, no scent of blood. Like a phantom, he emerges from the shadows by the entrance of the building, an unlit cigarette dangling from his thin, anemic lips. The poseur. If he actually lights it I'll die of shock. I'm not in the mood for *this* kind of mingling. I want new faces. I know I'm trapped. The worst part is I know he'll lay on the spiel about "just being in the neighborhood," which is such a transparent crock. I'm nobody, yet I have a stalker, sort of. Shelley's the one "friend" I still have from back a ways and he won't take the hint.

"Hey, Shelley."

"I was just in the n-n-neighborhood having a d-d-drink with a lady friend, and as we j-j-just p-p-parted company and I knew you g-g-got off work this t-t-time of night I thought I'd swing by and t-t-take a chance on c-c-catching you as you left."

"Why didn't you just call?"

"I wanted t-t-to s-s-surprise you."

There's nothing worse than a surprise with no element of surprise to it. He's "surprised" me this way so many times I've considered changing jobs just to avoid him.

"Consider me surprised. How long have you been waiting down here?"

"Oh, not long. M-m-maybe half an hour."

At least an hour, then.

"You're looking well, as always," he says, his thin smile masking something. Maybe jealousy. With bald head, sallow complexion, deep-set eyes, and long black trench coat flapping in the winter breeze, he looks more like an incorporeal being, a creature of the night, Nosferatu, than I do. But he's pathetically human—a wan Byronic figure, full of Eighteenth Century melancholy. Byronic Shelley. He was born too late. He should have been born in a time when you could go out in a slouch hat and velveteen cape and fit right in. I've thought of buying him that ruffled "Ultimate Poet's Shirt" from the *International Male* catalog as a goof, but I didn't think he'd get it. He'd just thank me with sincerity and that would slaughter the whole gag.

"Obviously if you're t-t-tired and want to g-g-go home or wish t-t-to be alone after a hard night's work, I'd underst-t-tand," he says, eyes brimming with slightly suspect amity. "Especially since I w-w-was just in the n-n-neighborhood. But if you're up for some c-c-company, perhaps we could sally forth t-t-to a local saloon for a libation?"

That's the way he talks, and I'm not referring to the st-st-stutter. That I could deal with. Sometimes it's hard to remember him before the stutter. That's a long time ago. When I think about the origin of the stutter I kind of remember why I put up with Shelley.

"Yeah, okay."

Maybe this won't take too long.

Maybe my shot at mingling isn't scuttled.

Maybe the heartache and yearning in his eyes will go away.

Maybe he'll just have a drink and be on his way.

Maybe he'll finally catch a clue.

Maybe a lot of things.

• • •

"How is that even possible?"

My tone of voice is judgmental and incredulous with a soupçon of peevishness, but I can't help myself. I find myself at a splendidly dark, unfortunately trendy saloon in Soho, seated at the bar opposite Shelley, watching him drink too much, listening to him complain about how often his girlfriend obliges him with fellatio. My disbelief stems from the nature of the complaint; she blows him *too* often. She's *too* libidinous. *Too* preoccupied with Shelley's package.

These are the kind of problems you want to have.

"I'm p-p-perfectly serious," he says, between pulls on his third or fourth gin and tonic. His breath smells like rotting meat with honey on top, exacerbated by the stink of gin and the occasional puff of a Newport. What kind of white man smokes menthols? The kind who kvetches about too many blowjobs from his girlfriend. At least he actually lit up.

"She goes down on you too often." I'm trying to remember the last time I had an orgasm that wasn't self-originated.

"We were in my car d-d-driving along the Van Wyck after doing some shopping, yes?" Shelley pauses and gives me this look, so I nod. What? Does he think I'm not listening? "I'm letting her d-d-drive. She loves to d-d-drive, so I'm t-t-trying to b-b-be accommodating. We're talking, having a p-p-perfectly amicable, reasonable adult conversation—I don't remember the p-p-particulars; they're not important. Just t-t-typical stuff, how her day was, maybe. Th-th-that kind of thing. Out of nowhere she veers off onto the sh-sh-shoulder. I ask her if there's motor t-t-trouble, not that I'd be any help. 'No,' she says, with this glint in her eye. 'Not motor t-t-trouble. Female t-t-trouble.' And she slides c-c-closer and begins to undo my t-t-trousers."

I'm sure my eyes glaze at this point.

"So I gesture out the window. Cars are whizzing b-b-by with great regularity. I mean, it's not l-l-like we're on some secluded c-c-country road at m-m-midnight. It's mid-*evening* on a b-b-busy expressway. And she begins to fish out my p-p-penis and . . . " he slams back the rest of his drink, his face taut, traumatized. "Well, you c-c-can imagine the rest. She engul-gul-gulfed me with her mouth and there was n-n-nothing I could d-d-do about it. My protestations fell on d-d-deaf ears. Only when I produced my d-d-dollop did she relinquish my little fellow and resume d-d-driving."

His "little fellow." He sometimes calls it his "John Thomas" or "Percy." He wishes he was British, and the more he imbibes, the more British he becomes. It's a control thing. He drinks, he loses control, he attempts to regain control by affecting a British accent to make sure he pronounces his words with care. Sometimes he goes with a posh English accent, sometimes a lilting Irish brogue, sometimes a wry Scottish burr. If he's tried Welsh yet it was too subtle for me to recognize. The drunker he gets, the less he stutters, though. When he's completely shit-faced he speaks perfectly. Still, it's very annoying. I might have to cut him loose soon. Between his rampant alcoholism, his mawkish disposition, and his barely closeted sexuality—he's batted bedroom lashes at me more than once—he's beginning to wear on me. For the last twenty-odd years. With his l-l-lamentations and confessions. *Oy*, enough with the confessions already. Even Catholics in remission love to confess; it's a sickness.

All my friends of yore gave up on me or I moved on from them. It's impossible to maintain friendships when you are what I am. Don't kid yourself. Most have gotten married, had kids, gotten fat and old and boring. Some have died. Most I just lost track of. Preserving himself by mostly eschewing food and drinking way too much, at fifty-two Shelley is getting thinner, older, and was always a bit boring. His face, the skin taut and translucent, exudes physical and psychological lassitude. At six-foot-three he weighs about a hundred and fifteen pounds. I survive on blood alone, am five-foot-ten and weigh twenty-five pounds more than he does. He's paler than I am, virtually albino, yet walks among his fellow humans in the sun, for all the good it does him. At least I assume he does. Maybe it's the raw diet. Cooked food never passes his lips. Nor meat, or so he says. Actually, I never see him eat, just drink, drink, drink.

He could seriously use a burger and fries.

Why does he hang in there? He might have to down a distillery's worth over the course of a night, but he hangs in there. Is it because my company is so good? I don't hang on his every word. I don't fake interest that well. I don't even pretend to like him anymore. He's human, more or less. He can mix whenever he wants but I think he's got fewer friends than I do, and including him I don't have any. He didn't just stroll over from some assignation with a "lady friend." He might have been waiting out there for me for hours.

It's a terrible burden to play nursemaid to a sad, lonely, inveterate alcoholic. He once told me, during a drunken confessional jag, that there were only two men he ever wanted to bed—which is two more than I could name. "One," he said, doing a sort of trembling Richard Harris impersonation, "was a sm-sm-smoldering, opal-eyed Egyptian boy in my sophomore English literature c-c-class in c-c-college . . . "

The other was me. If he wasn't such a sad sack it might even have been flattering. But it wasn't. It was just uncomfortable and gross. I seldom return his calls. I never initiate getting together. Why won't he let me alone?

"So I said to her, 'Okay, you got your way. Are you *happy* now?' And she gives me this astonished look like *I'm* way out of line just for being a t-t-tad snarky." He takes a sip of his drink, his stutter fading, his Britishness blossoming. "She's just sexually assaulted me and *I'm* to feel like *I've* done something wrong? I was the v-v-victim. I let her have her way. What? Am I not allowed t-t-to have *feelings*? Am I not supposed t-t-to make clear my feelings on the m-m-matter?"

I sigh audibly, even in this loud taproom.

"Oh, surely *you* can see my point."

"Why should *I* be able to see it? Like I wouldn't like a piece of that action? It's kind of stupid to complain about getting blown too often. It's ungracious. Decadent, even. A lot of guys would kill for a girl like that."

"I thought maybe you were a t-t-tad more evolved. People only think they know what they want. Trust me, if you had some ravening wolverine of a g-g-girlfriend who was always slavering for your t-t-tackle you'd grow disenchanted and resentful, t-t-too."

Shelley orders another gin and tonic and I drift for a moment. I've grown disciplined in my brand of imbibing and can limit my feedings to twice a week. Still, it's been a couple of days and I'm feeling thin and antsy. This joint is crawling with tasty morsels that fit my ethical criteria, these preppie date rapists and their moronic, over-privileged female counterparts. I count white-rimmed nostrils exiting the restrooms and marvel at the lack of subterfuge. These people just don't care. They're untouchable.

Well, maybe.

The longer we linger the less I care for the establishment, stygian or not. This isn't the type of crowd I wanted to consort with. Crisp pleats and conspicuously placed designer labels, hair arranged with much expensive product. Shelley fits in rather well. He's always dressed just so, his clothes fashionable if a trifle loose on his spindly, concave-chested pipe cleaner physique. I'll admit that fashionwise I stopped moving forward around 1964, just before the Beatles hit these shores. I favor the coffeehouse all-black beatnik uniform. I even donned a beret for a while, but that was high school, so cut me some slack.

In this bar I stand out like a gangrenous thumb, my working class genes creating currents of status static. But I'm comfortable in my discomfort. As indomitable as these assholes may think they are, they don't scare me. No one does. I find that the one emotion that made me most human is the one that no longer dominates my life: fear.

Fear motivated, dominated, and influenced virtually every decision I'd ever made when I was a regular human person. I was always afraid of something or someone, some situation, some confrontation. I'd do anything to avoid circumstances that were thorny. If someone spooky was coming along I'd cross the street. If someone was smoking nearby and was making me cough I'd move. If someone was talking too loudly in a theater or museum I'd bite my tongue and ease myself away to safety. Almost everything people do is motivated by fear. They choose the wrong mate but stay together because they're afraid of being alone. They stay in jobs that leech away their quintessence for fear of trying something new, branching out, taking a chance.

I've come to the conclusion that fear is probably the most basic human emotion, and I think I miss it.

I miss fear.

Shelley gets up to use the can and I rotate the barstool around to get a good look at the crowd. Sometimes I hate having a code, but it's a survival tool. These assholes all have parents and jobs and people who'd make a fuss if their precious darlings went missing and got themselves expired. This joint is bringing on some seriously Coleridgean pangs of "Water, water, everywhere, Nor any drop to drink." It would be a nice change to feed from an unblemished throat. I've grown so accustomed to sucking sustenance from scabby, filthy, furry, leathery necks that I might keel over from shock if I got my lips on a smooth, pampered, pedigreed one.

A finger jabs me hard on the shoulder and I swivel back to see the bartender squinting at me with clear disdain.

"Your friend is our kind of customer, but *you*, you haven't ordered anything all night. We don't make money from loiterers."

"Like this place isn't minting money. My boozy buddy's doing enough damage to his liver for the both of us. Besides, I don't feel like shelling out four bucks a pop for seltzer. That's criminal."

"You better order something or I'm gonna have André evict your malingering ass, wise guy."

"The place is hopping. Why you gotta bust my hump?"

"'Cause I don't like your looks. You don't belong here."

"That I know."

"We like a certain kind of clientele here and you don't fit the profile. We're very particular."

"I see you've got no problem slinging drinks to underage chicks."

"They've got proper I.D."

"*Sure.*"

A couple of tiny teeners with newly sprouted booblettes—the kind gravity hasn't even figured out how to get a grip on yet—sidle up to the bar and pout with impatience.

"Hey," I say, "you're ignoring some of your 'certain kind of clientele.' Those little gals aren't going to pour their own drinks and take advantage of themselves, you know? The sooner you get 'em potted, the sooner these preppie assholes can lure 'em into an alley and rape 'em."

"That's it." He jerks me off the stool by my collar, pulling my face closer to his. His breath smells like the inside of Big Tobacco's rotting lungs. What a shock. I smile and he calls for the bouncer, just as Shelley emerges from the men's room.

"You're a real cutie pie when you're angry," I grin.

Like I'm ever coming here again.

André trudges over to the bar and sees the barkeep and me. I'm still in his clutches, still smiling. I've learned to smile with my lips tight, masking my teeth, masking my nature. It would be so easy to take this creep down—permanently. It would be impossible to explain it.

Or escape from it.

One of my many immutable rules: If at all possible, don't make a scene.

What this is, this little unpleasantness, isn't really a scene. It's a hiccup. It's a bar. They get this kind of thing all the time.

"Is there a problem?" André asks as he nears the two of us.

"Is there a problem?" Shelley asks as he nears his seat.

"You two ladies can take it on the road," the bartender says. "We don't need either of you coming around here."

"Now see here," Shelley says, full of indignation. "Unhand him," he says, pointing at me. Like I need him to kick into Galahad mode. Or is it Lancelot? Whichever. I've attracted attention. Jeering from the well-coiffed lunkheads, giggles from the females. They grin at me, the unfashionable lowlife that's about to get evicted from their turf. The scene has already been made. This isn't my fault. Do I let it go or do I make it worse? The bartender still has me in his grasp, so smug, so sure he holds all the cards. The bouncer also smirks.

• • •

I stumble out the door, the bouncer's meaty mitts ejecting me onto the pavement.

Scene avoided.

I won't even allow myself to look back in anger. I walk straight ahead, eyes on the sidewalk, playing connect-the-dots with the constellation of hardened gum blotches and cigarette butts. Shelley lingers at the exit as he exchanges stutter-free unpleasantries with André, protesting about the barkeeper's "bloody cheek" for treating patrons like this. He's tanked up, imprudent. I look back. André, fists clenching and unclenching, fast depleting his limited verbal arsenal, is losing his patience. He's got slaughter in his thuggish eyes. Shelley persists with his recital of grievances, moving on to the inadequacy of the drinks themselves, the paucity of gin in his gin and tonics, the bartender's brusqueness and inefficiency. Shelley's about one pussy hair away from sucking down a major knuckle sandwich. But that's okay. Let Shelley take one in the mouth for a change.

Why should his girlfriend have all the fun?

6

I'm picking lint off my tongue.

At least I hope it's lint. It could be anything. It could be this degenerate's peel. Why do I subject myself to this? All those able-bodied boozy coked-up children of privilege and I feed on stuff located several layers beneath the dregs. It's hard to enjoy your meal when it smells like shit dipped in vomit wrapped in something even worse. These fucking homeless bastards. The crazies. Don't they ever go to the shelter and get deloused? Take a shower? Anything?

Oh Jesus, it's gummy flakes.

This guy's got psoriasis on his eczema on his leprosy. Dandruff, worms, you name it. Dropsy. Gangrene. But there was no one else tonight. This was the guy. This was the guy and I was hungry and that's all there is.

I spend time with that sad sack Shelley—who didn't even have the good grace to catch a beating from that irate bouncer—and the hours evaporate and I don't get to go mingle and so I drown my sorrows in this meatball's blood. Food is *supposed* to be comforting. That's why so many people have food issues. They take comfort from their meals. Yummy candy bars and delicious richly seasoned full course dinners temporarily lift their spirits.

I get *this*.

I get to suck on a bum in the bowels of the city. I suppose I should be grateful that there are plenty of subterraneans to feed on, but come on. Can't I just once suck a clean neck? Is that too much to ask for?

After stashing his body in a nook I make for the platform and wait for my train. Thank goodness for Purell hand sanitizer. I squirt a big blob into my palm and massage it in deep, savoring the germ-killing lemony alcoholic tang. This is what it comes down to: a disgusting meal and a strong antiseptic lotion. My body's energized but I'm completely nauseous.

Twenty-seven years of sucking on lowlifes.

At home I hang my keys on the ring by the door, take off my boots, and make for the bathroom to brush my teeth and gargle Listerine. I'll watch TV for a couple of hours, try to decompress, veg out, try to forget who I am and what I'm not doing with my life. I used to have ambition but I'm not sure what it was. Something to do with photography, but I don't even own a camera. And what am I going to take pictures of? And for what purpose would I take them? To sit and look at them? It's not like I'm going to sell them or have anyone to show them to. So I watch TV. I go to the toilet. Maybe I read a little and then go to bed.

And this is my life.

Sound familiar?

7

Thursday, January 11th, 2001

The club and bar scenes always left me cold as an active participant, but as a spectator they can be fabulous. Let's face it: most people who frequent clubs tend to be assholes. The women—mercenary, shallow, vapid hedonists who wield the power between their legs and stuffed into their bras—while superficially attractive on the outside, are usually monsters. The men—desperate, smug, anxious, vain, arrogant, and preternaturally priapic (but, let's face it, often coke- or whiskey-dicked)—are sad brutal losers. Plus, most men—at least the straight ones—don't really like to dance; they go to clubs to find females to fuck or to suck their cocks (see previous). They're not looking for a potential spouse, they're looking for a potential lay. They want a one-off repository for their reproductive junk.

The females, on the other hand, *do* like to dance, and even the heterosexual ones find most of the men repulsive but will gladly accept free drinks and drugs until it's time for the well practiced yet seemingly off-the-cuff rebuff. The men, their low opinions of the fairer sex confirmed, tromp off in a misogyny-fueled snit looking to pick a fight with one of the weaker members of the herd. And bad music pulverizes everyone.

Throbbing with illicit substances and activity, the filthy over-stuffed bathrooms are where the plotting really happens. The women powder the insides and outsides of their noses. I can smell their nosebleeds. They change their tampons and pads—wings or not, I can smell that, too—and hatch stratagems. The men pee, pretending not to look at their urinal neighbors' wangs, comb their hair, powder just the insides of their noses, and shoot vaguely threatening glances at each other.

Women are tasty morsels I rarely allow myself to dine on; they just seldom fit my criteria for acceptable eats. Call me sexist but I have a rough time dispatching the fairer sex, even when they're total creeps.

Men are just gross idiots.

I finish my night of scanning—tonight it's all parades, and I hate a parade, so I need to unwind—and it's off to observe the low rent glitterati. On what I make I can't afford the cover charge for the highfalutin joints. And besides, their patrons give me a pain. Call me classist, but in general I hate the fucking rich.

AbSINthe, on Tenth Avenue and 18th Street, is often a good spot to observe and grab a quick meal nearby. It's a huge nightspot, formerly a disco roller rink, before that a plain old roller rink, and before that I had no knowledge of the joint. Probably something industrial. But it's cavernous and always packed. I just hope it's not gay night. Don't get me wrong, either. Gays are fine by me; I'm just in the mood to observe some of those unidimensional hotties with the souls of slate tonight. No matter what the weather they arrive bare-midriffed with pullulating décolletage. After I feed I want to see bouncing bosoms and material stretched tight across round asses. When you're old enough to remember *Playboy* before it showed bush, this "Girls Gone Wild" world of ours is not without its charms.

Right now, however, it's the environs surrounding the exterior of the club that interests me. There are always dubious characters girdling the periphery, lurking in the shadows behind chain link and parked cars—different kinds of predators than me. Ones, if you'll indulge some elitism on my part, with a lower purpose. Above the club a section of the derelict West Side High Line hovers, a pitted relic of a time when this section of town was vital beyond just a spectral nocturnal street life. Once upon a time those tracks saw heavy freight being shuttled from place to place. Even though it's been out of commission for over two decades the line isn't officially classified as abandoned. That's bureaucracy for you.

Now vagrants and runaways camp up there.

See? Not abandoned.

Back in the days before they built the elevated line, when the freights were running along the surface streets, they referred to it as "Death Avenue." Where I live in Queens they refer to Queens Boulevard as "The Boulevard of Death." The more things change, right?

Just a couple blocks south of the club the High Line blocks out a big patch of sky above Tenth Avenue—not quite a tunnel, but desolate and dark. I scope out the terrain, looking beyond the chain link that cages the Edison Properties parking lot. Nobody back there, which means the guard is probably actually awake. That's a sort of good news/bad news situation because I've got to be more furtive. No guard on duty really brings out the scum, so dining is less of a challenge. Okay, so the lot is empty save for the guard and some cars.

As I pass under the High Line it grows darker, no streetlights here. Seeing just fine, I begin to ape an inebriated stagger, the echoes of my steps ricocheting off the cold, striated walls. On the drawn industrial gates and shutters a shedding membrane of tags and pieces by long-retired bombers coats every available surface, the temporary lamination of spray paint flaking away; sad stabs at immortality.

Midway I stop and listen.

I'm not alone.

Good.

I force up a burp and feign undoing my zipper to take a drunken whiz, tunelessly crooning early Depeche Mode. That's *gotta* make me seem a real easy target. There's no lure more tempting than a urinating dipsomaniac to bring out the ne'er-do-wells. With my coat open, fanned out to mask my pantomime, I stage grumble to myself, chastising my uncooperative bladder.

"Oh, sure, now you're pee shy? Come on." Affecting a grating whine, "Come *onnnnnnnn*! Ya fuggin' *dick*!" I let out a fake, braying laugh at my totally retarded drunken bon mot. See, I'm yelling at my penis and using the word "dick" both as a pejorative and literally. Hilarious, right? I press a hand against the scabby wall and lean, head bowed, looking down toward my sham uncooperative groin. I look as vulnerable as possible.

"*When I'm with you baby, I go out of my head, and I just can't get enough, I just can't get enough . . . Aw, c'mon, pee!*"

A scritch of flat sole on wet cement.

A poor imitation of stealth—even poorer than mine of a drunk— as my attacker nears. Even with all the competing stenches down here I can smell his sour breath. And then I hear the snick and feel the pointy tip of something press into the small of my back.

"Don't fuckin' move."

This is the nervous-making part I hate. I just hope he doesn't get skittish and cut my goddamned coat. Me I don't care if he cuts, but avoid the haberdashery, dude. I'm not made of money and when you weasels get nervous and wreck my clothes I get really sore.

"Oh, come on, fella," I stammer. "I'm just trying to take a leak."

"Yeah, well this is a *pay* toilet. Gimme your wallet, real easy."

"You're gonna mug a man when his dick's in his hand? That's low."

He gives me a hard shove into the wall and growls, "Don't make me fuck you up, buddy. I just want your money is all, but I'll fuckin' kill your fuckin' ass if you gimme static."

I'm so grateful that he used his palm to shove me into the wall instead of sticking my frock I go along with the scenario for another moment or two. I let him push aside my coat and dig into my back pocket, which only has my key wallet. He's getting irritated, which isn't so good. I've got to remember to put my wallet back there when I'm trawling; make it easier for my marks to get their grubby little mitts on.

"Where is it? Where's your money?"

"In my front pocket."

"Turn around," he says. "Real slow. Try anything funny and I'll put some fuckin' steel in your guts."

This guy's a real poet. I love the adrenaline and testosterone-stoked bravura.

"Can I put away my . . . you know?" I ask, a slight tremolo in my voice. "I mean, I was about to piss, so . . . "

"Yeah, yeah. I don't wanna see that fuckin' shit," he says, sounding somewhat appreciative that I asked. I pretend to tuck it away then cooperate and turn around real docile like.

I hand him my wallet and as he reaches for it I yank him toward me and sink my teeth into his throat. Over the years I've determined that my saliva has some kind of anesthetizing toxin or some such, because my dinner always goes limp after the first couple of sucks. No muss, no fuss, just quaggy and obliging. I ease him to the ground and squatting with him splayed across my loins like some blasphemous imitation of Michelangelo's *Pieta*, I drain him. Dee-lish.

Until he looses his bowels.

I can't tell you how many potentially delightful meals have been ruined by this disgusting denouement. As I'm slurping up the last few mouthfuls of the red stuff the fetid splort of the brown and yellow stuff issues from south of the belt line. The hell with those last precious drops; I stand up and let him fall to the ground, relieved that his colonic discharge didn't get on me. After all these years you'd think I'd be smart enough to never rest one on my lap, ever. Always feed with them to the side or underneath, because a good three-quarters of them shit themselves, the bastards. Death, contrary to what you might have heard, has very little dignity. Want my advice? When you're relegated to the deathbed, *stop eating*. You'll leave your bereaved a much more genteel final image than the one of you stinking up the joint in poopy sheets.

Seriously.

Clothes intact and fully revitalized I drag the guy around the corner and take his knife, stab him a few times, then kick his face in. The more it looks like a run of the mill violent street crime the better. I hack at his throat a bit and pare out the section of neck I worked on, throw him into a dumpster, and then split and make for AbSINthe. With his fifty-eight dollars and thirty-eight cents in my wallet. Waste not, want not. If I leave the money behind when and if they do find the body it looks way more suspicious if the guy still has his loot. I know that sounds like a rationalization for stealing, but it's true.

"You're like an angel and you give me your love, and I just can't seem to get enough . . . "

"Yo, sugar, wanna date?"

As I walk past a small passel of working girls, a tall bosomy black one sporting an open lime trench coat, fuchsia fishnet body stocking, and six-inch platforms mimics my walk from the opposite side of the street. She wears an outlandish blond wig piled high on her head and way too much makeup. Were it not for the fact that I can practically taste her menses from here I'd think she was a trannie.

"Yo, serious! Wanna date good-lookin'?"

"That's a real sweet offer, but no thanks."

"Y'all don' know whatchoo missin'," she says, haughty but sweet. She's proud of the merchandise.

"That's probably true."

"Y'all look like y'all could use a dose of Vitamin 'P'!"

That and a dose of something else, too, were I still susceptible.

"That's 'P' for *pussy*, 'case y'all di'n't follow my drift!"

"I did. Thanks anyway. Have a good night."

"Y'all are missin' out on some *goooooood* pussy!"

"I'm sure. Nighty night, now."

"Mm-*hmm*." She turns on her impressive heel and struts back to her spot. The street, devoid of traffic, is silent but for the clatter of her heels clacking on the pavement and under her breath I hear her mutter, "Muhfuggin' *faggot*." When she rejoins the others I hear clucks of commiserative censure.

How sweet. Those gals have got a real sense of community.

I slink up to AbSINthe, unnoticed by the beefy doormen who huddle together for warmth. These big men in big leather coats shiver by their space heater and I can't help but wonder how the hookers up the block wearing tiny strips of cloth and strands of ass-floss never look cold.

"Hello?"

"Oh." He looks at me, eyes tearing from the cold. "Let's see some ID."

Carded at fifty-four. It stops being flattering after a while. I show the guy my passport and he looks back and forth from the birth date and my face. He rubs a thick fingertip over the photo to make sure it wasn't tampered with. That spot has been worn pretty thin. His mouth draws into a thin line of doubt and then he does the usual and attempts to catch me off guard.

"How old are you?"

"Fifty-four."

"What year was you born?"

"Forty-seven."

He narrows his eyes, then hands me back the identification, smiling.

"Damn, bitch. You must be taking all the right drugs."

"Must be."

He ushers me in. Even with my less than glamorous duds, these guys always let me in out of respect. In the land of the superficial, the best preserved shall rule.

The music, if you want to call it that, throbs. For a Thursday it's pretty packed, the dance floor bouncing under the straining feet, calves, and thighs of a hundred revelers. Multicolored lights flash on and off. The whole purpose of these establishments seems to be the sustained derangement of the senses. Between the booze, drugs, sound and fury—signifying *less* than nothing—the overall effect is both zestful and deadening. Gay night or not, there are still plenty of boys dancing with boys, well oiled and syncopated, like live-action Tom of Finland drawings. Even refueled I get tired just looking at all that pumping and gyrating.

But the girlies. They're out in full force this morning and looking like exotic yet poisonous flowers. I'd very much like to get acquainted with their pink, glistening Georgia O'Keefes. No matter the season, the pants are worn lower and lower on the hips. Some are so low that the pubic mound is the only thing keeping them from slipping down to their knees. Many of these girls have both frontal and dorsal cleavage, yet their hints of ass crack are luscious, not evocative of squatting plumbers' fuzzy bike racks. Sweat shimmers on the small of arched backs, the precious salty liquid gathering in sacral dimples. Blood is good food, but a concupiscent honey's perspiration is an epicurean delight. No nutritional value, but edifying nonetheless.

I guess what I'm saying is, I'm horny.

But here's the rub. I never mastered that whole Bela Lugosi sex vibe. I don't stare into eyes and breathily seduce with Eastern European charm. I'm still a Queens-boy, through and through, which blows. You'd think after all these years I'd just turn the knob to "smolder" and the ladies would come running. That's my problem: I'd turn the *knob*. Who uses *knobs* these days? How retro. I work in front of a computer every night but when I think computer I still picture some Irwin Allen fridge-sized monstrosity with punch cards and blinky-buttony lights flashing on and off. I'm fifty-four but look twenty-seven. That does not compute.

I elbow my way through the throbbing gristle, the plangent booming of the speakers—which *are* fridge-sized monstrosities—controlling bouncing bodies synchronized with the beats, coalescing into one big cologne and perfume drenched sweaty beast. The scent is heady and overwhelming. As I press through, small anonymous contacts are made. A stray elbow clips my sternum. A wobbling buttock brushes my crotch—down, boy. Hair is whipped in a feral arc and falls across my field of vision.

THRUM-THRUM-THRUM-THRUM!

This is not a place to meet a "nice girl," but a nice girl is not what I'm looking for. Nice girls end up being people you want to get to know and spend time with; maybe even make a life with. I can't do that. In all the years I've been doing this I've never turned anyone. I'm not *that* selfish. So I'll have to settle for maybe getting laid. Maybe. As if. It seems my life is just hunting for one damned thing after another. That doesn't make me any different than the next guy, but it gets old. Other than work acquaintances I have no friends. Not any more. Shelley doesn't count—he's just *the thing that wouldn't leave.* I don't bother cultivating new connections. I used to think I was a loner, but that was with the cushion of having friends available when I needed company. Now I angle for brief encounters that will lead nowhere.

Junk food.

Junk interaction.

Empty calories.

I used to think I was nocturnal, but even I have to admit I was a dilettante compared to what I became after the change. Staying up late because you want to is a lot different than getting to bed at the crack of dawn because you have to. When survival takes choice out of the equation it ceases to be groovy.

Seated at the bar is a pale Goth chick with straight dyed black hair, black lipstick, PVC corset and leggings, and stiletto heeled ankle boots. Her breasts are Grade-A, the size of honeydews, and appear to be natural. She's drinking a dirty martini. Since she's not drinking the commonplace Goth Bloody Mary I decide I'll give her the benefit of the doubt. She looks bushed and bored. She isn't looking expectantly this way and that so she might be alone.

I hate this.

The comedian Chris Rock had a bit about how you don't want to end up being "the old guy at the club. Not old, just too old to be at the club." That's me. But I'm the old guy who looks like a young guy. So I'm ostensibly this twentysomething single guy who doesn't follow popular music. Most pop music stinks. It always has only now even more so. I keep up with movies and literature. But music? Fuck music. And fuck the inflated windbags who make it. This isn't helping. I have to get my game face on. Just a hint of Bela and maybe I'm in there. But young Bela, not creepy old junkie Bela.

"Julia?" I ask, my face a pastiche of uncertainty. Sometimes this gambit works.

"Excuse me?" She looks at me askance.

"Oh, I'm sorry, you just look like someone I went to high school with, but the accoutrements threw me a little. Sorry."

"No, no, *I'm* Julia. And you are?" What are the odds? This isn't how this play goes. She's not supposed to be a Julia. She's supposed to be an Iris or Stacey or Brie or Cathy or whomever.

"Oh, sorry. I'm Phil." Why lie about my name? Why complicate things further?

"Phil. Phil? Did we have any classes together? I mean, you look familiar, but . . . "

I look familiar. That's so great. I'm sure I do, too. I probably look like a dozen guys she had nothing to do with in high school. Before she refined the whole creature of the nightlife persona I'm sure she was the dark teen temptress that all the boys wanted.

"*Waaaaiiiiit*," I stretch it out as I scrutinize her face, deep into the bluff. "Julia Dolan?"

"*Ohhhh*," she says, now smiling. "No, no. You've got me confused for someone else. But that's so weird." She's smiling now so I take the stool next to hers. "I mean, what are the odds that you'd think I was your Julia and I am a Julia but a different Julia, right? That's so freaky."

"Yeah, it's a little odd. You've got the same basic bone structure but on closer examination you're much better looking." Smooth.

"*M-hmm.* So, this Julia of yours, was she a girlfriend?"

"No, just a classmate that I had the hots for."

"So you figured maybe you're a little older, she's a little older, why not try to connect now?"

"Something like that."

"But I'm not *your* Julia."

"You look like Julia two-point-oh. The upgrade." Double smooth.

"I have a boyfriend."

And with a Samantha Stephens-like twitch of her nose her stumpy boyfriend shows up, wearing a floor-length maroon PVC duster, ruffled collar, platform boots, mascara, and a dyed-black waxed handlebar mustache and, for his age, advanced male pattern baldness. What a moron. As Julia and her sawed-off swain stalk off to the dance floor I turn and lock eyes with a tall, thin guy at the far end of the bar. He's smiling, but not come hither–style. It's the very definition of an enigmatic smile; Mona Lisa would be jealous. In fact, with the *sfumato* effect of cigarette haze clouding the background, this guy's evocation of *la Giocanda* is uncanny, gender notwithstanding. I stare right back. I'll be damned after the Julia 2.0 snubbing if I'll shrink from some wisenheimer.

And then he gets up and starts coming my way. Oh, goody. Maybe it *was* a come hither smile. I hate inscrutable expressions. Smile like you're mocking me, or smile like you want to fuck me, but don't confuse me. This asshole reminds me of Shelley, only scary. He sidles up to me and puts a hand on my shoulder. I don't mean to, but I flinch.

"Hey, I'd have hit on her, too, my man. That chick was finer than frog hair."

"Listen, I'm not in the mood to . . . "

"We have something more in common than an appreciation of fine ladies, though, and I'm not talking about high school. That's a cute bit. Does it ever work?"

"Listen . . . "

"So simple. 'You just look like someone I went to high school with . . . ' It's very cute."

"Listen, *seriously*, I'm not . . . "

"I saw your routine out on the avenue. Tasty, but so much work."

Fuck me. I didn't see anyone out there. Behind the fences, the parked cars, the lifeless weeds. No one. Sloppy.

"You normally feed on predators? That's hard work. I prefer the crowd in here. All these decadent, stupid children."

Maybe I'm a little slow on the uptake, but is he what I think he is? I haven't run into one of my kind since the one of my kind who made me one of my kind did his number on me. I wouldn't know to recognize one if he was right in front of me. Which I think he is.

"Can I get you a drink?" He smiles, this time in a recognizably friendly manner.

"I don't drink."

"Now *that's* funny," he says. "It wouldn't kill you to have a belt of something they intentionally serve here."

"Alcohol . . . "

"Gives you diarrhea? Sure, of course it does. It gives all of us the trots. It's all *sooooo* enchanting."

"'All of us'?"

"Did you think you were the only one? Does that even make sense? Let me ask you something. When you look up at the stars, as I'm sure you do, do you have the brass to think we're alone in the universe or do you ponder the myriad unimaginable life forms out there?"

My head is spinning.

"Are we talking about the same thing?"

His expression changes and he looks put out, his patience evaporating. Even with the plashes of indigo then magenta then orange then chartreuse light playing across his features, I can see how pale he is. Pale like me. Not powder pale, not artificial like the wannabes. He's not seen the sun in many a moon. His eyes are wide set and clear, the pupils contracted, as are mine. Everyone else here has dilated pupils combating the general murk. There's an aphotic quality to him, like those deep-sea creatures that live forever in darkness.

"I think you know what we're talking about."

I think I do, too.

Suddenly I'm not so sure I want a friend.

8

His name is Eddie Frye. It doesn't go. At Eddie's suggestion he and I leave AbSINthe in favor of someplace more tranquil. He wants to talk. The thing is, when you don't eat food or drink drinks, except for water—every living thing, even living dead things, drink water; you've got to stay hydrated—it's hard to find venues in which to hang out. You can't just go to Starbucks or the diner. Bars are about it, and they're no good either. Unlike me, Eddie's got the Bela thing in spades, and even though I'm reticent to follow, I do. Call it charisma. Call it whatever you want. He suggests we go back to his place, which is in the Village. Christ, if this is all a pickup, so help me.

We walk south along Tenth, past the group of pros. The tall trannie-like one with the blond wig hollers, "Found a boyfriend, huh, *faggot*? I knew you was a faggot, *faggot*! No straight man passes up this good pussy!"

"Friend of yours?" Eddie asks, bemused.

"Yeah." For some reason I feel a flush of embarrassment and guilt.

Eddie looks over his shoulder at the jeering hookers, all of whom have joined in, hurling epithets.

"Jesus, you put those walking petri dishes on HBO and suddenly they feel empowered enough to get lippy with the gentry. Lippy in the wrong way, at any rate. Although I can't imagine ever being desperate enough to slip my business into one of their gnarly grills. You ever get a close up gander at the dental work of your average streetwalker? My, my. Not pretty. Not like ours." Eddie curls his lip and runs his tongue over his pointy-pointies like the Pearl Drops gal. *Mmmmm.* "One shudders to imagine the shape of their cooters. Yikes."

In spite of myself I snigger.

"I used to do like you, too," Eddie says, "but only at the outset. That is, if I'm assessing your MO correctly, which perhaps I'm not." He smiles that pitchman's synthetic smile again. "Correct me if I'm wrong, but you're approaching the whole need-to-feed aspect as a sort of cut-rate vigilantism. You go for petty hoods, the homeless, persona non grata. Types who won't be missed by polite or even impolite society. Correct me if I'm mistaken."

I make a face.

"I didn't think so. So skanky to live that way. Excuse me." He reaches into his pocket and pulls out a small bottle of artificial tears. "I've got these awful dry eyes. It's a real nuisance. You'd think you'd leave this kind of picayune bullshit behind, but no." *Plip, plip, plip.* Three drops in each eye, then the bottle returns to the pocket. Wiping the corners of his drippy orbs with a hankie he rolls them then continues. "Honestly, dry eyes. So, the subterranean cattle, with the bad hygiene and all. *Ucch.*"

"Blood is blood."

"And a good thing, too. You're very lucky we're immune to everything hominid, disease-wise, or you'd be in trouble big, mister. What's your name, anyway?"

"Phil."

"Just Phil?"

"For now."

"I can dig it. *Ucch,* I am so not in a walking mood. Let's head over to Ninth and get a cab."

After a nearly silent ride—neither of us wanting to "talk shop" with a captive audience, even an ESL one—we get out on Christopher Street in front of a B&D specialty shop called *Die Lederne Faust*, which Eddie is quick to translate.

"It means The Leather Fist. Don't let the 'Faust' fool you; there's nothing literary going on in there. Unless you consider getting paddled by leather-bound books a belletristic pursuit."

In the display window a male mannequin wearing a black leather thong, handcuffs, engineer boots, and a full-head black rubber mask with no ear, eye, nose, or mouth holes kneels before a standing male mannequin wearing a studded codpiece, leather chaps, lug-soled boots, some kind of harness with lots of metal rings and straps on the torso, and a peaked Nazi commandant hat, all in black leather. The dominant mannequin holds a long lethal-looking black truncheon with a tip shaped like a massive glans. I pause and look at the mask on the slave's head. Grooved and bulblike, it looks like a toilet float.

"How's he supposed to breathe in that get up?" I ask.

"Maybe he isn't," Eddie says. "Come on."

Hoping the window diorama isn't prophetic I follow him into the vestibule. It's a walkup. Naturally he lives on the sixth floor. As I catch my breath on the top landing he undoes the final of his five locks and pushes open the door, standing aside to let me in. He's shifted from Bela turf into Max Schreck territory and I feel my balls tighten up, my scrotum doing the cold-water cinch. As I step into his foyer he closes the door behind us and for a moment it's totally dark. Not the usual city dark, either, which is never really that dark what with the exterior light provided by streetlights, store signs, marquees, etc. This is real dark. Country dark. We both can see fine and he knows it, but the effect is intimidating.

"You forget to pay your electric bill?" I ask, hoping to seem flip instead of apprehensive, which I am.

He turns on a low-wattage lamp and gestures toward his small living room. The windows, naturally, are covered with heavy drapes, in Eddie's case, thick plum velvet. A trifle fussy for my taste, but what can you do? I'm sure my window treatment would seem awful banal to him, judging by his décor.

I stand by the entrance to the room and wait for Eddie to sit down, which he does in a Queen Anne–style wing chair upholstered in material that matches the drapes. Purple is the dominant color in this room, the walls papered in deep heliotrope, a subtle Japanese pattern printed in faded gold almost subliminally visible atop the sea of deep color. The furniture is old and expensive-looking, all dark wood and more mulberry, orchid, perse, plum, pomegranate, violet, wine pigmented fabric, all atop a rich, no doubt hand-woven Oriental rug. Looking at these antiquarian trappings I wonder how old Eddie is. He looks no more than thirty-five but he could be centuries old, if the immortality thing isn't just a load of horseshit. I figure I'll wait to find out how old he is. I don't want to just ask. Maybe that would be crass, like asking how much something cost or how much your salary is. Let it come out organically in conversation.

"Sit down," Eddie says, pointing at the empty chair opposite him. "Don't worry, I didn't bring you here to rape you or anything."

"Uh."

"So, how old are you?"

So much for tact.

"Fifty-four," I say, smiling. "And you?"

"How old do you think I am?" He smiles a Cheshire cat smile and flutters his lashes, fishing for a compliment. I don't know which way the blade cuts. Is it more of a compliment to say older or younger?

"I don't know," I say, casting my eye around the room. "Uh, let's say, one hundred and twenty-five."

"Christ, do I look *that* bad?" He looks crestfallen and whips his head in the direction of a large elliptical mirror with an elaborately carved gold frame. "One hundred and twenty-five? *One hundred and twenty-five*? I'm forty-six," he says, sounding wounded.

"Well, fuck, I don't know," I stammer. "I mean, I thought you were fishing. I'd say a hundred and whatever and you'd pooh-pooh it with a limp flourish of your wrist and tell me you used to hobnob with Voltaire or some shit like that."

"First he tells me I look like Methuselah, then he's calling me limp-wristed. Need I remind you you're a guest in my home?" He crosses his legs tightly, then grins and says, "I'm kidding, don't get your panties in a bunch. It was a perfectly reasonable thing to assume. So neither one of us kicked it with Napoleon. So what? But I could introduce you to some folks who have. If you're into Eurotrash, that is."

Suddenly I've got a social calendar. My eyes drift away from his face and take in the room. High bookcases built into the wall filled with old leather-bound volumes. The classics. They look like first editions, but what the hell do I know? Maybe they're just good facsimiles. Maybe the furniture is ersatz antiquity, too. Maybe this whole thing is a sham.

"How old were you when you got turned?" I ask.

"Turned? You make it sound like milk that's gone bad. Thirty-two. But I did a lot of reckless living in those thirty-two mortal years. I admit it. I reckon I've got that preserved waxen look of a former junkie. Young yet hoary. I can dig it. So, you up for meeting some other bloodsuckers?"

"I dunno. I'm kind of used to being on my own." I sigh. I fidget. "I dunno, it might be nice to fraternize a little. It's not like I've gotta join some club or something, right? No hazing or membership dues or whatever."

"It's not a rotary club, Phil. Listen, next time there's a get-together you can come along with me if you want. Or don't. I'm not going to twist your arm. The wolf hunts alone and all. I can dig it. But the cheese stands alone, too. Know what I mean?"

• • •

On my trip back to Queens a sorry-looking double-amputee on a dolly tugs at my pants leg and gives me the doleful moocow eyes. I give him the fifty-eight dollars and thirty-eight cents. His eyes go wide and he farts in surprise. Speechless, he wheels away.

• • •

Back at my apartment I ponder cheese standing alone. I know exactly what Eddie means, but I'm so used to it. The thought of a social life with like-minded, like-afflicted allies is tempting, but it could also be a big mistake. I've never been a joiner, and whether it's the Shriners or Knights of Columbus or the Elks or Trekkies or whatever, when a group all sharing some fundamental link gather it's already too homogenous and stilted. Whenever I see events like that, like a Star Trek convention or a peace rally, I always think that those folks like what I like but they don't like it the same way. They take it way too seriously. Their misguided enthusiasm completely fucks it up. Couldn't this be the same thing?

I glance at my window coverings and they do look mighty bland. While I'm not ready to blow the nut on rich velvet, I think maybe it's time to spend some loot and gussy the place up a little.

Especially if I might be entertaining.

9

Friday, January 12th, 2001

How many pictures of businesspeople shaking hands can there be?

I've done six boxes already of every conceivable variation on that one stultifying theme. Young white male go-getter shaking hands with venerable white-haired white male captain of industry. Young white male go-getter shaking hands with other young white male go-getter. Venerable white-haired white male captain of industry shaking hands with other venerable white-haired white male captain of industry. Black young go-getter. Hispanic young go-getter. Asian young go-getter. Indian or other non-white, possibly Middle Eastern young go-getter. All wearing smartly pressed suits and power ties. Then the female counterparts. Then the "differently abled" counterparts. Then the "differently-abled" non-white counterparts. So far no retards, though. I guess mongoloids don't climb the corporate ladder. Not yet.

Mix and match.

Season to taste.

There are twenty-three more boxes of this stuff. Some are posed in front of seamless paper. Others are interiors of offices. Some are boardrooms. Some are lobbies. Some are employee lounges. Then come the blue-collar variations. Young white male blue-collar go-getter in hardhat, plaid or blue work shirt, jeans, and leather tool belt shaking hands with venerable white-haired white male captain of industry/foreman. And so on.

Power haircuts.

Power ties.

Powerful handshakes.

All posed by models.

The construction workers' fingernails are manicured and buffed, with not a trace of dirt underneath. No cuticles or hangnails. Please. Normally I don't get saddled with this kind of characterless stock photography.

Where are my actual events?

Where's my succession of accident photos?

Where's my succession of crime scenes?

Where's my illustrated menu?

Hell, at this rate I'd even take a parade or two.

Every brochure you've ever perused, whether it was for auto insurance or a medical policy or a timeshare in Barbados, was peppered with photos of models pretending to be something they're not. "Hi, I'm your friendly neighborhood pharmacist." "Hi, I'm your friendly neighborhood mortgage broker." "Hi, I'm your friendly neighborhood fill-in-the-blank." You get the picture. There are photographers whose entire stock-in-trade is shooting simulated laborers, models playacting at actually working for a living. Those are the photographers whose path took a dire turn— the ones who the musicians who do Muzak look down on. No one, and I mean *no one*, set out to make a career of being the best documenter of soulless android-like fake office drones.

No one.

I've made plans after work with Eddie, who said he'd meet me in front of the building. I'm praying that Shelley doesn't pull a "sur-

prise" visit tonight. I'd like to keep my human associates segregated
from my new bloodsucker acquaintance. Who knows, Eddie might
find Shelley irresistible. He has, after all, been marinating ever since
I've known him. But is gin a recommended marinade? I doubt it.

• • •

"You enjoying the change of pace tonight, Phil?"

Kate Abernathy enters my workspace wearing the wary expression of someone who expects the answer to follow to either be de-
servedly sarcastic or willfully insincere. I don't dislike Kate, but
she's hard to warm to. She always looks like she's on the verge of
tears, what my mother dubbed a "slap-able face." She's a collection of bland tics and mannerisms. If Kate were to bark at the
moon or go into some Tourette's-like bout of spewing obscenity
and make inappropriate pokes and gropes I'd be much more in
her camp. Instead she nibbles pencils, leaving flecks of classic
Dixon Ticonderoga yellow on my work area. She endlessly twirls
her mousy brown hair. She simpers. I don't trust people who don't
really have a laugh. She lets loose the simper after every sentence,
a discomfited little through-the-nostrils closed-mouthed tee-hee.

I respond with a curt, "No comment," and she twirls a lock,
makes the not quite giggle sound.

"At least it's not like the other night, you know? Or the night
before that, huh? I mean, all that carnage." *Simper*. "I mean, that's
a little hard to endure, right?" *Simper*? "I mean, all that blood and
guts?" *Simper*?

"It beats the heck out of specious corporate ladder-climbers.
Criminy, Kate, get real."

She titters, which is annoying but better than the simpering.
"Oh, *you*." Oh me indeed. "I mean, at least everyone looks like

they're getting along in those pix, you know? I mean, that's an improvement over death and destruction, isn't it?"

"No comment."

I'm not finishing this tonight. There's no way I can endure over twenty more boxes of this shit. After a few more hour-like minutes of dreary "good-natured" chitchat with Kate, she leaves and I resume slogging through. I complete eight more boxes, not bothering with color correction or any of my other quality control niceties—these pictures, bland as they are, tend to be perfectly exposed, in focus, and color correct. Grabbing my coat I head for the door, half an hour earlier than my usual departure time. Fuck it, I've suffered enough for one night.

I share the ride to the lobby with one of the other anonymous late-night drones. The same one I see several times a week and have never bothered to introduce myself to. In silence we ride downward, staring at our feet or expectantly up at the dwindling floor numbers. In the lobby he arranges his collar up over his scarf, nods a brisk adieu in my direction, and heads out the revolving door. The guard snoozes behind his massive granite station and I head out.

I realize I've told Eddie my usual time, so there's the better than average chance Shelley will materialize, if he isn't already lurking in the periphery, biding his time, lying in wait to ruin my night. I sit on a standpipe and fumble in my pocket for a paperback I've been reading and remember my mother's constant admonitions that if I read in the dark I'd get terrible eyestrain. Now I get terrible eyestrain if it's too bright. Mother isn't always right.

"Any good?"

I look up, expecting to see either Eddie or Shelley, but instead it's the security guard, out for an unauthorized smoke. He lights up a Salem and smiles in appreciation as he sucks the vapor deep into his lungs. Though the substance is different, I know the feeling and I return his smile.

"Yeah, it's not bad," I say, closing the book.

"I never been much for reading. The occasional magazine and whatnot, you know, *Sports Illustrated*, *Consumer Reports*, *Hustler*," he winks, "but books never grabbed me. Not that I got nothing against them, you understand."

"Sure."

"Be better if I did enjoy reading. Make the time pass faster doing what I do here which is basically nothing but sitting on my ass and grabbing the occasional smoke." He chuckles. "Don't be narkin' on me, now. Man needs his smokes."

"You're in the clear," I hold up my hand, middle and ring fingers pressed down to my palm with my thumb, my index finger and pinky up. "Scout's honor."

"Shit, that ain't the scout salute. That's the sign of the devil." He sniggers, taking a deep draw. "'Less you went to some scouts I never heard of. Maybe you one of them Webelos and shit." He laughs and I do, too.

"I never was a scout and never went in for the devil. What the hell do I know?"

"Yeah, me either."

The levity dissipates and that awkward silence between chummy strangers descends. He smokes in silence and I open the book again. A few minutes later he flicks the butt into the gutter and makes for the building, adjusting his belt, the holster hanging heavily over his right hip. He sees me eyeing the gun and he smiles again, this time ruefully.

"Fifteen years I been toting a piece and I never got to shoot no one."

"Maybe someday," I say, trying not to sound too encouraging.

"Yeah, maybe. Well, back to the grind," he says, pushing into the doorway. "You know, you're gonna get a eyestrain you read in the dark too long."

"Thanks, Mom."

He laughs as he goes back in.

I read another fifteen pages, periodically looking up for signs of my anticipated company.

"Philip."

Fuck. The surprise that never fails to not surprise. What assignation ended conveniently nearby tonight? With what imaginary lady friend was he partaking libations? I should just let him suck my cock and be done with it. It's the unrequited aspect of this whole farcical friendship that keeps him coming back for more. It's got to be. If I just gave in and did the nasty with him he'd lose interest. Wouldn't he?

I'm not willing to take that risk.

"Shelley," I exhale. "*Quelle surprise.*" Do I sound sufficiently sardonic?

"I know what you m-m-must be thinking, but I had d-d-drinks with that self-same l-l-lady friend tonight and once again g-g-gambled on running into you. Lo and behold . . . "

Yeah, right.

"So, are you f-f-free for a n-n-nightcap?" His chalky mien sends ripples through my alimentary canal.

"No, not tonight. I'm expecting company."

"*Aaaahhh,*" he says, drawing it out sinuously, "a tryst with the f-f-fairer sex, yes?"

"Not exactly." Christ, if Eddie shows up while Shelley's here . . .

I'm pretty sure Eddie's gay, but I can't really tell. He could just be terminally droll. But Shelley will want to latch on and come along. It's inevitable. Like some overprotective spinsterish chaperone he'll want to probe my new companion, check his fingernails to see if they're clean, look under the hood, kick the tires; *is this Eddie character good enough to hang around with his precious little Philip*? I shouldn't have to feel this way. So some of it is my own neurosis, granted, but come on. Am I going to have to change jobs?

"Not exactly," Shelley echoes. "*Not exactly*. How abst-st-struse. Well, I d-d-don't wish to be a third w-w-wheel."

Yes you do. That's why you didn't follow that sentence with a cheery toodle-oo and leave. That's why you keep standing there, a slyly insinuating leer forming on your thin lips. Ever since my marriage dissolved over twenty years ago you've lingered like a not-so benign tumor. All those years ago, when I spilled my guts to you—holding back a few choice details like the fact that I disappeared from my marriage bed to go hunt for street scum on which to dine—unburdening myself of as many truths as I could to help explain why my marriage had disintegrated, I saw you. I saw you, furtive as you might have thought yourself to be, rolling your eyes like my personal catastrophe was old hat. Smiling that condescending smile, that above it all superior smug smile, as if you'd always known it was a doomed relationship and its end was inevitable. Like I was the last one to figure it out.

You saw us fight. So what? All couples fight.

You eavesdropped on us making love when your evening visits would lapse into overnight stays that would then sometimes lapse into weekend sojourns.

So when I told you about my impending divorce you were rather blithe about it. You'd always made yourself a good companion to my wife, but once she was out of the picture you never jeopardized your relationship with me by keeping up with her, even though there was no acrimony from me toward her. How could there be? Her reasons for leaving me were quite reasonable. I'd been secretive.

How does one tell one's spouse that he's become a parasite who hunts and feeds on human beings? An unprofitable one, at that. I always took the money as a cover—make it look as much like a routine mugging gone awry as possible—but always gave it away to some needy-looking unfortunate sonuvabitch. It's always been my way of making amends. Keeping the loot in the family of the downtrodden.

And how does one explain that he's lost his job because he can't go to work during the day like normal people?

How does one explain not being able to go out for a stroll in the sunshine?

Or to never keep the drapes open?

How does one explain fangs, for Pete's sake?

That the marriage endured three whole months of my then new "lifestyle" is a testament to her patience and understanding. That no one believes in . . . let's just say it. Let's just get the word out. That no one believes in . . .

That no one believes in those *things* in a modern North American city is the only thing that kept our marriage going as long as it did. Insanity is a lot easier to swallow. So yes, we fought occasionally. And yes, you were a witness. But we gave it a go and when it collapsed your sympathy was insufficient. And yes, I bear a grudge.

"S-s-so w-w-when are you expec-pec-pecting your company?"

Are you still here?

Behind Shelley Eddie emerges from between two parked delivery vans, silent but deadly as Xyklon-B—*der überfart*. I could learn a thing or two about stealth from Mr. Frye. Even though the street is as quiet as a street in Manhattan can get, his footfalls make no sound. His smile is toothy, playful, his eyes glinting with bottled mayhem, and the cork is loose. One foot behind Shelley he speaks, and Shelley, ever-composed Shelley, has a knee-buckling spasm.

"And *you* are?" Eddie breathes, his voice liquid.

"Good grief," Shelley stammers, "y-y-you startled me."

"Oh, I'm sorry," says Eddie, who clearly isn't.

"Quite all r-r-right. Shelley Poole. And you are?"

"Phil's date." I wince, but I'm pretty sure Eddie's just fucking with Shelley, so I smirk. "Are you thinking of tagging along?"

Shelley beams with pleasure and says, "Well, if I'm invited."

"You're not," Eddie says, now serious. "I'm sorry," he says, again not meaning it, "but this is a private function. I'm afraid you wouldn't fit in."

"T-t-try me," Shelley says, hackles raised, dignity at stake.

Eddie leans in close and sniffs Shelley, who winces and recoils, uncertain as to the proper etiquette when a stranger—or anyone for that matter—takes a whiff off you in such an obvious manner. Eddie grins and says, "*Mmm*, don't think so. Not my brand."

"Hey," I say, trying to seem casual, friendly-like, "Like I said, Shel, it's a private thing. We'll hook up another time. Maybe you'll call first and we can make a concrete plan." Or at least give me the chance to worm out of the situation for once. Shelley, the ever obliging martyr, nods and wishes us well, and I believe he means it as much as I believed any of Eddie's apologies to Shelley. All this distrust can't be good for the soul. Good thing I don't believe in them. Souls, that is.

"Well, he's ghastly," says Eddie, hopefully out of Shelley's earshot. Actually, what the hell do I care if Shelley hears this indictment? "Do you work with that cadaver or what? *Ucch*, his breath smelled like a compost heap. Shelley Poo, indeed."

"Poole."

"If you say so. He's got an odd scent. Firewater plus something else. I dunno."

"So what's all this about your being my date? Let's get something straight between us . . . "

"Now *that* smacked of double entendre."

"Seriously, if we're to keep . . . "

"Listen, you're not my type, Philbo. You're a little too much of an ectomorph, you dig? I like 'em brawnier with a little meat on 'em. You know, real hairy-bearies, broad of chest and thickly befurred." He eyeballs me, brow knitted. "If we're going to hang, if I'm going to let you into my world, you've got to lighten up, buddy. I like the ladies. I get so tired of people assuming I like the cock. I have no problem with menfolk who yearn for the high hard one, but I happen not to be one, you dig? It's so boring. *Ucch.* Okay, so maybe I'm a little delicate looking. Maybe I'm a little more epicene than your average *Monday Night Football* couch-warming gridiron enthusiast, but cut me a fuckin' wedge. I like to bivouac at Fort Bushy, *entienda*?"

"You live on Christopher Street above a gay bondage boutique."

"So? I don't operate the fuckin' joint, Philip. Hop on the clue bus, bitch. I have a great rent-controlled apartment."

We both laugh.

"Okay, so can we get on with the evening? You feel secure that your dokus isn't in peril? Good. Taxi!"

Cutting across two very active lanes a cab swerves over and Eddie opens the door, gesturing for me to slide in first. The driver, an impatient looking Arab, chews his lip as he eyeballs the light that he's going to miss as I make to enter.

"Come on, get in," Eddie says.

"Yes, please to get in," the cabby chimes in. "The light we can still make."

I get in as the traffic signal turns red and as the cabby mutters under his breath in his native tongue. I'm glad I'm not multilingual. He drums at the wheel as the long seconds tick by until green returns. When it does he goes Indy 500, barreling back into the center lane, cutting off a *Times* delivery van. I look at Eddie and he smiles, saying, "One man's reckless is another man's eager."

"You want I taking West Side Highway or what?" the cabby barks.

"Whatever is fastest," Eddie says, egging him on. He looks at me and whispers, "If we're in a wreck *we* won't die, so live a little."

The cab races along Hudson Street and as our maniacal driver veers west to make the left for the highway another cab cuts him off and we're treated to the squeal of rubber on asphalt. Our cab misses the light and the driver bellows through his open window, *"How many moments you lose? You should live like a homeless, you idiot!"*

A loud thump on Eddie's window startles us and for a split second I think we hit someone. But we're not moving so that means something hit us. We jerk our heads to see what's what and Shelley stands there, eyes wide, a sphinxlike sort of not-quite smile on his face. We've traveled several blocks at high speed and there he stands, not winded. Eddie rolls down his window and in a courtly bow Shelley leans forward and pronounces with nary a stutter, "Enjoy your night, gentlemen."

Green. Go. The cab peels away and we both look back through the rear window to make sure Shelley isn't following. He stands there erect, immobile as the black slab in *2001* and twice as eerie. We're supposed to be the spooky ones, not him. Not mortal Shelley. Neither of us saw him following us. Did he run? Did he fly? Did he project himself from one location to another? Can he bi-locate?

"Your friend is a bit of a freak, isn't he?" Eddie says.

"No duh."

"Is he going to be a problem?"

"I don't think so. He's probably just a little jealous. Anyway, I hope not."

Seriously.

10

After another near silent cab ride we arrive on the Upper East Side at a modern apartment building, just off the FDR Drive. The concierge announces us and we walk across the bright lobby, both squinting as we pass under the four thousand watt chandelier, its heinous luminescence reflected from countless beveled mirrors and other polished surfaces. The lobby is just one shiny expanse after another. Gleaming brass fittings. Polished pink granite floors. When the elevator arrives we practically collapse into it, enervated. Mercifully, the elevator is dim, with dark faux wood walls.

"Even if I liked it bright, that lobby would give me the whim-whams," Eddie says with disgust.

"Amen."

The car rises to the fortieth floor where we get off and walk over to another elevator, this one to the penthouse. The operator is snoozing by the door, a lumpy little man of dubious ethnicity. He has a mole on the side of one nostril that is the size of a quarter. Eddie makes a face and points at it, silently mouthing, "Malignant. Dead in a month, tops."

"Raul," Eddie says gently, prodding him on the shoulder. "Wakey-wakey."

"Huh? Wha'? Whozzat?" Raul rouses himself, batting at the air like a demented kitten hopped up on 'nip. "Oh, it's you, Mr. Frye. Sorry, I was just catching a few zees."

"No prob', Raul."

Raul fishes a key ring out of his snappy uniform jacket and opens the door, rubbing sleep boogers out of his eyes with his other hand. The picture of refinement he is not. When I see someone like Raul I wonder what he sees when he looks in the mirror. We all view ourselves through our own disadvantage point, usually seeing someone less attractive than we actually are staring back. Just ask any woman. A woman with curves thinks she's fat. She doesn't realize men like those curves. A meaty ass is anathema to a woman, manna for a man. Is that nature or nurture? Who's to blame? So what does a troll like Raul see? Does he know that growth on his face is cancerous? Does he care? Maybe he is aware and anticipates the day he'll drop dead as a sort of liberation day. It's possible.

In the private elevator Raul adjusts himself in the indiscreet manner of a little boy and I wonder if perhaps he might be retarded. Eddie finger combs his hair and pops a mint, offering one to Raul who needs it. I suspect Eddie carries them with the sole purpose of dispensing them to those who offend his senses.

Mental note: start carrying mints, the curiously stronger the better.

"Penthouse," Raul announces, as if he didn't know.

As we step out of the box he begins picking the nostril that isn't partly collapsed by the nodule. Poor Raul. Poor soon-to-be-dead Raul.

"Okay, a little background," Eddie says as the elevator doors close, Raul safely ensconced out of earshot behind them. "This bunch doesn't play by your rules. They aren't out to cleanse the city by feeding on one bum or mugger at a time . . . "

"I'm not on some campaign to . . . "

"*Shh-shh-shh,*" he says, dismissing me with a fervent wave. "Don't get sniffy. This isn't about you. This is about *them*. In *there*." He jerks his head at the closed double doorway, eyes wide. "These are the, I don't know, the high rollers. They don't follow an ethical code. They're of the 'if it feels good, do it' school of philosophy. They do what they want, when they want, to whom they want, whenever they want."

"They sound charming. Why am I here? We have nothing in common." Eddie raises an eyebrow. "Okay, but that's only one thing."

"It's a pretty significant thing, you gotta admit."

"Maybe so, but that's like assuming just because you're black you'll . . . "

"I'm not black."

"You know what I'm saying. Like all blacks have something in common, by virtue of their skin color. But after that, what? You expect some black Wall Street guy to have anything in common with some dirt farmer in Mississippi? Not likely. Or . . . "

"Yeah, yeah, yeah. Don't hock me to China; I got your point. But they're an interesting group in there."

"Okay. You didn't make that clear. And it's *hock me in chinik*. A gentile like you misusing Yiddish gives me *tsuris*. Feh."

"So you wanna go in or what?"

Eddie presses the bell and after an elaborate series of chimes a painfully thin woman answers the door. Her face is like a mask, creaseless, the skin too smooth, with no visible pores. Is it a liberal application of base or is she really this unblemished? The burnished quality of her dermis makes my stomach emit an embarrassingly audible growl.

"Sounds like someone's hungry," our hostess says with a mild European accent, smiling in a way that displaces none of the skin around her mouth. I imagine when she steps into a bath the water level remains unchanged. "There's a buffet inside."

Eddie and I step into a round grand foyer replete with statuary recessed into alcoves in the curved wall. Above the double door- way is a recessed tympanum featuring an elaborate bas-relief sculpture of orgiastic revelers engaging in many variations of the nasty. Anthropomorphized mythological animals are involved, many bearing John Holmesian love-batons. Though I'm certain this isn't the intended effect, the entranceway reminds me of Disneyland's Haunted Mansion—corny. There's a forced deca- dence to the decor, like the bygone swing club Plato's Retreat in the heyday of New York's sleaze boom. I'll say this for Ms. Thing's antechamber, though: none of this is cheap. The floor's real mar- ble, as are the pillars, the lintel, the sculptures, the whole deal. What isn't marble is gold or bronze. Eddie waggles his eyebrows at me as if to say, "Don't judge them. Give it a chance." I prune my mouth, turning it into a little sphincter, but nod. We both follow our hostess through a thick ultramarine velvet curtain.

Again with the velvet.

"Welcome to our humble gathering," she says, her voice also velvety.

Enough with the velvet already.

Velvet is to bloodsuckers as fried chicken and watermelon are to stereotypical Negroes, or hooknoses and niggardliness are to the Hebrews, and as with any stereotype there will be plenty within a group's membership who'll be happy to live down to it. I step through the curtain and for a moment I think I'm tripping, having an unwelcome flashback to the time I suffered through Bob Guccione's explosive bout of cinematic diarrhea, *Caligula*.

"Oh come *on*," I blurt, my voice incredulous and more than a trifle judgmental.

Eddie shoots me a look, but it's too late. Our hostess turns on her heel and actually laughs, her face softening somewhat.

"It is a bit much, isn't it?" she says in her honeyed voice. "Take a minute to acclimatize. We'll get you settled, don't you fret."

She extends a long leg and steps down into the sunken living room, Eddie elbowing me in the chops. "You trying to embarrass me?" he hisses. "I extend myself and get us invited and you've got to be gauche? Show some decorum, Phil."

"Don't *hock me in chinik*," I say, grinning, and Eddie elbows me again and laughs.

"You asshole."

The scene is retarded. It's like these idiots are going out of their way to embody every preconceived notion of debauchery possible. Some are completely naked—more shades of Plato's, not that I ever went—others in partial states of undress. Some are even fucking. Many have blood dripping down their chins onto their bare chests. Maybe they could give out bibs only instead of a lobster they could have a human being printed on them. It's an obscenely large room—you could fit a couple of my entire apartment into it—the drapes open to display a panoramic view of the city, lit up and picturesque. This city, like many things, looks great from a distance. It's up close that the illusion is shattered and the endless blemishes come into focus.

In stark contrast to the foyer—Philippe Starck, to be exact—the interior design of this dwelling is crisp and modern to the extreme. No gothic overtones or even undertones, except for the use of velvet in the upholstery and drapery. The place oozes affluence.

"Can I get you *someone* to nibble on?" our hostess purrs, gesturing to a gilded cage full of gagged naked teenage boys and girls of every shape, size, and color. Gee, what's the age of consent in this state for being sucked dry by prodigal immortals? The teens gape at me with narcotized eyes. There's something very unappetizing about making eye contact with your dinner. The only reason people can pick their lobster is because lobsters have those blank black orbs on stalks. If they had live cows and lambs flashing those big expressive peepers at restaurants, only the most committed carnivores would eat meat.

"Uh, no thanks," I say, looking away. Cached reserves of PETA-like pity swell in me and I tamp the urge to swing into activist mode and liberate the livestock. Hell, looking at some of those nubiles, I'd rather fuck them than sup on them.

"Well, if you change your mind," she says, dangling a key from a thin gold chain. As she glides away she drops her robe and reveals a naked body so thin I can practically see through her. People at Auschwitz would've looked at her and said, "Quick, somebody get that girl a sandwich." Famished Third Worlders would be asking Sally Struthers to send *her* a CARE package. You get the picture.

I look at Eddie and he shrugs. "What, you don't dig the scene? Come *onnnnnnnn*. You just got here. Listen, I'm going to mingle. I'd like to make some introductions, but if you're going to be a stiff prick about it I'd just as soon go solo and let you handle yourself."

"Lemme catch up with you," I say. "I wanna check out the view. I'll be on the terrace."

"Idiot."

Eddie bounds into the fray and I slide open the glass door and step onto the flagstone terrace, closing the door behind me. Seated at a long rectangular polished steel patio table in the shadows a pair of well-dressed guests feed on a naked Middle Eastern-looking boy. They look up from their meal long enough to regard me with minimal curiosity then return to their repast. In another milieu the table and chairs would just be contemporary patio furniture. Here they're a pastiche of an operating theater.

At the rail I peer out at my hometown. I've wanted to leave for so long, but travel is difficult when you have to worry about different time zones. By the time you get to your destination, the sun might be coming up. One delay at the airport and you're well and truly fucked. While seeing Europe has been a dream for ages, I'm not willing to take the chance of mechanical failure on the tarmac. I'd risk dying in a plane crash, but a sunrise incineration? No thankee. I have to play tourist in my own hometown, keep reinventing how I see this burg. I've never seen it from this neighborhood at this altitude.

I can pretend it's new to me.

I can allow myself to think it beautiful.

Peering straight down I see another large terrace about ten or so stories below, and several floors beneath it another one, the building stepped like a high-rise ziggurat. Some deck furniture is there covered in tarps. I wonder if the tenants ever go out and enjoy the space they're paying a premium for. So often I've looked up enviously at balconies and penthouses and seen the decks vacant. It seems such a waste. The folks rich enough to have them are also rich enough to usually summer elsewhere. I think of all the great apartments in this city that remain unoccupied probably more than half of the year. Criminal.

Only dumps are occupied fulltime.

I turn and look back through the window at what's going down inside. A roomful of villains and rotters. No morals. No scruples. Twenty-seven years of sucking on dirty necks and like some sad voyeur I watch two ravishing beauties slurping the dregs from either side of the pristine neck of a runway model—at least she looks like a model. It's like sanguinary porno, a bloody *ménage à trois*. The slurpers, in sharp—or should I say curved—contrast to our hostess are both Junoesque lovelies, and I feel my own blood surging south into Groinsville. Now I really feel like some pitiable peeping Tom.

Fuck. I really want to hate this bunch.

Twenty-seven years with the possibility of innumerable more. Maybe a few hundred. Maybe even immortality, whatever that means. How many thousands of dirty necks belonging to the lowest of the low does that add up to? How many have I already had? Maybe two or three feedings a week. Let's call it two and a half. That's two-point-five times fifty-two times twenty-seven. You do the math, I'm no good at it. But that's got to be at least three thousand. I've killed at least three thousand of society's dross. And not one of them made the papers. That's how unimportant they were. I know. I used to scour the papers looking for my handiwork, always terrified that someday they'd come looking for me. But they never have. No one misses the invisible people. How long can I cleave to this self-imposed moral imperative?

I'm tired of massaging palmfuls of Liquid Silk into my pocket Graf Orlok.

I want to play slap and tickle with those buxom bloodsuckers.

I'd like to suck a clean neck.

With resignation and a weak attempt to reconcile what I'm about to do, I slide open the door and step into Sodom.

11

"So our coy mystery guest has decided to join the party. *Trés* cool." The emaciated naked hostess rises from a velvet—yes, *velvet*—divan and drifts across the marble floor. Though her feet are nestled in glittery high-heeled bedroom slippers her footfalls make no sound whatsoever. "I've not had the pleasure of learning your name, precious. I'm Adélaïde Sigismund." She offers a hand so delicate I'm afraid to touch it, but when she takes mine her grip is unexpectedly firm. "Don't worry, wall flower, I'm sturdier than I look."

"Uh, Phil Merman." My name sounds gracelessly Jewy and I feel weird saying it to this undead *shiksa*. Don't get me wrong, I'm an atheist, through and through, but around acutely non-Jewish types I feel self-conscious. My nose, while decently proportioned—thin, even aquiline—suddenly feels like it belongs on Goebbels-approved anti-Semitic propaganda.

"Like the great songbird, Ethel," she says without a hint of derision.

"Uh, yeah. No relation."

Though I've worn decent clothes—nice stuff, Banana Republic— I feel disheveled. Maybe, what with the clothing-optional atmos', I feel overdressed. Who can say? I feel clammy is all. Out of my element. This should feel like a homecoming yet I feel like the foreign exchange student arriving in class and hiccupping, "So solly, me no speaka de Inglese."

A few inches shorter than me, Adélaïde places a hand on my chest and looks up into my eyes, her smile growing on me even if her anorexic body makes me more than a little uneasy. "I really do wish you'd join the party, Phil." From her lips my name sounds like a sly accusation. "Really, dearest, pull up a davenport and rest yourself. You'll see. You'll get comfy and then you'll be all about the banquet." She presses my chest, pushing me back and my knees fold over the edge of a seat I didn't know was behind me. Maybe it wasn't. Maybe some unseen servant slipped it behind me, silent as his mistress.

Eddie, spotting me from across the room, claps his hands and hollers, "Philly Cheese-steak finally makes nice with the party girl. Atta boy, champ!" He waves me over and I excuse myself from the company of my nude hostess. "Phil," Eddie says as I join him in a conversation pit, "these are Winston and Jackie. We're just discussing the best names of TV shows of all time."

TV trivia I did not expect. My God, bloodsucker parties are the same as regular people parties. The horror. Winston and Jackie, both seated together, practically entwined, mercifully clothed. Queens-boy that I am, all this casual nudity is discomfiting. I'm not used to seeing strangers' breasts and penises flapping around. The couple on the sofa—a massive burgundy leather number softer than a baby's skin—is dressed in latest haute couture. It must be haute because it's hideous but radiates costliness. Clothing this ugly has got to be expensive. Winston is thin, but not Holocaust thin like Adélaïde. He's about as skinny as Shelley who, sad to say, would fit in here better than me. Winston's lank jet-black hair hangs over one eye and he affects the world-weary dissoluteness of a veteran rock star. Maybe it's not affect. Maybe he is a rock star.

Like I said, I can't be bothered following every pop act to come down the pike.

Jackie's legs are draped across Winston's lap and she looks well gorked, though not as bad as the teens in the pen. Those poor doped up cattle are probably better off not knowing what'll be hitting them soon. What promises lured them here? Drugs? If so, fait accompli. Sex? Fame? Money? Immortality? Sorry, Charlie.

Maybe they're real punks, the bad seed. Maybe they deserve what's coming. I know what kids are like these days. Maybe they're too stupid to live. Maybe.

"Best name for a TV show, ever?" Winston says, pausing to do a "you're-not-going-to-believe-this" face. "That's *easy*. *Coke Time*, back in the fifties."

"There was a show called *Coke Time*?" Eddie says, not believing it.

"Yeah, but it wasn't like that, obviously. Not in the fifties. It was this fifteen minute musical show hosted by Eddie Fisher, you know, Carrie's dad."

"Carrie, the telekinetic chick?" Jackie says. "You mean Sissy Spacek?"

"Nah, nah. I mean Princess Leia. Carrie Fisher."

"Oh, right. She'd liked to have been on *Coke Time*, I bet. Didn't she used to be a druggie?" It takes one to know one.

Eddie chuckles and I feel dizzy. This is some mundane shit. Where are those buxom honeys who were doing the tandem slurpity-slurp-slurp number on the model? If I'm going to get into the party vibe here I'd rather take my chances on those Rubenesque twin suckers. I hear the clink of metal on metal and look over my shoulder to witness one of the teens, a short-bobbed Asian girl, being led out by a muscular naked man. He's presumably one of "us," though I'm not feeling much kinship for those gathered here. The Asian girl comes out of the cage on her knees and the man slips his semi-erect penis into her mouth. From the zombified look on her face I gather her response, which is to suck on it, is just preconditioning. Twelve-year-old girls blow Bar Mitzvah boys in the limo on their ways to becoming men at the bema, so why am I surprised? Blame MTV. Fellating on autopilot. The man closes his eyes and grins toothily.

"First you suck me," he says, patting her head, "then I suck you. Fair's fair."

Seeing this actually quashes my ardor for the twins. They're not really twins, but you know who I mean. This is all so juvenile.

"Is it always like this here?" I ask, speaking to anyone who cares to field the question.

"Yeah, pretty much," Winston replies, patting Jackie's thigh. "Just business as usual at Maison Sigismund. Pretty great, yes?"

My lack of response is my response.

"You don't like? Maybe it's because you're sitting on that couch like you're waiting for a reprimand from the boss. Or nun. Or principal. This isn't Sunday school. Are you a prim prude or a seditious libertine? The latter is much more satisfying."

Behind me the man comes. In a flash he pulls out of her mouth and bears down on her, sinking his fangs into her throat, his dripping erection vibrating like a diving board. All that's missing is the cartoon sound effect: *BE-DUGGEDA-DUGGEDA-DUGGEDA*! She makes no noise. Her eyes register no surprise, no horror—just mindless acquiescence. I get up and walk in the opposite direction, my appetite for clean neck, dirty neck, any neck, ruined. Eddie makes to get up and follow me but I shake my head and gesture for him to stay put, keep talking trivia. If immortality means an eternity of this shit, include me out.

I spot a wet bar and make my way over to it, the bartender smiling in a way I'm unaccustomed to. Welcomingly.

"What can I get you, sir?"

"Just some water."

"Nothing stronger?"

"Booze and me don't cozy up."

"No, something *stronger*?"

He draws a curtain and behind glass are more naked teens bearing the same somnolent expression, shackled in an upright position with hoses affixed to their necks, held in place by silver bands, IV drips in their arms. The bartender produces a tap and shoots a rubicund sample squirt in a crystal goblet.

"Some prefer the Senegalese, but it's a bit piquant for my taste. I'll admit I'm not the most well-versed sommelier."

I follow the line of the tap back to the throat of a boy darker than any you'd find locally. This is pure African black. There's no miscegenation here.

"Senegalese?" I say, my voice cracked.

"Of course. All our selections are imported. Perhaps Vietnamese is more to your liking, or maybe the Peruvian? The Ecuadorian gets raves, I must tell you. As a newcomer, perhaps you'd like something less cheeky. The Romanian is practically like domestic stock. Very mild."

I don't know what to say. The bartender drinks the sample himself, licking his lips.

"Waste not, want not," he says, smiling warmly. "So, the Romanian?" He nods his head at a pale ash-blond girl and my stomach lurches. This is not what I expected. This is not juvenile. This is major league fucked-up shit.

"Are all the, uh, are all the victims . . . "

"Tut-tut," the bartender says, irritated. "There are no victims. The livestock are not victims. You can't look upon them that way. That's naïve. We treat them well, very humanely. Far more humanely than they were treated in their homelands. When we send our produce buyers out to replenish our stock we make sure they are liberating the livestock from intolerable circumstances. We keep them comfortably numb, as the song goes."

"They're human beings."

"And you feed on what?" Adélaïde sidles up to me, still nude, still grinning. "Are you judging us? How long have you been a member of our caste? If you're some rank buckwheater then this naïveté is permissible, but if you've been at it for a while you can't afford this kind of outlook. It's hypocritical at the very least."

"But . . . " She's right. I got nothing.

"Listen, precious, the Third World is our Costco, only when we buy bulk it's young adult human beings. You think they're being taken from good homes? You think if we didn't take them that their futures would be bright? These youngsters are just being emancipated from predestined drudgery and ugliness, ethnic cleansing, systematic rape. Eddie's told me a little about how you prey on the canaille."

"The what?"

"The riffraff. If that's your poison, so be it. But don't come into my home and act like you're better than us. Okay, precious, maybe you sing harder for your supper but your supper is human, too. We all know that sucking a rat or a cat or dog or a monkey doesn't do the trick. For better or worse, humans are our source of sustenance, and I for one would rather take nourishment in refined and convivial surroundings. Fine if you like hunching over some filthy miscreant in an alley, but what does that make you?"

"But does it all have to be so . . . baroque?" I gesture at the tapped teens. "That's grotesque."

"I think it's whimsical. To each his own." To the bartender she says, "The Ecuadorian, s'il vous plaît."

"See, very popular," he says, filling Adélaïde's glass. She takes a dainty sip and closes her eyes with pleasure.

"Just have a glass," Adélaïde says, her voice sibilant, hypnotic.

I've made a life of rationalizing what I do to survive, but this is different. But is it that different?

"Just have a glass," Adélaïde says, her voice sibilant, hypnotic.

I look around the room. Naked bodies. Blood dripping down their faces. Blood on their chests. They have such a surfeit of the stuff they waste it. It's so American it's practically patriotic. You never see blood on my clothes, unless it's my own. The beautiful people are always so fucking heinous. Why is that? I want to fuck those two voluptuous girls I espied from the terrace. I want their flesh pressed against mine. I want to knead their buttocks, gnaw on their nipples, caress their faces and breasts. They might be twenty years old. They might be two hundred. I want them. I hate them. I hate everything. My head is pounding and the universe feels too small to contain the hatred welling up in me. I want to tear a hole in the universe and let some of it out.

"Just have a glass," Adélaïde says, her voice sibilant, hypnotic.

So I do.

This is not good.

12

Saturday, January 13th, 2001

"You pounded us good," Sheila says. Sheila. She's the redhead. Ribbons of her long, elaborately curled hair fan out across my chest like an exit wound. My head is swimming, drowning. What the fuck did I get up to? What's the brunette's name? With effort I push myself up against a padded headboard. I'm in a gargantuan, ornamentally carved canopied bed. More fucking velvet. I'm naked. So are my two bedmates, Sheila and what's-her-name. So I bagged them and I can't even remember it. Story of my life. I hope I had a good time.

"Did I?"

"He doesn't remember. I guess when you said you were going to fuck our brains out you fucked your own out instead."

"I said that? That doesn't sound like me. I mean, I'm no poet but I'm not usually that . . . coarse."

"Oh, we liked it. It was refreshingly workmanlike. We're so used to the effete ninnies who frequent Chez Sigismund. They fuck like they're afraid their dicks'll break off. Granted, if anyone's pussies could snap off a joint . . . "

What's-her-name guffaws. It's not a musical laugh.

"I think somebody had more than their limit last night," Sheila continues. "Besides, until you build up a little resistance to the shit Adélaïde pumps into the vittles' veins, you'll get knocked for a loop every time." Sheila laughs and hers is more pleasant, more feminine.

"The vittles' veins? I've drained heroin and crack addicts to no ill effect. I mean, what kind of additive are we talking here?"

"It's like a preservative or something, but not. I don't really know. It's like the Colonel's secret recipe. It's some herbal organic blend Adélaïde uses. Her staff cooked it up decades ago. Adélaïde's been at this for a long, long time. Like scary long. Anyway, crack, heroin, LSD, booze, all that stuff, we know that filters out, but Adélaïde's house blend is a potent concoction. It's a little psychotropic. Very disorienting for newbies. Like you."

I get out of the bed and don't bother looking for my pants. Not right away. I figure my companions are acquainted with what I'm packing, so why cover up? Contempo low-wattage wall sconces light the room softly, the walls covered with textured mauve suede. The windows are completely hidden by steel shutters.

"What time is it?"

"It's like maybe elevenish?" Sheila says, tapping at her bare wrist.

"In the *morning*?"

"Those shutters really do the trick, don't they?" what's-her-name chimes in.

I regard the shutters; brushed steel and completely impervious to sunlight or anything else, I'd imagine. Adélaïde has major bucks, that much is certain. I reckon from the sounds of it she's been in the blood-sucking game for a mighty long time and knows a thing or two about a thing or two. Creepy thin though she may be, she's got the secret to longevity, and from the looks of this joint, fine living at that. I can't say as the honey-dripping dissolution of Maison Sigismund does much for me. I finally realize the adolescent sex fantasy of nailing two inarguably hot chicks and can't even remember it.

I'm not sure how, but for now I'll blame the Republicans.

Sheila steps out of bed, sliding into a red satin kimono. Now, with what's-her-name still under the duvet and Sheila covered up, I feel stupid naked. I'm about to pull on my pants when I notice how flaky my crotch is, the dried physical evidence of my tri-une boinkfest. Looking like a panko-coated turkey neck my crusty Johnson reminds me of recent throats I've sucked, and I feel sorry for myself. Crusty Johnson. Sounds like a bayou bluesman with crotch rot. I ask where the shower is and Sheila points. My head pounds and I realize I'm hung over. Great.

The bathroom. What can I say? Another huge chamber. My life is looking less and less palatable. Fucking Eddie. I wonder if he's still on the premises or whether he booked. After a luxurious half-hour shower in a quintuple-wide glassed-in stall with benches and massaging jets coming from every conceivable direction—this is the best thing about my visit here, let me tell you—I dress and groom, brushing my teeth with my finger and a blob of sparkly Aim. When I reenter the boudoir, Sheila and her companion are gone.

Scattered about the living room like crippled refugees, Adélaïde's guests slumber, some clustered together entwined, others solo, all *au naturel*. One couple still engages in the mechanical act of intercourse though both appear to be fast asleep. Plashes of blood stain the floor, pooled, coagulated, wasted. I bust my hump to feed on society's castoffs and these spoilt degenerates just let the blood fall where it may. Call me an old-fashioned socialist, but come the revolution. That's all I'm saying.

Fully dressed, Eddie taps me on the shoulder and grins. I frown and his grin evaporates.

"*What*? Oh come *on*, you must've had a good time. I saw you scamper off with Sheila and Brianna."

"Brianna?"

"Brianna. Anyway, how can you be pulling a puss after canoodling with those two spicy numbers all night? I heard some of what was going down in there and the joint was jumping."

"Don't get me wrong, it was nice getting my dick wet, I guess . . . "

"You guess? He guesses. *Ucch*, you're impossible. I take you to the nicest place and you get all shirty with me."

"I don't even remember what happened . . . "

"Ah. Adélaïde's *spécialité de la maison*. Strong medicine for the inexperienced." Eddie chuckles.

"Whatever. Listen, Eddie, I'm sure I had a wild time, even if I can't remember a damned thing, but this group doesn't exactly bingle my bongle, you know what I mean?"

"Ingrate. I try to introduce you to greener pastures and you spit in my face. There's another group you might fit in better with, but I'm not sure I should bother hooking it up."

"I don't mean to seem ungrateful, honest I don't, but I dunno. Maybe I'm just not a society type. I'd love another crack at Sheila and Brianna, maybe one I could actually remember, but . . . "

"Okay, okay. I'm sure you're welcome here any time, but maybe it was too much for your plebian little mind to absorb all at once. Especially that house blend. I've got to admit, first time I had a snootful I was *non compos mentis* for two full days. You're made of sterner stuff to be up and about a mere few hours later. That's hardcore, dude."

"Where's Adélaïde? I should thank her for her hospitality."

"Such a nice boy. Such good manners. Hey, we're not going anywhere, champ. Sundown's not for another . . . " Eddie consults his watch, "about four and a half hours. Wanna watch some tube? Sixty-inch plasma screen."

"How apt."

"Maybe a little hair of the dog?" Eddie gestures at the glass case full of stupefied Third Worlders. The curtain is pulled aside, the bartender nowhere to be seen. I feel that latent activist urge again, wanting to spring the poor bastards. Who knows, though? They're probably all brain damaged from Adélaïde's herbal preparation.

Fuck 'em.

Eddie shrugs and sprays himself a snifter of blood from one of the taps. No one in the case reacts in the slightest so I have no idea whose he's consuming. Vietnamese? Romanian? That Ecuadorian everyone's so gaga over? He takes a sip, smacks his lips in a theatrical manner, and toasts me lofting the glass in my direction and throwing a TV pitchman's wink my way. Clearly this is Eddie's home away from home, his comfort zone. Here the guests roam free, doing whatever they want to whomever they want whenever they want—a precinct for total abandon.

Silent as ever, Adélaïde slips unnoticed into the room and presses her hands into the small of my back, startling me.

"Sleep well? Or did you sleep at all? There was quite a ruckus before the quiet returned."

"I, uh . . . "

"I'm just glad you settled in and allowed yourself a good time. I feel inadequate as a hostess if even one guest has an unsatisfactory visit."

"No, no. Everything was just dandy."

Dandy?

I don't want to be trapped here for another four plus hours. My hostess, my alleged brethren, kind of give me the creeps. Okay, so some of the females are extremely hot, but the venue is icky. For all its pricey, ostensibly tasteful accouterments, Maison Sigismund feels as sleazy and confining as a cum-spattered peep booth in the glory (hole) days of Times Square.

Me want out. Now.

Damned sun.

Taking Eddie's cue I follow him into the entertainment room and we settle in to watch Cronenberg's adaptation of *Crash*. It's a good movie, but I must admit it feels too familiar, like I've just lived it. These thrill-seeking perverts, these James Spaders and Holly Hunters and so on, I'm surrounded by them. They're bored with life eternal, whatever that means. Life eternal? *Life eternal*? Pretentious much? Eternal life. Please don't let me slip into cloying Goth-speak. *Life eternal*. Somebody kick me in the nuts, quick. But eternity? Eternity?

Eternity is like those Powerball lotteries. I mean, if you asked people to consider—and I mean really truly utilize their gray matter and consider—what eternity meant, the idea of so-called capital "P" Paradise would be nightmarish. Most people can't figure out what to do with themselves for a long weekend. Can you imagine what they'd do if confronted with the actuality of eternity? Any eternity? I'm not talking damnation. That's a no-brainer. Anyone would say that's for the birds. But even the nicest, best, most wonderful things in the world would get old after, what, a few hundred years? And we're talking infinity here. We're talking the great boundless unending forever.

That's not enticing, that's terrifying.

So, like those mega-lotteries where, let's face it, most people who win don't have a clue as to what to do with the winnings— they'd be just as happy with a million or even a few hundred thousand—eternity is something they'd have no idea what to do with. It would be torment. I mean, scientists, brainy, deep-thinking scientists can't wrap their heads around the concept of the boundless universe. It's too hard. It's too big. It's so big that big isn't even the right word to describe it. Because big indicates it's still got an end to it. But it doesn't. If the universe actually had an end it would mean something even bigger existed, because something must exist within something else, right? So that would mean the universe was contained within something even larger. So wouldn't that be the universe, too?

So *that's* eternity. And no sir, people would not like that one bit. But most of the bozos who believe in an afterlife, who believe in eternity and Paradise, they don't have the cerebral prowess to consider the bigger picture. They envision Heaven—eternity—as sitting around stuffing Doritos into their faces, not gaining weight, and watching their favorite sports or sitcoms or soaps forever and ever. These are people who are incapable of introspection or deliberate nonlinear thought. If you asked a rational person which they'd rather have, either one hundred and fifty years of guaranteed satisfaction and pleasure or eternity in Paradise, they'd choose the former. No contest. Eternity is a long fucking time. Longer even than the lines at Six Flags Over Buttfuck.

• • •

Back in the confines of my apartment I consider everything I've seen in the last few hours. Eddie tells me he knows several more groups of our kind scattered throughout the boroughs. He thinks maybe I'd fit in better with a less high-flown group. I don't know whether that's a dig or not, but in spite of myself my appetite has been whetted for companionship. And clean necks. Looking at this snug little dwelling I've been calling home for the last fifteen years is as depressing a sight as I've laid eyes on in ages. This is my microcosm. It's not like it's a bad apartment, really. It's fine. It's adequate. I've got a nice big bedroom, likewise living room, an eat-in kitchen I've never eaten in, good foyer. Bathroom. It's tidy. I like the furnishings I've chosen, though I should spring for a new sofa. I've got my books and movies and home entertainment setup, even if my TV is only a twenty-seven-inch plain old CRT.

This is comfortable.

This is familiar.

Uh-oh, has contempt been bred?

And now I'm on an eternity kick. I'm considering my own possible immortality. It's not the first time. But here I am, fifty-four, a middle-aged man in a young man's body. My brain works fine. My body's tip-top. I've got a nice complexion, tight pores. I'll never need Viagra. I fucked two shapely honeys and I can't remember a goddamned thing. Ain't that a bitch.

So, for the time being I guess Eddie can continue to be my Virgil.

I'll take another tour of Hell, reconnoiter, see if any of its other denizens float my boat. If not, something's got to give. I'm thinking immortal though I may be, I might choose a shorter life than that of Joe Average.

And in the meantime, I've got laundry to do.

13

Monday, January 15th, 2001

Back to the carnage. The ordinary whir of the scanner stirs up images of my equivalent of comfort food: dead bloody humans. Unlike the caged teens at Maison Sigismund, these folks spent their hemoglobin the old-fashioned way. No high-tech gimmicky neck-nozzles, just plain old death by misadventure. I love that euphemism. *Death by misadventure*. It sounds so much zippier than "accidental death," don't you think? It conjures images of Kilimanjaro more than slipping in the tub.

Label: "Maureen Dooley. Cypress Ave./East 138th St., Bronx. 6/16/00, early morning; 7th St./btwn. Ave's. A & B, Lower East Side. 6/16/00, late morning. ©2000 Metropolitan News Media, Inc."

Ah, Maureen, the gorilla my dreams. No-fucking-around Maureen. The first sequence is a gruesome connect-the-body-parts string of images of a romantic little South Bronx double subway suicide. Seems these two lovelorn Latinos might've had some problems, maybe disapproving families. *West Side Story*, Bronx-style. Capulets versus Montagues, only in this case Riveras versus Rodriguezes. Maybe one was Dominican the other was Puerto Rican. Bad blood there. Who knows? The frustrating thing about these images is that there's no accompanying text other than the label with the time, date, and location. Sometimes you luck out and there's a newspaper clipping, but mainly it's just the pictures. I've made up many tales of proletarian intrigue to go along with these gory pix.

Anyway, the sequence starts on the platform, then descends and travels along the tracks one chunk at a time. These two were obliterated; must've been caught under the wheels because they were dismembered like they'd been through a massive Cuisinart. Legs here, torsos there, bits of head, brain, teeth, eyeball, etc. Maureen, bless her sour lens, ends on two of the most morbidly poetic images I've come across to date, one the setup, the other the punch line. The setup is a close-up of his left and her right hands held in a permanent romantic clutch, the fingers interlaced, her red nail polish offset by the spatter of small droplets of blood across their palms. Then comes the kicker, a pulled back shot revealing both hands leading up to arms severed midway to the elbow. Oh, Maureen.

In the words of ol' Shaky, "Where civil blood makes civil hands unclean."

The second Maureen Dooley documentation is of the aftermath of an autoerotic suicide. Is there anything less dignified than one of those? Poor schmuck with his head in a clear plastic garment bag, his face obscured by vomit splattered across the interior, his shriveled gray putz still clutched in his contorted dead fingers. Dry spooge clumped across his fuzzy belly. On the grubby bed linens just the hint of colonic discharge—oh how I *hate* that postmortem colonic discharge.

In these shots the cops make no attempt to hide their equal parts amusement and disgust. One holds up to Maureen's unforgiving lens the material our departed onanist was abusing himself to and though it's a close-up of the stroking matter you can make out the cop's mouth contorted in a hideous chortle. It's an image torn from an—I'm just guessing here—early-sixties vintage catalogue, maybe Sears, of a lady with a bouffant wearing a girdle and bullet bra.

In the backgrounds it's obvious this guy was a packrat hermit type. Piles and piles of books and periodicals. The windows covered by cheap, tattered, discolored plastic shades. You can practically smell the staleness of the air in the room, the air quality now further diminished by the soiled sheets and moldering cadaver. One hopes the bag over his head contained the barf smell.

And this is Maureen Dooley's life.

Maybe she set out to be a photojournalist covering wars abroad. Maybe she wanted to do catalogue work. Maybe there's a double irony in the Sears girdle model image—maybe Maureen shot that early in her career. Maybe that's why the cop is laughing. Doubtful, but you never know. The world is choked with coincidence and cliché.

Consider this: you're walking down the street in Manhattan, minding your own business. Suddenly some whacko comes over to you with an aluminum colander on his head. He stops you, his eyes urgent; he pleads for you to take care, that the aliens walk amongst us. It's his duty to spread the word. It's yours to heed his warning. He moves down the street repeating this spiel to anyone who'll listen. And you think to yourself, that was such a fucking cliché. Every bad movie you've ever seen where bumpkin comes to the big city has some montage of the protagonist encountering wacky city archetypes. You, urbane city dweller that you are, roll your eyes and think what a hack the filmmaker was to include the nut with the foil hat.

But now you've encountered him in the flesh and you forgive the filmmaker, at least for the moment, because this shit happens all the time. It's one cliché after another out there. The riven Rican

Romeo and Juliet; how cliché is that? So Lover's Leap in the Big Apple isn't as picturesque as a rugged, windswept promontory; it's still Lover's Leap. It's banality incarnate. Same goes for the masturbation demise. You think he intended to die while yanking his pud to Miss Bullet-tits of 1962? He was just experimenting. His mother cried when she found out her baby boy was dead, and worse yet she had to make up a lie as to how he passed on to his final reward.

And the cops laughed.

You wonder how the call to the next of kin went down. Did they show sensitivity? Did they just treat it matter-of-factly? Did they stifle chuckles or seem judgmental? Jesus, people are always gilding the lily. Isn't a normal orgasm enough? Now who's judgmental? Sue me.

• • •

Several such boxes later I call it quits for the night, tucking Kate's note of apology into my file. I keep them. They amuse me. I have dozens. Maybe a hundred. There's no shortage of grisly slides for me to scan. Not in this world. Not in this city. And this is always local stuff. There are photos like this taken in every burg in the country. Maybe the whole world. Millions of gruesome death scene photos. They say death is a part of life, but isn't it really that life is a part of death? I mean, which lasts longer?

Think about it, then you tell me.

14

Saturday, January 20th, 2001

Used to be a time I could sit in front of the boob tube stuffing my face with donuts or sandwiches or cold cereal. TV is often better when you're eating. Maybe mastication takes your mind off how passive and stultifying your relationship with the idiot box is. It's not like I keep blood bags in the fridge. I don't even know if cold blood would be satisfying. I miss chewing. I haven't chewed in decades. I don't do gum. Sometimes I wish there was a blood substitute—actually, I wish that quite often—or something to mitigate the bloodlust. A Nicorette kind of product. Or a patch. Maybe if I was working the jaw, chewing my cud like a good couch potato should, I'd find watching television, doing nothing, somehow gratifying.

So sometimes it's the theater of life that provides the diversion; that passes the downtime between work and foraging for consumables. For the last fifteen minutes I've been sitting in my unlit living room watching this plug ugly Latino guy across the street fucking his lady. His face is contorted by exertion and concentration, both of them standing, he nailing her from behind, she clutching the window sill for support. The way he's gripping her hips in his white-knuckled hands, the way he's slamming his pelvis against her ass, his expression, all I can think is, *he doesn't love her*. Maybe they've been married for fifteen years and the familiar sight of her aging flesh repulses him. Maybe each ripple of her haunch-meat horrifies him. Maybe he just hates women. Maybe he's wishing she was a guy. Honestly, what difference does it make? Who cares if he loves her or hates her? So it's a hate fuck. So what? What difference does anything make? Why bother caring? Why bother doing anything?

This is unacceptable. Fifty-four years old and I sit in the dark, a sad misanthropic voyeur making up personal histories for strangers I couldn't care less about.

As a finale he pulls out and dribbles a few sad globules onto her buttocks, squeezing them out like the dregs from a tube of toothpaste.

This is my life?

My downstairs buzzer rings and I convulse in alarm. I look at the clock. Six thirty-six in the evening. Saturday. No work. Too late for a package, and besides I get all my parcels delivered to work. I can't make it to the post office if I miss a delivery. *Duh*. Eddie still doesn't know my last name or where I live, so it isn't him, even though we've got plans tonight. Should I play dead and not answer? I hesitate then decide to let it go, not answer. Ten minutes pass and I've moved from the window to the couch succumbing to television-induced torpor when my actual doorbell rings, followed by a series of knuckle knocks. Whoever this is they got into the building. They've shown determination. Maybe it's the cops. Maybe one of my meals finally proved to be somebody someone else cared about. Great. I need this like a hole in the head.

"Who is it?" I shout, trying to sound threatening.

"It's Sh-sh-shelley. I w-w-was in the n-n-neighborhood and th-th-thought you m-might like some c-c-company."

Oh *JESUS*.

"Yeah, uh, okay. Gimme a sec', I gotta just . . . " I pantomime needing to get dressed even though I already am. Midway through the gesticulations I stop and chastise myself for being a complete idiot. With my chin on my chest I slink to the door and unlock it.

"I hope I'm not int-t-truding," Shelley says, his thin lips drawn like a curtain over his bad teeth. In the thirty plus years I've known Shelley, ever since our student days, I've only seen his teeth once or twice and they were terrible. Maybe that's why he affects the British accent when drunk, which is invariably. Like now.

His breath precedes him through the door.

"Well, you are, but it's okay. It's not like I was splitting atoms or anything." I gesture feebly at the mute television and Shelley nods with a languid smile—his only kind.

"Yes, I w-w-was visiting an ailing r-r-relative over at Elmhurst Hospital and th-th-thought I'd drop by to s-s-see you, if it's convenient."

"Yeah, yeah. Sure, whatever. I mean, I'm in for the time being so why not. I'm heading out in a while, though, just so you know."

"A date?"

Why is he always so interested in my love life?

"Yeah, maybe. Not really. No. I'm just getting together with a friend."

"A friend," he echoes, skeptical.

"A friend. Right."

"Your n-n-new confrere Edward, p-p-perhaps?"

"What, like I've got to clear my social calendar with you? Okay, so Eddie was a little brusque with you the other night. I apologize on his behalf, but . . . "

"You n-n-needn't ap-p-p-pologize for the w-w-way your chum addressed m-m-me," Shelley says, full of noblesse oblige. "He's a

grown m-m-man and chose his w-w-words intentionally, I'm sure.
I was intruding on your date . . . "

"*It wasn't a date.*" I sound too defensive so I notch it down. "Why
does everything coming out of your mouth have to sound so
insinuating? It was two guys getting together. That's not a date. A
date comes with all kinds of baggage and implications. Date is a
sexual lovey-dovey romantic term."

"Okay, Philip." Sounding wounded. Oh, to wound Shelley. To
put him out of my misery. Would anyone really miss him?
Methinks not, but I'm not willing to take that chance. Mental
images of cops at the door. "You mind?" he asks, producing a bottle
of his favorite poison from deep within his seemingly bottomless
coat pocket.

"Why would I mind? You gonna swig straight from the bottle
or you want a glass?"

"Please."

I go into the kitchen and Shelley follows, taking a seat at the
small breakfast table I've never used—at least not for breakfast.
The occasional crossword puzzle, maybe. Though I keep the place
clean I'm sure there's a thin layer of dust on the tabletop. I sit
down across from Shelley and he pours a generous tumbler of gin.

"You wouldn't happen to have any t-t-tonic, would you?" he asks,
knowing the answer. I shake my head. "Maybe a wedge of lime?"
Again I shake my head, adding a shrug. I don't even keep my
refrigerator plugged in. Why pay to keep the air inside cool 24/7?
"So be it," Shelley says. He gulps a mouthful and my throat burns in
sympathy. Gross. After polishing off the tumbler and pouring another in silence he looks up, his eyes moist, and says, "I tell a lie . . . "

Uh-oh, confession time. And the Brit accent. Is that Glaswegian
I detect?

"Do tell."

Don't, *please* don't.

"I weren'a visiting an ailin' relative in hospital." The stutter gone, Scotty just beamed in. Fabulous. "Ach, I feel a right prat tellin' ye this, but I've been feelin' a wee bit out of the loop lately anna you're the only one I kin rely on to be a good ear." Lucky me. "We don't fraternize the way we used to, Philip. Not any moore. Not for a long time now. *Ach*, 'tis been such a long time since I felt we really connected and I wonder what I've done to alienate ye."

I've got to leave soon. I've got to primp and get ready for my "date" with Eddie.

Shelley stares at me, looking up past his nearly hairless eyebrow ridge, eyes supplicant, lonely, dejected, dispirited, doleful, forlorn, funereal, gloomy, grieving, lugubrious, melancholy, mournful, piteous, pitiful, rueful, sad, sorrowful, woebegone, wretched. Out, vile jelly. I have no answer only because the answer comes too readily. Why do I suppress it?

"Hey, people hit fallow periods in their relationships, Shel. It happens. We've known each other a long, long time. It's bound to happen. It'll get better. Give it time." A kind lie or uncharacteristic optimism?

"*Ach*, I know, I know. I'm just bein' a wee bit sensitive on accounta me ailin' relation in hospital."

"I thought there was no relation in the hospital."

"And ye'd be right. Forgive me. I am feelin' a right bastard, though. I'm all messed up t'night. Truth be, and I swear it's the honest t' God truth, I hit me lass an we broke up."

"You hit . . . ? You hit Little Miss Blowjob?"

"That'd be the one. I'm a shite an' I knows it. I hate meself. *Oogh*. Ye'll be excusin' me for a tick, I've got to visit the bog."

He staggers out of the room clutching the walls for support.

Tragic Shelley. Misbegotten Shelley. Why, when I find him so off-putting, do I still associate him? *Because he's my last tie to my human life.* I guess that's it. That's what he has to offer. It's not the pleasure of his company; he's just the only tangible thread that leads back to when I could get a tan.

I'm a fucking sentimentalist.

It's ten after seven. I said I'd meet Eddie in Union Square Park by the statue at eight. I've really got to get ready and Shelley is taking his sweet—or should I say sour—time. From behind the bathroom door I hear the unmusical trumpeting of a championship bout of the Hershey squirts. Dear God, the man shows up uninvited then paints my porcelain with his muddy feculence? God damn it. I putter around the kitchen killing time, sponging the dust off the tabletop, recapping Shelley's emptied bottle, tossing it, hoping that the bathroom will air out before I go in to freshen up. Fat chance. After several flushes Shelley emerges looking even more washed out than usual, daubing his eyes. He's been shitting *and* crying.

"S-s-sorry about the pong."

No such luck.

"Well, I just needed to talk," he says. "I know ye'll be needin' to gussy up for your assignation, so I'll be toddlin' off then. Thanks for bein' an ear. You're my good friend."

He hugs me and I can feel his ribs through his shirt. If he and Adélaïde ever got nude together . . .

Okay, I just made myself throw up in my mouth.

Shelley departs and warily I enter the john. The stink of Shelley's diarrhea sets me gagging, the latent mental image of his and Adélaïde's kindling-like bodies still stoking my nausea. Hand clutched over my nose and mouth I manage to throw open the window to let the fresh air in, the foul air out. Thanks Shelley. Thanks for the visit. Thanks for the stenchful olfactory souvenir. The

Union Carbide Bhopal disaster has nothing on the toxic effluvium left in Shelley's wake. How can such a skinny man create such a funky miasma?

• • •

On the subway a young black woman sits down next to me, her thigh brushing up against mine. Though I've done nothing she glares at me like I've just molested her. She clucks loudly, sucking air between the wide gap in her front teeth. She's reasonably well dressed in a sort of vintage brown collegiate plaid pantsuit, loafers, very bright red lipstick, and a retro-styled wig—very Supremes. Her head keeps making little jerks, her blazing eyes following everyone who gets up or gets on or off. In an angry, flat, hateful monotone she says, "Don't touch me. Nasty. Nasty fucker. Nasty fucker. Nasty fucker. Buncha whores."

I keep reading.

To a homeless black woman begging for change my nutty neighbor says, "Slut. Whore. You sing? You gonna sing and dance? Nasty. You need to go to church. Big fat ho. Nasty. Slut."

To a homeless black middle-aged man who announces himself as being in his late fifties, cold, hungry, and having no benefits, she says, "You gonna sing? You gonna dance? Nasty."

I scootch along the bench away from her and she shifts her glare back to me. "Don't touch me." She brushes off her shoulder like she's whisking away cooties. "Nasty fucker. No. You're not doing that. Nasty ho." I begin to smile, wanting to laugh at her. "What are you smiling at? Nasty. Slut."

I bet her blood is bitter as gall.

• • •

Eddie waits by the statue of Gandhi and when he spots me he taps the crystal of his watch and shakes his head. I'm twenty minutes late.

"*Tsk-tsk,*" he tsks. "You're lucky I'm a patient fellow, otherwise you'd be hightailing it back to whichever godforsaken outer borough you live in, robbed of an evening on the town courtesy of Eddie Frye."

"The subway . . . "

"Whatever. It's okay. So, tonight. *Tonight, tonight, won't be just any night . . . *" His singing abates and he grins. "Tonight should be more your cup of tea. No society types, just plain folks who happen to be like us." He stifles a laugh and I wonder what the hell he has up his sleeve. "No, seriously. These are good folks. You'll like them. They're a diverse group."

We walk west across the park and go up 16th Street. Midway to Fifth Avenue we stop at a commercial building and Eddie presses the video intercom. A crackly voice asks who's there and Eddie announces us. The camera raises and lowers, settling on a view it likes. Satisfied, the buzzer sounds and the door unlocks. We step into the lobby and Eddie rings for the elevator.

"What, no preamble?" I ask.

"Last time I said too much. Let's just let this one happen more organically. I don't want to color your opinion."

"Okay, fair enough."

We arrive on the fifteenth floor and get out. The hall is plain, the plaster in need of patching here and there. Dulled semi-gloss hospital green paint covers the lumpy walls. This is a far cry from the dripping opulence of Maison Sigismund. I feel more at home, and relax a little. Maybe Eddie got my vibe and has tailored the evening to fit. It might be nice to rub elbows with others like us who aren't decadent bastards. Eddie rings the doorbell and a small woman opens it a crack, then, seeing Eddie, throws it open wider and beams.

"Eddie, you haven't come round in ages!" She hugs him and then acknowledges me. "Who's your friend?"

"Deirdre Callahan, this is Phil."

"Just Phil?" she asks.

"For now," Eddie says, smiling.

"Hm," says Deirdre. "Well, come in, come in."

We step into a plain foyer with some stains on the wall. Between the foyer and the next portion of the space is a steel security door with a small window of safety glass webbed with chicken wire. Above us are two strategically placed video cameras, one facing the outer hall door, the other the inner one. Eddie raises his eyebrows and says, "Can't be too careful, right?"

We're buzzed in again.

"So," Deirdre says, tentative, looking me up and down. "You're joining our little group? You *look* normal enough."

"Yeah, well, all things considered, I guess." Normal enough?

We walk up a bare hallway and as we round the corner I could kill Eddie. I suppose I should have guessed such things exist. I mean if we can exist, why should we be exempt? Our kind? But to see it in the flesh? I want to laugh and cry at the same time. Seated in a semicircle doing kindergarten activities—coloring with crayons, making macaroni pictures, weaving dream catchers, stringing lanyards—are a group of befanged mongoloids. Where's Diane Arbus when you need her? Mixed in with the Down syndrome cases are a few other defectives, some physical, some mental. Deirdre looks at me and her comment sinks in: "You're joining our little group? You *look* normal enough." What the fuck did Eddie tell her about me? That he found me wandering around Times Square drooling and picking my ass?

"I'm not a retard," I say, my tact temporarily on hold.

"Maybe a social one," Eddie says, and any pretense to hold back levity dies. He cracks up, bending over, slapping his knees.

"Oh. Eddie," Deirdre says, schoolmarmish, disappointed. "You're such an," she lowers her voice, "*asshole*."

"Remind me to murder you later," I growl, channeling Moe.

Eddie keeps laughing and Deirdre looks up at me, embarrassed.

"I had no idea," she says. "Eddie told me he was bringing me a new potential resident. Clearly he thinks what I'm doing here is some kind of joke."

"Oh come on, Deirdre, it's funny. If you weren't so close to it you'd see the humor."

A tug at my jacket casts my glance down on a tiny crone with a large light bulb-shaped noggin, her forehead huge and swollen, her little birdlike nose hooked and pointy. Her eyes, clear and intelligent, lurk between puffy lids and massive eyeglasses—the kind favored by old Hollywood leading men, like Gregory Peck or Robert Mitchum. Her small mouth is pursed and nearly lipless. Perched atop this huge cranium is a thrift store wig and I think back to the crazy foulmouthed black woman on the subway.

"I bet this wigged out scene is fuckin' your shit up big time," she says in a high, Munchkin voice. "Fuckin' madcap low-rent *Cuckoo's Nest* bullshit. Ken Kesey can suck my withered cunthole, the hippie rat. You tryin' to catch flies, bitch?" she says, nodding at my gaping maw. "For serious, this is one motherfucker of a scene."

I feel helpless. Who is this creepy off-color wizened creature? I notice her clipboard.

"That's right, a-hole, I work here. What, like I'm ever going to mix in polite society or get invited to any of Eddie's faggoty society clambakes? Yeah, maybe as the entertainment. Maybe so's they can charge a nickel to poke me with a stick. So this hideous little bitch has got Progeria. So fuckin' what. Like you're any bargain. Like I asked for your blessing. You're not the fuckin' Pope of me, bitch, so kiss your own rings."

"That's enough, Connie," Deirdre says, voice stern. "Don't make me give you a timeout."

"Timeout? Give me a timeout? Just 'cause I got turned when I was eight don't mean you can treat me like a fuckin' child! I'm a hundred and fourteen years old, you scrawny-assed dyke. Fuck! You think any of these bent-headed cocksuckers would do anything you said without me backing you up? You ever seen *Freaks*, bitch? 'One of us, one of us,' my *ass*! We *don't* accept you! Just 'cause you suck blood doesn't mean you're down with the pack, missy. Not by a long shot." She throws down the clipboard in disgust and storms out of the room. "Show me some respect, you skanky-assed whore!"

"Progeria?" I ask, flabbergasted.

"Yes," Deirdre says. "She looked a hundred and fourteen years old a hundred and six years ago. They practically burned her at the stake. They thought she was the devil's child. She's from *Maine*."

"Oh," I say, nodding as if I know what the hell she means.

A door slams and in the arts and crafts group a small scuffle breaks out between two of the mongoloids, one male, one female. The male, fists clenched, grimacing, takes a swing at the female and connects with her nose. The sound is like a ping-pong paddle on a slab of beef, sharp and moist. The female yawps in dismay, covering her face, the usual collection of exaggerated concave and convex extremes. She lets out a peal of such high frequency my ears pop, and Deirdre scoots over to break up the fracas.

"What is this, Rico?" she shouts.

"She stole my . . . *something*," he says, words thickened, eyes narrowed, obviously lying, oblivious to his obviousness.

"Lisa, did you take something that didn't belong to you?"

The female, Lisa, shakes her head vigorously, like a dog drying itself after frolicking in the ocean. She holds up her palms, which, save for a smattering of blood, are empty. Rico's eyes go wide at the blood on Lisa's palms, as do Lisa's. "Food," Lisa says, marveling. She licks her palm and Rico rocks back and forth, eyes wide, greedy. Lustful. He lunges at her and begins licking Lisa's muzzle, tonguing her nostrils. He begins sucking them, drawing blood and snot, but not yet biting into the meat and cartilage. Deirdre flips.

"What have I said about this kind of thing? Rico! *Rico!*"

Nothing. Rico's not interested in a lecture. Dinner is served and Lisa is pulling away from her ravenous compeer. She's making awful noises, muffled and wet as Rico sinks his fangs in, not wanting to stop. Lisa's eyelids flutter as she pounds at Rico's head, stubby fingers a motion blur as her panic rises. She's suffocating and so am I. So is everyone in the room, all eyes on hers, even Eddie's. I look at him for a second, and though he's not stricken dumb like me, he's not laughing.

"A little help," pleads Deirdre and I pull the "who, me?" move, looking over my shoulder at Eddie. I must remember to have words with him when I regain the ability to speak. I flap my arms helplessly and Deirdre tugs me by the elbow toward the melee. Nearer my God to thee, and all that jazz. *I want out.* Gimme the lair with the teens of every flavor hooked up to taps. That's looking a lot more my speed right about now.

"What the hell am I supposed to do?" My voice is whiny and I feel embarrassed at the sound of it, but really, I'm a little outside my element here.

"Rico's new. Just grab him and pull him off without damaging her face too much. Regeneration or not, why make a bad scene worse? Let's try to keep her nose on her face. I'll try to pull Lisa away from him."

"I . . . uh . . . I . . . Okay."

Lisa's eyes are bulging, in jeopardy of popping out. They're wide, but unfocused. Swimming. She doesn't seem to be breathing, in her hysteria seeming to have forgotten how. I place an arm around Rico's thickset chest and a hand over his nose, trying to both pull and suffocate him. His mouth is adhered leech-style to Lisa's nose, so maybe if I cut off his breath he'll relent. Deirdre is hectoring him about not attacking our own kind, never to feed on our own kind, etc. I flash to snippets of the Sayer of the Law's speechifying in *The Island of Dr. Moreau*. "Not to go on all fours; that is the Law. Are we not Men? Not to suck up Drink; that is the Law. Are we not Men? Not to eat Fish or Flesh; that is the Law. Are we not Men? Not to claw the Bark of Trees; that is the Law. Are we not Men? Not to chase other Men; that is the Law. Are we not Men?" Add, "Not to suck Blood of a Bloodsucker; that is the Law. Are we not Men?"

We are Devo.

Rico's not hearing any of it, so Deirdre is just venting, reciting the rules for the room's benefit. I wonder, though, as I tug and pinch this wriggling man-child, if drawing blood from one of us is even beneficial. Does our blood have the same life-sustaining properties as human blood? I've considered this once or twice over the years, but I've always concluded ours was no good. I imagine ours is somehow corrupted. Maybe that seems judgmental. Okay, not corrupted, but altered. Definitely. How could it not be?

Rico's mouth comes away from Lisa's snout, gulping air. Mission accomplished? Not hardly. He turns on me with a fury I haven't encountered before, mouth open wide and terrifying. He looks like a baboon, blood streaked all over his face, teeth huge and sharp, the spaces between them wide and disturbing. Ropy strands of blood-thickened saliva loop down from his lips and make contact with my face, creating a web as they stick. Is it just my imagination or does it burn? He's making sounds but if they're words, I don't recognize them. Somewhere beyond the enraged man-mountain I hear Lisa sobbing, but all I'm thinking is, *The hell with that retarded bitch! Someone get this monster off of me! Now!*

Rico lays a forceful open-handed swat square onto the center of my face. Over my internal roar of heightened distress I hear something crunch inside my skull. What's Rico have against noses? I feel mine fill up with everyone's favorite liquid refreshment and squirm. Rico is fucking strong. Like, crazy strong. Stronger than me, that's for goddamn sure. It's all I can do to keep his face away from mine, his jaw snapping at me. He's like a bipedal pit bull, bred to fight and maim and all that shit. Oh yeah, this is classic Moreau. Where's the Sayer of the Law when you need him? With a freakin' Taser, too, please. I can't keep Rico's ocean of teeth away for much longer. Uh, Eddie? Oh, Eddie? A hand? Any time will do, but mainly *now*. Deirdre's comment about regeneration sinks in as I envisage myself leaving this establishment sans schnozzola. Sure it'll grow back, but shit. How long does that take? I don't want to take a personal day to grow back my nose.

That'd be wicked lame.

Hands appear on Rico's heaving shoulders, thick knuckled and strong. These are not Eddie's hands, nor are they Deirdre's. I don't care whose they are, they look formidable and they're keeping Rico's yammering mouth away from me. Those teeth! Thick globules of his slobber rain down on me as I fall over onto my back, his knees and feet pummeling me as he runs in place. Finally he's off me and I roll away from him, crabwalking to a far wall to collect myself.

"Jesus mother of fuck."

I take in the scene. Deirdre is petting Lisa's head, which is folded into Deirdre's breast. If reentry to the womb was possible, I think Lisa would attempt it. Any womb in a storm, you dig? I envision Charlton Heston in his filthy loincloth screaming, "It's a madhouse! A *madhouse!*"

A burly man dressed in outerwear restrains Rico, coldcocks him with a large, bricklike fist. Tough love, I suppose. Rico's eyes dim and he drops to the floor with a soft thud. Deirdre's and my eyes meet and she apologizes silently. I nod. What am I going to do, make a federal case out of it? It's not her fault. Eddie, though. Hoo-hoo, he's got some 'splainin' to do.

Two more burly men come into the room with large moaning canvas sacks slung over their shoulders. Quickly sizing up the situation, chuckling, shaking heads, they drop the bags that on impact with the floor emit muffled *oofs*. I've gotten off my ass but haven't lifted a paw to help Deirdre up. My nose is bleeding and I'm attracting looks from the rest of the pack of Deirdre's charges. From the hunger in their eyes and the licking of their chops I'm reckoning the concept of feeding on one of their own isn't unique to Rico. The bags are opened and the squirming, terrified, bound, and gagged folks inside don't even have the chance to ponder the nature of their demise. Maybe they thought this was a kidnapping, plain and simple. There was hope. The ransom would be raised. Maybe they were being packed off into white slavery. They never figured on being the main course.

As the orderlies cart away insensate Rico and wrest Lisa off Deirdre, the rest of their fellows crowd the wriggling flesh troughs and dig in. Lots of wagging behinds accompanied by slurping and sucking sounds. What would Miss Manners say? *Don't slurp your soup.* They look like anthropomorphized giant piglets suckling the teats of their mama. The pack makes contented yummy noises.

I stumble over to Eddie and give him a light punch on the arm. His eyes are red from laughter and some other indecipherable emotions, tears running down his cheeks. I drag the back of my hand across my nose and mouth, staining it with my own blood, which mercifully is no longer of interest to the room. I want to be pissed but I laugh, too.

"Yeah," Eddie gasps, "it's funny, right?"

"Yeah. Yeah, it totally is."

• • •

After she cleans up in the bathroom, Eddie gives Deirdre a check and she forgives him, accusing him of leasing a conscience to which he replies, "Why own when you can rent?" She pats his cheek and smiles, her face softening. "No hard feelings," he asks. I can see she's sweet on him and she shakes her head. As we make to leave a young-looking redheaded guy in a wheelchair blocks our way in the hall. He smiles and in a heavy New England accent begins talking, telling us his life story as if either of us asked.

"Oy gawt back from th' wah in nineteen fahty-fah," he says, his voice eerily similar to that of the Pepperidge Farm guy, "some Jap having rawbed me of the use of both moy legs. Oy don't hahbah any resentment to the little yellow menaces, awnest Oy don't, but as Oy was wheeling moyself ahcross the hahbah in the dahk, Oy foind moyself undah attack again, only this toime it's no kamikaze poylet, it's a *cursed thing of the noight*. So, the hawrrible curse begins. Fawrevah young in a crippled bawdy. That's moy rewahd faw service to moy country. Oy ahsk you."

"You got turned and . . . "

"If yaw crippled when yaw turned, as you put it, that's the way you stay. Oy ahsk you. If it weren't faw Ms. Callahan's good works

Oy'd have burnt up aw stahved years ago. It's mighty hahd to hunt when yaw stuck in a wheelchayah."

"Yeah, I'd imagine so." What else am I going to say? I'd never considered the possibility of handicapped and retarded blood-suckers. It just never crossed my mind. How much does that suck? So, Deirdre is a good woman. I'd never think to do this, to run a clinic or home or whatever you want to call it, for differently abled bloodsuckers, but I guess it's needed. So on the one hand you've got Adélaïde Sigismund and her ilk, and then you've got Deirdre Callahan and her do-gooders. Sure the orderlies came in with a couple of sacks of human cargo, but they're the hunter-gatherers. They probably have some kind of code, like mine, not that I'm anyone to judge.

"Oy did things of which Oy'm nawt proud," the crippled vet says, eyes moist, "but that's behoind me and Oy troy to make up for it with prayer. Perhaps this extended loif is moy hell on Earth, moy penance. Awl paht of the good Lawd's plan. Mayhaps when and if Oy do meet with moy end in this loif Oy'll foynally be rewahded by joining Him boy his soyd. Praise Jesus."

"Excuse me?" I'm dumbfounded.

"Praise the Lawd. Have you accepted the Lawd as yaw personal savior?"

"I . . . Huh?"

He holds up a small bible, and something else that never occurred to me does: just because someone gets turned doesn't mean he stops being a devoted little Christian. Like anything that's built to survive, adaptation is necessary, and religious fealty is no different. So I'm an atheist. So what? I was before and I still am. I don't chalk up the change to anything supernatural. Early on, once I'd gotten a grip on my situation, for shits and giggles I'd walk into churches and fondle the odd cross, tickle Jesus on his crucified tootsies.

Nothing. I'd poke into baptisteries and take sneaky sips of holy water from the fonts. Not that refreshing, but totally harmless. Empirical evidence is manna for the faithless.

There's a condition called Erythropoietic Porphyria which can cause acute allergic reaction to light, resulting in severe burns. Critical photosensitivity. So what I am—what we are—it's explicable in rational terms. It's a mutation. I'm certain there's a scientific, biological explanation for it, but to the best of my knowledge the Discovery Channel hasn't done a show on it. Yet. But this guy in the wheelchair, this is like some kind of purgatory trip for him.

"I gotta go," I tell him. "Good luck with your whole whatever."

Before departing I also make a donation to Sister Deirdre's Mission for Wayward Retarded Misfit Bloodsuckers. I'm being flip about the name. There isn't one, really, it's just a supervised group home, but she's doing good, selfless work and for once I don't feel ashamed of what I am. As we ride down in the elevator Eddie grins and pats me on the back.

"Did *that* bingle your bongle?"

"Eddie. Eddie, Eddie, Eddie."

"How's the proboscis? That Rico kid pasted you but good."

"It's fine. But maybe a dose of our favorite potent potable would make the pain go bye-bye."

"*Hmmm.* You've never hunted with a partner, have you?"

"Hunted? I thought maybe we'd swing by Adélaïde's place and . . . "

"No, no, no, "Eddie chastens. "One doesn't just swing by. There's a little thing called protocol. See, you *are* a social retard. No, Adélaïde needs a little notice. It's not one nonstop bacchanal up there, in spite of what you think. We'll forage for porridge on our own, okay?"

"I dunno, man. That's a little suspicious. It's easier to hide one's tracks when there is only one."

"That, my friend, is where you're wrong. Unlike you, I have hunted with chums before. Think of this as an urban safari, only we don't have to dress in tacky orange hunting vests or camouflage."

"Remind me again about how straight you are."

"You're *hilarious*."

"I know."

"Adélaïde's place. You fucking hypocrite."

"I know."

"You're having fun, aren't you?"

And it hits me. I am having a good time. I'm actually having a good time. I forgot what it felt like.

Cool.

15

Instead of some boggy blind in the woods, Eddie and I hunt in Williamsburg, Brooklyn, near the Domino Sugar factory. Plenty of lowlifes, plenty of abandoned lots, burnt-out auto carcasses, very near the water. So near the East River, in fact, that the air is cold and damp enough to even give me a bit of a chill. The street is seemingly abandoned but I know this turf, sad to say, and there's always some tasty morsel lurking in the shadows. Refuse is liberally strewn about, most of it affixed to the cobblestones by glutinous substances best left unconsidered. Too unappetizing. Other than the streetlights, the majority of which are broken, there's no illumination for blocks. Sandwiched between residential enclaves of various ethnicities and classes the area is purely industrial, one dark factory-type building after another.

I can tell Eddie hasn't done this kind of fieldwork in ages because he's chattier than usual, nervous. For once I'm taking the alpha position in this nascent relationship and I like it.

"You're in a good mood," Eddie says. "You seem more relaxed. You've always seemed a little tense around me, you know? You don't seem like a really easygoing type of a guy. But maybe not. Maybe it's just me."

"I dunno, I guess I resented you or something. You seem so damned comfortable in your own skin, like being one of us is no big thing. I mean, I didn't even like myself *before* the change, so now, with no support, no friends, a crappy job . . . "

"Not to go all *After School Special* on you, but you've got a friend."

"Okay, now it's getting sappy. Let's go kill someone."

"Can our quarry at least be clean?" he asks. "I don't mind slumming, but . . . "

"Listen, here's a good opportunity to put your flamboyance to good use. I usually take the quiet approach, but here's a chance to have a little fun by drawing attention. Hold my hand."

"What?"

"Hold my hand. This isn't a great area for a male-male couple to be strolling after dark. Or any time for that matter. We don't have to smooch or anything, but I guarantee the sight of two well-dressed . . . " Eddie looks at what I'm wearing and raises an eyebrow. "Oh fuck off. I'm dressed perfectly reasonably, especially for what we're about to do. I'm not going to put on Armani to hunt."

"Like you own any."

"Like I'd want to. Anyway, two men holding hands on a midnight stroll by the waterfront ought to work like deer estrus on a stag."

"*Deer estrus*? How the hell does a city boy know about deer estrus?"

"It's a thing called reading. Ever try it?"

"Shut up and hold my hand, egghead."

Stifling mirth, Eddie and I saunter along, Eddie humming a show tune, me casting my eyes lazily along the periphery, looking just nervous enough to be further enticement to your shier mugger or hate criminal. It shouldn't be hard to ensnare suitably ignoble prey. And Eddie should be pleased by one thing: muggers and hate criminals tend to be cleaner than derelicts.

Making our way toward the river via South 2nd, we near the

Domino plant, crossing Wythe Avenue. The air has a weird smell and it's hard to tell whether it's a sweet stink caused by the sugar plant or just rot. Eddie slips and almost loses his balance, but it's not the wet cobblestone; it's a juicy condom. Both of us make a face. Midway between Wythe and Kent we pass a couple of ne'er-do-wells ensconced between a couple of dumpsters and Eddie's clasp on my hand tightens.

"I know," I whisper.

Throwing in a bit of cheesy improv, Eddie bleats, "I don't know, Bryce, maybe this *isn't* the way to the party."

I elbow him, telling him not to overdo it.

"I'm *scared*!" Eddie squeaks, laying on the mincing shtick a little thick for my taste. But apparently not everyone is such a critic because from behind us the dumpster bushwhackers begin their lamentable attempt at a sub-rosa attack from the rear, their shoes making squelchy sounds on the gluey pavement.

"Oh, Bryce," Eddie vamps, "Estébàn would *never* live in such a *godawful* area as *this*. I told that cabby he was way . . . "

And they're on us, but without the usual preamble. Prepared for a threat or two prior to actual engagement I stupidly leave myself open and take a shiv in the right lung. Fuck, I totally wasn't expecting that. I won't die, but it still hurts like a motherfucker. Plus, dressed to meet what I thought would be more of Eddie's high-toned hoity-toities, I find my mood temporarily ruined, unlike my jacket which is permanently so. Okay, so it's not Armani. I don't make Armani bucks—maybe outlet, but not direct—and this shitbird has pierced my jacket. Yeah, now I'm pissed. I was all prepared for the back and forth of genuine threats from my attacker and feigned wheedling from me, but no, this guy skipped the foreplay and busted my hymen. So he's got to pay extra. Normally I don't play with my food, much, but tonight?

Eddie's on his own. He can do what he wants, but I wheel around and punch my attacker in the throat. Nothing says, "Hey, asshole, you've really frosted my strawberries," better than a fast knuckle punch to the esophagus. It hurts like hell and debilitates instantly. Eyes wide in disbelief my assailant drops to his knees, his weapon clattering on the stones. What'd he get me with? A sharpened screwdriver? No class, no class at all. Still, maybe the hole in my jacket is small enough to mend. I decide to take it easy on him, somewhat mollified by the notion of a reparable gash in my garment. Clutching his throat with one hand he grapples spastically at the road, trying to lift his weapon, which I kick away. All the while he's making this nasty sound, a sort of "*Guck . . . guck . . . guck . . . huccchhhh . . .* " It's unpleasant but I indulge it for a few moments to watch Eddie work.

I've got to say he's a bit of a sadist.

Eddie has a fistful of his ruffian's gonads, grinding the beans. And he didn't want to hold hands? The guy's got some nerve calling me a hypocrite.

"Want me to let go?" he taunts. The guy croaks an affirmative but Eddie holds on, his voice a purr of pure malice. "Beg me," Eddie says, smiling, his voice a smooth gravel driveway. The guy begins begging and Eddie releases the guy's batch only to deliver a brutal kick to the solar plexus. The guy doubles over and Eddie looks over at me, shrugging.

"This is fun," he says. "I haven't done this in ages."

A loud report echoes in the canyon of gray buildings and Eddie looks down at his side, which dribbles blood. In the hand of his mugger is a small .22-caliber pistol, which Eddie looks at with a combination of bemusement and rage.

"This little dope took a potshot at me," Eddie says, incredulous. "This little peckerwood shot me with a . . . " he snatches the gun out of the guy's hand, the guy even more astonished than Eddie. "A fucking Bernadelli Model 60. You expect to take a man down with a little wop peashooter like this? For serious? Oh, you kid."

"I . . . I . . . I . . . " the guy sputters.

"*Ai-yi-yi* is right. Now I've gotta fish a fucking slug out of my side. That's just super." Eddie looks over at me, annoyed. "You can't leave those things in there, you know? Catch enough lead and you're rattling around like some fucking meat maraca. Silly bastard."

Eddie pounds the top of the mook's skull with the wee gun, coldcocking him.

"And that, as they say, is that."

"Let's eat."

Eddie and I carry our game off the main drag—you never know when the stray car might trundle by—through a gap in a fence and into a nearby lot. Before Eddie digs in he sticks the thumbs and forefingers of both his hands into the bullet hole, widening the aperture.

"Hey, do me a favor and get the slug out? I'd do it myself, but I think you'd have better luck. If I had a needle-nose pliers or something . . ." he trails off. "You understand."

I poke my fingers in and the slug is just under the surface. I pop it out and hand it to Eddie, who lets the entry wound snap closed.

"*Merci.*"

"*De nada.*"

Soup's on.

After draining our attackers Eddie and I sit back and look up at the stars, burping, sated. I've never hunted with a buddy before. I've never had a buddy to hunt with. It's kind of nice. Though I always frowned on sport hunters, I can now kind of see the appeal.

There really is something very primal about sharing a moment like this. Of course, those cowardly pricks use high-powered firearms to take down ducks and deer just so they can feel like they've got balls, so it's different. But I get the gist. As I commence my ritual butchering of the corpse's neck wounds, Eddie chuckles.

"What's that all about?" he asks, wiping his mouth.

"I don't like to leave 'em looking drained. I always fuck 'em up a bit so it looks like an ugly, but human-caused death. 'Never leave fang marks' is my credo."

"Words to live by."

"No doubt."

"Just so you know: it looks really psycho, you perched there chopping away at a dead guy's throat. Very Ed Gein."

"Yeah, well."

Eddie chuckles some more and I finish my "embellishing," then ease back on the dank punctured upholstery of the torn-out car seat we're on. It's peaceful and quiet, and staring skyward we both hear the fast thuds of footfalls in the perimeter.

The cardinal rule: no witnesses.

"Fuck. Can't a guy digest in peace?" Eddie moans.

Eddie and I spring off the springless seat and give chase, advantage ours. We're faster and, more important, we can see. Our unfortunate buttinsky picked the wrong lot to kip in. His advantage is he seems to know the terrain better than we do and rabbits back and forth amid the debris, zigzagging his way through the yard toward the waterline. Keeping my eyes on him I don't pay enough attention to what's on the ground and stumble over an agglomeration of rusted auto parts. Good thing tetanus is a past concern.

"You okay?" Eddie hollers.

"Yeah." My shins throb, but I'm back on my feet and running, just in time to see Eddie repeat my misstep across the lot.

"Keep after him," Eddie shouts.

Like I need to be told. The guy peels out through another tear in the chain link and I follow, make a grab for him, miss. I slip again and stumble on Kent. The guy's really booking toward the Williamsburg Bridge. What, does he think he's gonna make it to the city? I right myself and tear after him, my legs pumping, finally feeling a bit more steady. I pick up speed as the guy abandons his first trajectory and makes a sharp left onto South 4th, back toward Wythe. I didn't expect this much exercise, and immortal though I may be, I'm not in shape for the decathlon. Eddie, nowhere to be seen, is no help at this point.

Up ahead the guy vaults up a short metal staircase onto a loading platform and begins pounding on a steel door. This can't happen. I'm not about to let this escalate. I race up the block and dive onto the platform, grabbing him by his ankles and toppling him off. His head hits the pavement and makes the sound of a melon being introduced to a mallet.

Winded, but in full-on survival mode, I sling him over my shoulder and run back toward the river. Above me a light goes on. Probably a converted loft building. No witnesses. I smell the guy's blood oozing out. This jacket is ruined. Why do I ever buy "dry clean only" items? Like I'm going to take this in. What kind of explanation could I possibly give for a blood-soaked jacket with a puncture hole? Who knew? This whole shebang was so impromptu. If I'd known we would go hunting I'd have dressed down.

It seems such a waste, but I'm too full to feed again. When I reach the gap in the fence, Eddie stands there leaning, looking perturbed.

"So, you got him," he says, stating the obvious.

"Yeah. I'm fucking gasping, man. I'm not used to that much running."

"Yeah, well, more bad news."

"Yeah?"

"Yeah. He wasn't the only one in the lot. When I got up—and would you look at my clothes by the way? Anyway, when I got up I figured you had a handle on the situation, maybe I should mind the fort. So I'm walking through the lot and whammo, somebody brains me from behind with a crowbar. I didn't even hear him on account of I must've still been a little shaky from my tumble, yeah?"

"Great."

"Right, great. So down I go, again, and I see him make for the same hole in the fence. Not gonna happen, right? So, I'm still a bit woozy, yeah, but I get back up and go after him . . . "

"And?"

Eddie points a few feet away and I see feet sticking out from behind a torched chassis.

"*Mazel tov,*" I say, patting him on the back. "Good work. Jesus, four in one night."

"Yeah, well . . . "

"Yeah, well what?"

"There was a fifth who got away."

I take a minute to let that settle in. There was a little fish that got away. I'm so stunned I momentarily forget I've got an unconscious—or dead—person slung over my shoulder. The weight of the situation and the body sink in and my knees go weak. I drop the body and sit down on a bald tire, head in my hands.

"This is bad."

"How much could he have seen? They don't see like we see."

"True, but this is still bad. We were sloppy. Overconfident."

"Agreed, but it isn't a catastrophe."

"Pretty close, though. Fuck, this is bad."

"Keep saying it. Mind over matter, Phil. Mind over matter."

"Fuck."

I look down at the guy I chased. Dead, no doubt about it. That part's okay. He'd have had to die anyway. But he's young. A teenager. Dirty blond whiteboy dreadlocks poking from under a wool hat. Patchy billy-goat beard. Eyebrow piercing. This isn't some seasoned vagrant; this is a runaway. I don't do runaways. I get up and walk over to Eddie's catch and my chest feels corseted.

"Eddie, your fucking *him* is a *her*."

"Oh yeah? So?"

A teenage girl, same basic deal: pierced face, dreadlocks. Another runaway. I'm sure under their coats they're tattooed. This is great. I look around the lot and see the rust-flecked carapace of a powder blue VW van, no doubt their home away from home. This is just super. These were kids squatting in a lot by the Williamsburg Bridge and we slaughtered them. I dump my victim next to Eddie's and again I'm reminded of work. The Bronx double suicide. What's that joke? "Murder is just an extroverted suicide." I don't normally feel like a murderer, but this is different. These kids don't fit my criteria for acceptable dining. And I didn't dine on them, so it is what it is. It's murder, plain as that.

"All they were missing was the requisite pit bull," Eddie says, looking at the bodies. "These types always truck around with a pit bull. I guess that's good. I hate killing dogs. So whattaya wanna do?"

"What do I want to do? Besides rolling back time and not having done this, what do I want to do?"

"I hope you're not blaming yourself. We were in the moment. We got careless. So what? Shit happens. Look at these two. Living in a fucking van by the river? *Ucch.* Consider these mercy killings. This wasn't murder."

"No?"

"This was euthanasia."

"It was murder."

"Maybe manslaughter," Eddie says, whisking dirt off his chest. "Anyway, we can argue semantics and ethics later, but for now we've got to focus and get rid of the bodies. Destroy the evidence."

"Death by misadventure."

Eddie smiles. "Exactly."

• • •

After lugging the bodies and several large chunks of metal and concrete from the lot onto a rotting jetty, Eddie and I bind them with some rope, weigh them down, and dump them. Suffice it to say the euphoria from earlier is long gone, just a pleasant, indistinct memory. Eddie and I walk away from the pier, conversation momentarily on hold. Finally Eddie speaks.

"You think we should look for the other one?"

"Did you catch a decent enough look at him? Or was it a her, too?"

"It was a guy. It ran like a guy. Chicks run different. Yeah, I saw him pretty good."

"Did he see you?"

"Like I said, it was dark. Keep reminding yourself that our dark and their dark are two different animals, you dig? He was a spooked little white dude. I was an indistinct dark blur. The nearest streetlamp was like a hundred yards away. Listen, for all we know they thought we were cops rousting bums and that's why they took off. Or maybe they were up to no good. You ever think of that? Trust me, this ends here."

"But what about the other one?"

"He never saw us. We were never here. Relax."

Filthy, bloodied, tired, we part company and go our separate ways. I look at my watch. It's four forty-eight; sun's up a quarter after seven. I take off my ruined jacket and trudge up toward civilization, hope to spot a cab, think the better of it, head for the good ol' anonymous subway. As I near it, a freezing rain starts. Marvelous.

Nathan Leopold and Richard Loeb.

Henry Lee Lucas and Ottis Toole.

Eddie Frye and Phil Merman.

This is why I work solo.

16

Monday, January 22nd, 2001

Eddie's called a couple of times to see how I'm doing, which I appreciate, but I'm not in the mood to socialize. He's blithely moved on, unaffected. I should be so lucky. Fucking latent Jewish guilt. Maybe I should be grateful I haven't entirely lost touch with my humanity, so to speak. Guilt and worry. Rationally I know that humans don't see like we do. It was dark. I have to remind myself that it was. Just because to us it wasn't doesn't mean it wasn't to them. Perimetric light from the city, the bridge, the one working streetlamp a block away; that's not enough for them. I *know* that. I rationally know that. But the doubt in my gut is festering away. The rational mind and irrational mind really shouldn't occupy the same real estate. The irrational mind should be located in the ass or something. It should be like the appendix—expendable. Removable.

More slides of carnage, some by misadventure, some extroverted suicides. Kate walks in as I'm color correcting a particularly vivid image and she gasps and about-faces right back out the door. That's okay. I'm not in the best mood and small talk wouldn't be my forte tonight. I've got other things on my mind. Bad things.

I bought the papers today.

I haven't bought a paper in ages, especially not to check up on possible reportage of my handiwork. For years I've been careful, methodical, unambitious in my hunting and gathering, so no need to consult the dailies. But Saturday night? Maybe my thinking is a bit off these days, since I've rejoined the ranks of those with social lives.

The Sunday papers brought nothing. Today the *Times* likewise has nothing, natch. Small time local nonsense they wouldn't bother with. *The Daily News* and the evening edition of *The New York Post*, however, both sport smallish items that nonetheless loom large. The *Post* reports on a freaked-out twenty-six-year-old, Duane Darrell Pyne, with a history of drug busts and assault charges, being picked up by the cops in the Williamsburg area early Sunday morning on a controlled substance and weapons possession collar. There's nothing about the runaways, but the location of Pyne's bust, Driggs Avenue and North 5th, is so close to where Eddie and I were it makes me wonder. The *Post* item, no more than a single column, sports a photo of Pyne, who it must be said is one creepy-looking sonuvabitch. I call Eddie and ask him to pick up the paper and look at the picture. He complains that I'm being too much of a worrywart, that I should just drop it. But I persist and he agrees to go out to the newsstand and pick up a *Post*. At least the *Post* is trashy enough to justify the trip downstairs in his robe and pajamas, a sartorial detail he lets slip to let me know that he isn't about to get dressed just to go down and get the paper.

Five minutes later he calls me back.

"That's the guy," he says, his tone neutral.

"It is? I mean, it is." My stomach hurts.

"Yeah. I mean, I'm pretty sure. It's hard to say for one hundred percent certain, but yeah, I'm pretty sure that's him."

"We are so completely fucked on this, Eddie."

"No we're not. These are little people, Phil. They're . . . " Eddie pauses. "Is this line secure? Do they monitor your calls?"

"Now who's paranoid?"

"It's contagious. You're a fucking carrier. I'll assume the line is clear. If not, *hello*? I know who killed JFK. I know who ate all the Frusen Glädjé." Eddie snickers at his own joke. "Seriously, Philbot, chill. No greasy dope-fiend drifter is going to topple the house that Eddie built. Or Phil."

"Even if it's a house of cards?"

"Don't get all melodramatic, sister. Just do your dreary work and relax. And call me when you're up for more wild and crazy times."

"Yeah, I'll do just that."

"Don't be like that. Seriously, just stash it away in the recesses. There's no need for anxiety. All is fine. Go to your quiet place and do some mental origami or whatever smoothes your ruffles. Vegetate."

I tell Eddie I'll try to comply, then disconnect and get back to my consecution of splattered walls and gunned-down humans. Jus' reg'lar plain ol' dead folks. Nothing to do with me. I glance at the two items about Pyne. On the plus side, Pyne was picked up in possession of an unspecified quantity of heroin and a ten-inch combat knife. He's under arrest because of his dubious nature and his priors. He's clearly a scumbag.

Duane Darrell Pyne.

That's a nice name for a serial killer.

• • •

In my living room I sit glued to the local cable news channel, NY1. I like this station. There's a very "let's put on a show in the barn" quality to their approach. Sort of a little-channel-that-could lack of gloss that I find comforting, even as they tell me what a shitty world this is. They have technical errors. Their newsreaders stumble sometimes. A couple even have what I'd call speech impediments. It's like the public access of news. It's very human, in the good sense. I watch the remainder of the overnight broadcast, forgetting that at that time of night it's mostly sports and talk format public affairs pap, the local news only in easily digestable headline form every half hour or so.

I stay up, safe behind my dull window treatments, and watch until nine in the morning, getting a large, concentrated dose of local *mishegoss*. Murders, rapes, scandals, traffic and weather, local affairs and politics, more murder and corruption. Business as usual in Fun City.

Pyne doesn't show his ugly mug once. No mention of missing teens.

Good.

I switch off, collapse into bed, and fade.

17

This is a good news/bad news situation. The bad news is that the teens Eddie and I ushered into the next realm have been reported missing. Russell Earl Ginty and Sage Thompson, both hailing from the Pacific Northwest, both nineteen years old. I don't like to think of them as having names. The good news is that they were reported as having last been seen in the company of Duane Darrell Pyne and that he's the prime suspect in their disappearance. Some of their runaway brethren reported them as having gone off with Pyne to score heroin and they never returned to the squat.

More has been brought to the fore about Pyne, too. He's wanted in connection with a few missing persons cases in the Midwest, having also been seen keeping company with several missing—presumed dead—teens in Nebraska, Kansas, and Missouri. This is very good news, actually. The more times I reread it the better I feel.

After apparently denying his alleged connection to Ginty and Thompson, Pyne changed his tune and his story now is that he and the youngsters were "camping" in the husk of a VW van—I *knew* it—when they heard what sounded like a gunshot. They hid in the van and when they saw some activity in the lot they were bivouacking in, they panicked and took off. The individuals involved in the gunplay and subsequent chase are not described in any terms other than that they were likely male. No race, no builds, no nothing detail-wise. His story is the unvarnished truth, but I have a feeling he's going to be railroaded, which suits me fine. He sounds like a real asset to society.

The authorities aren't calling it a murder case or anything very specific. Yet. According to Pyne's testimony he and the others just "disbanded." Pyne has good reason to be keeping them alive. The late Mr. Ginty and Ms. Thompson—as well as the two muggers, who no one knows about—are unaccounted for. Now that they've made the news their respective parents have emerged, all dewy-eyed with questionable concern. Maybe the authorities will find them. If they dredge the nearby shoreline they'll turn up. But at this point, I'm feeling a bit better about the whole affair. Scratch that. I feel a lot better. And the fact that we just killed them and didn't feed is a plus. There's nothing to link their deaths to Eddie's and my particular lifestyle. Just plain old murder. I regret killing those kids, but I think our Mr. Pyne is going to take the fall. As for the muggers? I did my bit on them. Fuck it. They're waterlogged and Mr. Pyne's worry.

I hope.

18

Thursday, January 25th, 2001

Okay, so maybe I'm not so certain about Pyne catching the heat for our misdeeds. There's been nothing in the papers today about him, but that worries more than soothes. I haven't fed for a couple more days than usual and I'm feeling a bit wired. I'm hungry but apprehensive about feeding. And I haven't slept well. I'm a winner. Eddie, I'm certain, sleeps the sleep of the innocent. What's that like, I wonder.

My scanner purrs to life and I gird myself for the blitz. Tonight I actually want stock photography. I want corporate hand-shakers and babies and orangutans wearing funny hats. I want kittens clinging to branches and grannies pulling hot pies out of the oven. I want to turn my mind off and just coast. Instead I have the illustrated menu and everything looks putrid. It's times like this I wish I smoked. I could go out for one and sit on my standpipe and watch the cars go by. Watch humanity go by. Watch life. Instead I've got death on parade.

It's funny all these thousands of photos of dead folks. I wonder sometimes whether anyone bothered to take their picture when they were alive. Some of them might only have become interesting enough for someone to document by croaking in some rotten way.

Anyway.

Label: "Vincent LaGombrianno. Parkchester, Bronx. September 13th, 1987 (1-2 a.m.). ©1987 Metropolitan News Media, Inc."

There's something otherworldly about flash photography of the dead. The colors are at once more vibrant but the flesh is more blanched out. This sequence is pretty surreal anyway. The setting is a project. I mean, call it what you want, an apartment complex, whatever. But it's a project. Plenty of gawkers in the background and though it might sound racist, due to the lateness of the hour and the effects of flash photography and dark skin, only the eyes and teeth and clothes of the background spectators are visible, lending an ethereal Magritte weirdness by way of turn of the century pickaninny advertising art.

Uniformed cops doing crowd control, taking statements, milling about, looking bored, as per. The fly-bait in this batch are several waterlogged homies, their bodies strewn about a large round fountain with bronze sculptural elements, none spouting water. Either they turned off the fountain because of the crime scene or they don't run it at night. Leaves and paper refuse float on the water's surface so maybe it hasn't been running for a while. Hard to tell. With lights on under the water everything is lit from below and tinted swimming pool blue. Even the living look dead, zombie-like.

One of the bodies is draped across one of the fountain sculptures, a squat, thick-legged dwarfish figure with a gaping, quizzical yet stupid face bearing vacant eyes—the sculpture, that is. Actually both of them, to be honest. The sculpture holds its hand to its chin as if wondering how this dead young black man came to be laid to rest in its lap. With the water off it's just as easy to imagine the stream coming from the gaping mouth or from between the splayed legs. It's not an attractive piece of art. In the background are five more of these cast monstrosities, but this is the only one cradling a dead body.

There are several shots of each of the four corpus delicti, all bearing gunshot wounds, a couple still clutching their guns, the others with their gats nearby. The crowd looks interested but no one looks surprised or upset. No one. In the illuminated water the ultra-vivid blood trailing away from the head wound of one of the bodies looks appetizing and for the moment I feel a little better. A cop, looking like he wishes he had rubber boots, steps into the water and turns a submerged body over, its eyes open but dulled by death, small bubbles collected around the nose, eyes, mouth. Water ripples distort the face. The body is lifted out and laid on the ground in a black body bag. Zip.

Similar sequences of each body removed from fountain, tagged, zipped up.

Next.

Label: "Trey Verbitsky. Sunnyside, Queens. After hours/predawn. 7/7/99. ©1999 Associated Image Bank Syndicate."

First shot is of the exterior of a titty bar on a side street in Queens. A garish lime green neon sign declaiming the name of the joint, B.J. McHoochies, sandwiched between glowing pink silhouettes of mudflap cuties. Not ten feet from the entrance is the body of a plastically attractive young woman with gargantuan fake tits lying face up on the sidewalk, blood pooled around her, a stab wound in the neck. Her shirt has been torn open and her breasts stand straight up, perfectly round. One nipple is exposed, the scar running along the areola raised, grotesque. I'll never comprehend men who find these mutilated women attractive. I mean the ones with fake breasts. Mutilated, as in stabbed in the neck, that's a whole other fetish I'd just as soon not contemplate.

Our photog', Mr. Verbitsky, seems to feel otherwise, exposure after exposure of her silicone mounds in close-up and long shot, some real tight shots of the neck. Plenty of that exposed nipple. A bit of a perv, I'd say. He goes in close between the legs, a hint of her labia peeking out from her threadbare denim short-shorts. Then come the shots of her face, calm, almost beatific. Her hair, short and tussled, is auburn, blending in with the darkening coagulating blood. A few feet away from her head is what looks like a flattened Pekingese dog—her wig. In the background the doorman is weeping, a Brobdingnagian bald black man with a brilliantly polished dome. His grief is palpable.

The cops in these shots have a broader variety of reactions. One shows an officer placing a hand on the doorman's shoulder, the policeman's expression one of complete commiseration. A plainclothes dick kneeling by the body wears a mask of world-weary pity. One uniform looks like he shares Verbitsky's kink, more than a hint of lechery in his eyes. This box of slides boasts an unusual bonus. For a change the perp seems to have been in the vicinity and the sequence ends with a handcuffed scabby little mustachioed bastard in a tan Members Only windbreaker being forcibly shoved into the police cruiser. Thinning hair, shiny knees on his trousers, bad shoes. Let me guess: the victim didn't want to become Mrs. Little-Rat-Faced-Shit so you showed her what for. Seldom do I see the killers, just the results of their handiwork.

Including my own. Right, Sven?

Next.

Label: "Duffy McDevitt. Jackson Hts., Queens. July 4th, 1998. Mid-afternoon. © Duffy McDevitt, Inc."

Yecch. Let me just state that for the record. *Yecch.* Here's a situation where nobody looks happy or amused or bemused or anything but disgusted and putout. The cramped room is furnished in classic Lonely Bastard, the milk crate bookshelves, all leaning, barely able to sustain their stuffing. Everything claustrophobic, piles on top of piles on top of piles, dirty laundry strewn about, porno magazines and videos in plain sight, stained jockey shorts, crumpled tissues, fast food and candy wrappers, thrift store/hand-me-down furniture. The centerpiece for the suite is the corpse, in full bloom. It's July, the windows are thrown wide open but I'm guessing they were closed tight before the team got here. In hot weather decomposition occurs very quickly. Bacteria thrive in the body, the body bloats with gas, maggots infest the body, consume the eyes, features, other soft tissue. In addition to the maggots, some mature bottle flies whiz around, being swatted at by the poor cops and EMS team.

Besides the hot rot, our cadaver owned a dog that chewed away a large portion of his master's face and forearms.

With that ghoulish cue a funny thing happens: the tone of the set changes. A slapstick sequence of two uniformed officers wrestling this massive blood-caked Rottweiler to the ground unfolds. At first the big brute of a canine seems like it's attacking one of the lawmen, but McDevitt goes in for some close-ups and suddenly we've got a sick pastiche of that Pepsi commercial from the seventies with that little kid being licked into hysterics by a pack of puppies. The beast's tongue laps the cop's puss, which goes from disgusted to gleeful. It's weird to see this kind of mirth in such a macabre scenario. They finally subdue the pooch—more with cuddles than force—and lead it out of the cramped space, its eyes twinkling with doggy delight. The drear mood of the beginning of the set is erased and everyone looks cheery.

See? Dogs can get away with anything. If *I* were ever caught in flagrante delicto with blood all over *my* face, no cop would be chucking me under the chin. He'd be chucking me in a cell. Cujo, here, probably became the precinct mascot.

All the same, *bad dog*. Definitely a closed-casket for your master. Next.

Label: "J. Peter Steinmetz. FDR Dr., N/B. July 23, 1973. ©1973 Associated Photo."

The scorched husk of a luxury sedan, a Mercury Marquis Brougham four-door, sits in the shoulder of the service road. Smoke has blackened the areas around the windows and singed the white vinyl top, which curls away from the metal frame in a scabby sneer. The car is burnt orange—burnt everything, actually—and so big that it doesn't need a license number; it needs a zip code. Thank you.

In addition to cops and EMS workers are several firemen. It appears to be early morning, just after sunrise, judging by the light. Or at least my memory of what the light would look like that time of day. There's no time indicated on the label. Very sloppy, Mr. Steinmetz. Traffic looks relatively light, though. Anyway, the car, while cooked, isn't wrecked. No dents, no skid marks (*tee-hee*). After twenty or so shots of the car's exterior, Steinmetz has the authorities open the doors to get some interiors and that's where the sequence takes a darker turn. Looking like those barbecued ducks that hang in the windows of Chinese restaurants are the vehicle's occupants. In the front seats are two what I imagine were adults, both cooked to the point where their genders are only manifest by the remnants of their clothes from the waists down, he in slacks, she in a skirt. From the midriffs up they're well done, all features and hair roasted away. In the back seat are a likewise roasted pair of small corpses, slight of build, kids I'd guess. Hard to tell when the models have been broiled. They could've been midgets. What do I know?

These images have a familiar feel to them, maybe because I've seen similar roadside cookouts before, at least on my monitor. Looking at them I get that weird sense of paramnesia. I didn't see this firsthand, but it's so familiar. The car. The model. I don't know from cars, so why did I recognize that it was a Mercury? And so precisely? A Mercury Marquis Brougham? I remember someone describing the model as "outrageously baroque" in design, though one man's "outrageously baroque" is another's "just plain hideous."

Shelley.

Like I should even have to strain to remember. Shelley's parents and sister were found roasted in the family ride, namely a 1972 Mercury Marquis Brougham. So things are weighing on my mind. Plus it was nearly thirty years ago. But Jesus, this is Shelley's family. I'm guessing it is. Like going through girlie mags hoping you'll see a girl you knew once upon a time naked, I experience a similar sensation every night I turn on the scanner. Will I recognize anyone?

It's been a banner month so far.

But wait a minute. The date is wrong. Shelley's family was killed in the winter. And those two figures in the back seat. There were only three in Shelley's parent's ride, and his sister was too big to pass for a child. Or midget. Only three. Like three wasn't enough. Like three wasn't enough to turn Shelley into the living ghost he's become. But Shelley wasn't with them. Then it would have been four. It's not them. But it's damned close. Wrong side of town, too. But Jesus, close enough to bring back the memories, even if they are a smidge fuzzy.

I stop my scanning activities and go through the three boxes of this batch looking for the chit. Sometimes there's a name. As usual, nothing. No elaboration. No details. It's so frustrating. But I seem to recall I kept a clipping. I'd like to find it. Maybe later, when I get home, I'll see if I can lay my hands on it to refresh my memory.

I can't imagine a worse way to go than being incinerated. My hands tingle with sense memory of my brief first—and mercifully only—post-change encounter with the sun. Roasted alive. When you see pictures like this all you can think is, *I hope death came quick.* Or that endorphins or whatever just eased the experience. Whatever that chemical in the brain is. Something. But probably not. How can you expect any mercy when this is the card dealt?

Anyway.

Another reminder of why I tolerate Shelley. Tragic Shelley. Orphaned Shelley. Once upon a time, so long ago it's hard to remember, Shelley was a fun, upbeat guy. He dressed in colorful clothes, very psychedelic, very arty. After his family got perished he cut his hair short, abandoned the colors and the lightness, and became the alcoholic mope he is today. I remember when this happened and I remember that was the death knell of his being fun to hang with. Not that I blame him, or at least I didn't for the longest while. He lost his family in such a horrific way. Talk about "outrageously baroque." I endured his stoic, tearless grief, bolstering him as best I could. We spent countless nights in bars, he drowning his sorrows, me watching, listening. Depression took him and he, too, became a creature of the night, but by choice. Day just ceased to have relevance to him. Though he never bounced back, his mordant humor eventually returned, augmented by the new stutter and the terminal pixilation. Then, come August of that same fateful year, my "situation" began and Shelley was of no use to me whatsoever. I'd hoped that my being there for him would be reciprocated, but . . .

I've been over this already.

These strolls down Memory Lane are a bummer. Smoker or not, I'm taking five.

On the standpipe I vicariously enjoy the security guard's cigarette. Now I remember why Shelley only eats raw food. Even with my lack of appetite I might need to feed tonight. I could use a little refueling, a little comfort food, and the rawer the better.

I bid the guard goodnight and he and I go our separate ways, he back to his drudgery behind the granite welcome station, me to my unspectacular sanctuary in Queens. I guess I'll pick up a bite to eat on the way home, but I'm so not in the mood for hunting. This must be how they felt in the Pleistocene Epoch. "Fuck, I'm hungry. Tired as I am I gotta go spear me a woolly mammoth." Life's easier when you can just *buy* whatever you need.

Grumbling, I step off the curb and get rapped hard on the knee by a passing car, the contact between the bony joint and the vehicle making an audible *thunk*. I shout an oath at the departing vehicle, which slows down to a stop for a moment, then speeds back up and turns at the corner. What? Was the jerk behind the wheel going to get out and start some shit with me? *He* hit *me*. Did my pointy knee damage his precious trophy wheels? It was a Porsche, so what should I expect but world-class small-dicked assholery? I pause for a moment to rub myself. The material is abraded and spotted with a small amount of blood. It was his light. Whatever. When I reach the other side of the street I roll up my pants leg and do a damage check. This isn't anything major, but it renews my desire to feed. I don't like wasting blood, especially my own.

As I limp toward the subway the throbbing in my knee intensifies. That jerk clipped me worse than I thought. I mean granted, this is just an inconvenience, but it still hurts. Fucking Porsches and Porsche drivers. Shelley drives a Porsche but I can't remember what color. He's gone through maybe a dozen over the years, so it's hard to recall, especially when I don't care. I think about him whining about his orally fixated gal pal blowing him in his stupid little car and my forehead gets hot. I'm limping along with a throbbing bloodied knee and he complains about . . .

Bah! Time to get something hot and wet in me.

They say soup is good food, but blood is better.

• • •

At home I start pulling down boxes from the dark corners of my closets. Cigar boxes, shoeboxes, file boxes. It's in here somewhere. Call me maudlin, or morbid, whatever, but I've kept little clippings over the years. Things I thought were important landmarks. Celebrity deaths. Technological breakthroughs. Ticket stubs to plays and movies I thought were the shit. Programs, playbills; just little souvenirs. Tangible reminders for when my memory would inevitably fail me in my latter years. Once upon a time I thought I'd get old. I can feel nostalgia for having such naïve thoughts. I spill out the contents of box after box onto the floor of my foyer. What a bunch of crap I've held onto. But you know what? It all goes back in the boxes and then back in the closet. If all I've held onto from my human days can fit in a few small containers I don't think I've been excessively sentimental.

But box after box reveals nothing. Where's my tragedy box? My divorce papers and so on? I find boxes with old snapshots of the good times and somehow those are so much worse to look at. Look, I'm smiling. And my teeth are just teeth. Look, my arm is around a sexy woman. Oh, it's my wife. My wife. Look, friends. Look, family. Look, shared moments. Look! Happiness. Monica on the front stoop. Monica leaning against a vintage car. Monica preparing some holiday meal. Monica sunbathing on the roof. Monica running her fingers through her hair. Monica running her fingers through my hair. With tenderness. Fuck. Tenderness was such a long time ago. Monica was such a long time ago. Wrong box. Wrong box after wrong box, and my memory starts jogging. Not in a box. Segregated from the other memories. Somewhere else.

I put everything away and begin pacing around the living room, running my fingers through my hair, without tenderness. With agitation. I stop and stand in the middle of the room, close my eyes and try a little tenderness, smoothing my hair, petting myself. Emotional masturbation. I pretend to remember what it feels like to have someone I love caressing me. If sex without love is an empty experience, what is love without love? Just sad, I guess. Maybe a little pathetic.

Blue Movie.

It hits me then. I was reading Terry Southern's *Blue Movie* when Shelley's folks got roasted. I used the record of their tragic demise as a bookmark. A mass-market paperback, sort of a salmon pinkish cover. That's not a front row book. I don't have tons of space so I double and sometimes triple row my bookshelves, oldest stuff in the back, hidden away, almost forgotten. I wish I kept stuff in alphabetical order, but nope. So I begin scooping out row after row of paperbacks. Five shelves later I find the book and flip through it. Sure enough, stuck between yellowed pages is an even more yellowed newspaper clipping.

MEAT INSPECTOR FOUND ROASTED

By SHELDON MARSCH, New York Post

NEW YORK, February 5—The charred remains of Eldon Poole, 58, his wife, Cynthia, 53, and their daughter, Alice, 17, were discovered inside their smoldering Mercury Marquis Brougham just before dawn near Exit 14 on the Henry Hudson Parkway. An unnamed motorist who spotted their burning luxury sedan on the shoulder reported it to the police.

Cynthia Poole, an inspector for the New York City Department of Health, had been embroiled in several investigations of local meat packing facilities.

Renowned for her integrity, Mrs. Poole had made outspoken enemies in the meat packing trade. Poole made a name for herself in 1965 with her well-publicized exposé of unsanitary practices at Farnese & Sons Meats, United Meat Services, and

Real-Good Meats. After her inquest, Farnese & Sons Meats and United Meat Services were put out of business for multiple code violations and non-compliance with Health Department regulations.

"Yeah, she was a pain in the a—," said Vincente DeBuonollarco, 62, proprietor of the still-operating Real-Good Meats on West 13th Street. "But she did her job well and although we'd had our differences it's a shame she went out like this. After our to-do in '65 I was all about compliance, but Aldo [Farnese] held a grudge. What can you do?"

When confronted with DeBuonollarco's comment, Farnese, 66, said, "Vinnie said that? I didn't harbor no grudges. That's bunkum. She was a tough broad. Tough, but fair."

Others in the meat packing trade, many of whom Poole had repeatedly cited for health code violations, expressed similar sentiments.

Dominic Pugliese, operator of United Meat Services, died in 1969, but his son Anthony, 36, stated, "After she put my pop out of business his health went down the toilet. I'm not saying she had it coming, but I'm just saying."

Son Shelley, 24, whose whereabouts at the time of the conflagration are not currently known, has issued no statement regarding the death of his family, but family lawyer Barry Hurwitz stated, "This is a time of great personal tragedy and loss for my client. Any insinuation Shelley had anything to do with this tragedy would be terrible. And that's what I told the police."

An investigation is pending.

Son Shelley.
Tragic Shelley.
Orphaned Shelley.

19

March 5th, 1974

Shelley has insisted that I accompany him on a joyride in his new toy, a brand spanking new Porsche 911 Carrera. I know zilch about cars, but I know I should be impressed with this showy aubergine speedster. It's very late and we're the only ones zooming along this desolate stretch of anonymous nowhere in some industrial district of New Jersey. The air reeks, even with the windows rolled up, like all these factories are mass-producing high-octane flatus, the smokestacks pumping their pungent bounty into the atmosphere. The road is smooth, though, and stretches out ahead for miles, devoid of other cars, which explains why we're here. This is the first time I've seen Shel smiling since the tragedy, so even if he is zipping around a little faster than I'm comfortable with, so be it. I wish he was a little more sober, too, but he keeps telling me he drives better when he's sufficiently lubricated.

"Driving sober is the w-w-worst way to drive," he says. "People have it all wr-wr-wrong. When you're s-s-sober you're m-m-much more aware of everything g-g-going on around you, so you're m-m-much m-m-more likely to be tense. After a few b-b-belts you relax and become one w-w-with the r-r-road." I don't drive so I have no opinion. All I know is I'd feel more relaxed if I was a little more buzzed myself.

"So, you're loving the new wheels, huh, Shel?"

"You'd b-b-better believe it."

He takes a sharp turn and I almost fly into his lap.

"B-b-better buckle up," he says, grinning.

It strikes me as odd that the first thing Shelley would buy with his inheritance money is a sports car—*any* car, for that matter. Maybe this is his version of getting back on the horse, even though he wasn't with his family when they . . .

He wasn't with them.

I can't imagine what's going on in his head these days. It's exactly one month to the day since their bodies were found nearly fused to the interior of the family ride. Unreal. I ate dinner with the Pooles so many times. They were always kind of stiff, formal. No elbows on the table when eating; real sticklers for the Emily Post routine. I think his kid sister had a crush on me, but maybe I was just imagining it. She'd look at me over her plate, braces twinkling, and when I'd return her gaze she'd turn away, blushing. She was nice in an awkward kind of way. Maybe a little dry, for a teen.

Dry.

Stiff.

These are not adjectives I should be using. They've become a bit too contextually literal. Desiccated. Charred. I get the heebie-jeebies thinking about it. The hairs on my neck and arms rise with the gooseflesh. If I lost my folks that way? Or Monica? Oh my God, I don't even like to think about it. I look over at Shelley and he's in hog heaven, swerving around, racing toward oblivion, and taking me along for the ride.

"Uh, Shel, maybe you could gear down a little or whatever. You're going a little fast for my taste."

"You ch-ch-chicken?"

"Yeah, me chicken. Cluck, cluck."

Shelley laughs and decelerates to a reassuring sixty-five miles per hour. It's good to hear him laugh. What a month. Jesus. Between the actual calamity and ensuing grief, the endless onslaught of reporters and officials and cops and lawyers and so on and on and on. Shelley's been drinking pretty regularly for the last few weeks, and I can't blame him. And this stutter. I guess it will pass, but it's unsettling. So far the cops know nothing concrete. They keep grilling him for possible leads. Grilling. I really need to consider my words, even when I'm just thinking. It seems likely that one or more of those mobbed-up scumbags Mrs. Poole was always investigating decided to get rid of her. The authorities think that theory holds the most water. I agree. The stories she'd tell about those meat trade knuckle-draggers over supper would often ruin my appetite. She'd be carving some rare roast beef, all the while rattling off sordid details of all kinds of health code violations and so forth.

"So there was a pile of beef carcasses this high, teeming with maggots, portions discolored with rot like you wouldn't believe, and they're hosing them off in preparation to butcher them and send the cuts off to market. I couldn't believe the audacity. And the worst part is they think *everyone* is for sale. I can't tell you the number of times I've been offered graft. I tell them, 'It's bad enough, Mr. Fill-in-the-blank, that your operation is corrupt, but if you think *I'm* for sale you're barking up the wrong tree.' Would you like some au jus with that, Philip?"

No wonder Shelley is a vegetarian. And now he's on this raw food kick. I guess the idea of cooked food is unappetizing. I understand. When your whole family looks like the main course at the *churrascaria* . . .

Enough.

It seems these days only booze passes his lips. I'm worried about him. He's sold off most of the family estate. He hired some broker to sell off their earthly possessions: the family home, the furnishings, all of it. It's like he's trying to erase their existence by shedding all physical reminders of them. No sentimental doodads, nothing. Between the insurance, the inheritance, and the divestiture, he'll be set for life. His lawyer advised him not to buy anything flashy, at least not right away, that it might look bad. Shelley said he wouldn't and then immediately went out and bought this dopey Porsche. His feeling is if the authorities look askance at his shiny new plaything he'll just ask them what they'd do to kill the pain if their families were roasted like chestnuts. What balm might they apply?

I hope he can buy himself some happiness.

He deserves it.

20

Friday, January 26th, 2001

Duane Darrell Pyne was charged today with the murders of Russell Earl Ginty and Sage Thompson and two unidentified males who were dredged from the East River early this morning. Once again, because it feels so good: *Duane Darrell Pyne was charged today with the murders of Russell Earl Ginty and Sage Thompson and two unidentified males who were dredged from the East River early this morning*.

Christ, I'm starving. What's that? My appetite—fully reinstated and ready for action. Halle-fucking-lujah. Welcome back. Nobody was available for noshing last night so I went to bed and lay awake all day on empty, veins burning like they were pumping Drāno. The hunger pain's mellowed a bit, but after five nights in a row of death scenes and apology notes, worry, lack of sleep, and lack of blood, I'm ready to unwind and I want din-din. Eddie said he had something special in mind tonight, assuring me that it could be good for me. I'm willing to take the chance.

Sitting on the standpipe waiting for Eddie to show up I realize Shelley hasn't been around lately. I was convinced he'd appear the night I did the slides of that charbroiled family I'd thought had been his, but sometimes life spares you the contrived coincidences.

Cosmic mercy or some shit. Actually, I haven't heard from Shelley since he reeked up my bathroom. Maybe he's embarrassed. Good. I'm sure it's just a temporary hiatus, but I'll take what I can get, especially in light of this trying week. Shelley pulls brief blackouts from time to time, going sometimes as long as a month or two without contact. I always appreciate those little reprieves.

"No loitering."

Eddie arrives, smile on face, not shy about displaying his keen-edged canines. I suppose ever since the Goth kids started bonding their teeth with fake fangs you can be bolder. I know I don't really mask mine and have made up lies to cover for my indiscretion. I've claimed to be a Goth many times—dressing in black helps—but don't expect me to listen to The Cure or Dead Can Dance or Miranda Sex Garden or any of that crap. I'll stick with Kenton or Coltrane or Mingus. Sometimes I claim it's a birth defect, that my mom had pointy teeth, too, so in her memory I don't have them corrected. I tell that one to people like Kate. They find it very touching, a boy's devotion to his late mother. But honestly, in a city where people get from Point A to Point B stepping over bodies sprawled on the pavement, fangs aren't even a blip on the radar. I hoist my keister off the standpipe and Eddie and I shake hands as we walk away from the salt mine.

"What a week," I gripe.

"Yeah, but now it's over. Our long nightmare is over. Well, *your* long nightmare, at any rate. You breathing easier?"

"Yeah, pretty much. But every time a batch of dead teens came up I felt that twinge of guilt and dread."

"A batch of dead teens? What is it you do again?"

"I . . . " I stop myself as Eddie grins, knowing full well what I do. We've moved past the mystery phase. Eddie knows what I do, where I live, what my full name is. You kill together and a little bonding is bound to happen. Punching his bicep I ask him what the game plan is.

"I thought after last week's debacle you might like something a little calmer."

"Yeah, true. I've had the guilts all week. Not constantly, but niggling away in the recesses. I haven't been sleeping well. I keep thinking about those kids' faces."

"Guy, seriously, they were too old to be milk carton kids. Forget them. They're what's-his-face's problem now."

"Duane Darrell Pyne."

"Right. They're gone now and all that's left is the fresh scent of Pyne."

"Did you at least feed?"

"On who?"

"On the girl. Did you feed?"

"We'd just had those two muggers. I'm not a glutton, you know. I had a taste. I couldn't resist. Does that make you feel better?"

"A little. Okay, onward."

● ● ●

We cab it to Madison Avenue in the high eighties, and get out in front of a small art gallery situated next to the polished brass entrance to a large, elegant old commercial building. In the window of the gallery are a few small to medium canvases of beach scenes. These are not the efforts of some Bob Ross-style hack. They're good, confident, boldly painted. The beach looks alluring, the clear azure waves capped in luxurious foam rushing onto clean white sand. Looking at these images I feel a slight tug of yearning for the days of weekends at the beach with Monica. So long ago. She looked good in a two-piece. She just looked good, period.

I sometimes wonder if I should have turned her. Would she have gone along with it? We could've been together forever, young, vital, living our clandestine life. She probably would have, but I couldn't bring myself to do it. I guess I did the right thing. I don't know. I'll never know.

"You done admiring the pretty pictures?"

"Yeah."

Eddie unlocks the door and we enter the Art Deco lobby of the commercial building and once again find ourselves in an elevator going up, the mysterious destination soon to be revealed to me. Eddie loves playing tour guide. *Loves* it. We stop at the thirteenth floor—actually labeled thirteen, even though it's an older building— and walk down a carpeted hallway, the lower portion of the walls wainscoted in dark oak, the upper portion papered in a bland traditional pattern. The doors are all painted black. We round a corner and make for the last door, which is painted dark red. Eddie rings the doorbell, which chimes expensively, and a small middle-aged Asian man opens it and admits us with a slight bow. I nod my head in acknowledgment of his time-honored gesture. He takes our coats, ushers us through two large, curtained French doors, and departs, closing them behind him.

The room is large and comfortably appointed. Big leather couches, a couple of large upholstered armchairs, soft light. For a change the upholstery isn't velvet. The walls are papered in a very womblike salmon pink with a subtle, amorphous pattern. Seated in a dark brown leather chair is a bespectacled silver-haired man, thin, academic. He's dressed in traditional hound's-tooth and sports a Van Dyke beard. Scattered throughout the parlor are a few neurotic-looking folks, one chewing her nails, another fidgeting with his shirtfront, picking off lint, one staring off into space. None acknowledge our presence. Eddie smiles at me, but it's not his rakish devil-may-care grin. This one is sincere, warm. For some reason it gives me the creeps.

"So glad you could make it, Edward," says the man in the hound's-tooth, his voice also silvery, baritone, professional. "It's been a while. I see you've brought a friend."

"Yes I have," Eddie concurs. "Dr. Ost, this is Philip Merman. Philip Merman, this is . . . "

"Yeah, Dr. Ost. Uh, hello."

"Philip," begins Dr. Ost, but I wave off the formality and suggest he call me Phil. "Very well, *Phil*, have a seat. Make yourself comfortable. This place is all about making ourselves comfortable, isn't it, Justine?" The nail-biter looks up, caught off guard, and stammers out an affirmative. Dr. Ost nods with a smile. *Where's this guy's pipe?* I wonder. What has Eddie dragged me to tonight? "We're still waiting for a couple of our tardier confederates to arrive," Dr. Ost says to Eddie and me, "so in the meantime why not find a seat and get settled?" We comply and find places on two separate pieces of furniture, Eddie seating himself next to Justine the nail-biter and I snagging an armchair. I need my own space.

After a few moments of awkward silence three more enter the room, courtesy of the silent Asian man, and join the group, finding their seats. One, a large dude in Con Ed coveralls, stands before me and grumbles that I'm in his seat. I'm about to move when Dr. Ost gently chastises the guy for being late and says that there's no assigned seating here, that it's first come first served. I look up at the guy and he glares at me, taking a seat near the lint-picker.

Is this what I think it is?

"All right, we're all here," Dr. Ost says. "Group can begin. Anyone want to start the ball rolling? I believe we ended last week with a dangling thread from you, am I correct, Beatrice?"

A petite young woman covered in flowing silk scarves of many vibrant hues nods and dabs a moist eye with a scalloped handkerchief.

"That's right, Dr. Ost," she says, voice quavering. "It's just, I can't seem to make peace with this whole business. If I just knew who did this to me and why I was chosen. I'd never do this to anyone, ever. When I feed I make sure my victims are dead. I refuse to let this cycle of suffering stem from me. I so badly wish I had the courage to just end it all. It would be so much easier, but I can't. Sometimes I just picture myself going up to my roof and waiting for the sun to rise and then, *poof*, I'd be . . . I'd be . . . " She bursts into tears and her neighbor, the Con Ed behemoth, puts an arm around her narrow shoulders, which, once she realizes it's there, she shrugs off like it's a thirty-pound bag of manure. "*Leon*," she shrills, "*I don't like you touching me!*"

"Oh sure, you think you're better than me because you got money! We can't all got money, Miss Moneybags. All a youse, you all lookit me like I'm some kinda jerk on accounta I ain't loaded. Well, fuck all a youse, that's all I'm sayin'! You think the sewers are self-maintaining? Fuck that shit. Jerks like me gotta go down there an' slog through your shit to make this city run. You should all be kissin' my puckered starfish!"

"That was very good, Leon," Dr. Ost says. "Very raw. But no one here thinks any less of you because you're a laborer."

The way Dr. Ost pronounces "laborer," doesn't convince me that he doesn't think less of Leon.

"Ah, banana oil," Leon grouses, staring into his lap, legs spread wide as he adjusts his bunched package. "I was just tryin' a little tenderness is all."

Beatrice continues to weep into her silken hanky.

This is exactly what I thought: group therapy. For bloodsuckers. Jesus H. Christ.

"You know how many times I spot bodies floatin' down the tubes?" Leon continues, taking the floor. "You jerks think you can flush 'em like baby alligators. You think the sewer is like some magic portal that makes your dirty work go away. Well, it ain't, I'm sure as shittin' tellin' youse that. It ain't and I'm the schmuck who's gotta make your bits of business go away but for permanent. I'm getting paid to keep things flowin' down there, not do a little extra maintenance for our so-called community. No one here's writin' me no checks, I'm tellin' youse that. I should be gettin' some kinda kickbacks."

"We all acknowledge the value of your work, Leon," Dr. Ost says, his voice soft, conciliatory, phony.

"Ah, nuts." Leon folds his arms and pushes his chin onto his expansive chest, which heaves with indignity and resentment. "I been down the sewers for over a hundred years dealin' with this crap. None a you fucks works. None a youse. 'Cept Desmond. Desmond's a fuckin' machine." Leon nods his head at the lint-picker, who returns a sheepish grin. "He earns his fuckin' keep, but that's it. Desmond's square an' the rest a youse can go fuck yourselves."

"That's poppycock," a prissy-looking black gent in a cravat and derby says. "I work, yes, you best believe I work." He shifts in his seat, bristling. His dress is completely anachronistic, the bowler hat, spats, the silver pince-nez. He looks like Henri de Toulouse-Lautrec, only black and of normal height.

"Yeah, so whattaya do?" Leon asks, confrontational.

"I'm not at liberty to say," Prissy McDerbyhat huffs, also folding his arms across his pigeon chest.

"Uh-huh," Leon continues. "How's about the rest a you jerks? Whattaya youse do?"

A chorus of variations on the "I'm not at liberty to say" theme is echoed throughout the room and then Leon's glare falls on me, the interloper.

"What about you, pal?" he challenges, a globule of spit flying out on the hard "P."

"Perhaps you have something to share with our group, Phil?" Dr. Ost coaxes.

"Not particularly. But I'll say this: I work a shitty job that I just came from, and while I'm perfectly at liberty to discuss it, I don't know any of you and don't feel any compunction to share anything whatsoever. Okay? I came with Eddie. You want me to wait outside I'll wait outside. No skin off my back."

Leon half smiles and says, "Answered like someone with a sac fulla balls. Stay put, pal. Maybe you'll like our little group. Plus it could use a little injection of testosterone. We got us a bunch a real overcooked noodles in this room."

"*Please*, Leon," says Dr. Ost.

I glance over at Eddie, who's clearly in Leon's noodle category, and shake my head. Eddie looks different here, less confident. I look around the room counting nine, including me. Justine the nail-biter, Desmond the lint-picker, the black Lautrec, Eddie, Leon the Con Ed guy, Doc Ost, Beatrice the scarf lady, and a silent Mediterranean-looking guy in the far corner who just sits and observes, his fingers steepled. Like all the others, except for Leon and me, he's dressed expensively and I, like Leon, wonder how the hell they've gotten all this loot. Eddie told me he made his money the old-fashioned way and inherited it, but do all these clods come from the lace-curtain crowd?

Eddie says, "Phil and I had ourselves a little adventure last weekend . . . ," but I cut him off with a brisk, firm, "I don't think we need to get into that."

"Oh ho," Dr. Ost says, "It seems we have a difference of opinion. Perhaps Eddie needs to share your adventure with the group."

"Perhaps that's too fucking bad," I say. "If Eddie felt the need to share he should've let me in on it first and given me the option of veto."

"That's reasonable," Dr. Ost allows, "but this is a group therapy session and what we say here stays here." He points at his multiple framed degrees and certificates on the wall. "I took an oath nearly a century ago, and doctor-patient confidentiality is taken very seriously here. As is patient-patient confidentiality, isn't that so, everyone? We've all confessed and purged in here, yes?" Everyone nods, even the silent Mediterranean. "We all share the same . . . condition here, and have all committed innumerable mortal felonies as a result. So if you please, let Edward speak."

"I don't please. I'm fucking chagrined."

"I understand your feelings," Dr. Ost says with a hint of condescension. "Edward?"

"I dunno," Eddie says. "Phil's right. I kind of shanghaied him here and he wasn't expecting this. I thought maybe, since he'd been feeling bad since our little faux pas, maybe he'd like to talk about it with a professional and . . . "

"*Faux pas*?" I sputter. "You're calling it a faux pas? We didn't topple a tray of hors d'oeuvres, *Edward*, we . . . " I stop myself. "We didn't topple a tray of hors d'oeuvres. Listen, you seemed pretty sanguine about our ordeal. As for me, I'm used to tending my own garden. No offense, gang, but therapy and group confessions are not for me."

"And, Edward, how do you feel about Phil's position?" Dr. Ost asks.

"Phil's right. What we did, it was no big thing for me. I'm mercifully unburdened by conscience."

"Quoth the bard, 'Conscience doth make cowards of us all,'" misquotes Prissy Lautrec, earning him a contemptuous "Ah, shuddup," from Leon. I'm liking Leon more by the minute. What he lacks in finesse he makes up for in refreshingly brusque straightforwardness and open hostility. Prissy bristles and I begin to laugh. "Fuckin' A," says Leon, who erupts in a throaty guffaw. If muscle cars could laugh, they'd make the same sound.

An hour passes, filled with gripes, petty complaints, self-esteem issues, therapy jargon, and many more tears from Ms. Lachrymose with the frilly hankies. I've never cottoned to therapy. My ex suggested it when I was becoming what I've become, laboring under the mistaken idea that I was just going through a phase and would snap out of it. I'd explained the burns on my hands and arms as a freak cooking accident, but my newfound aversion to the sun, my depression and confusion, my lack of intimacy with her? She thought some trips to the local headshrinker would help. I told her they wouldn't. She took it for a lack of willingness to help heal our relationship; that my general negativity had ballooned beyond her endurance. What can I say? She was wrong, she was right. Water under the bridge. I wonder what she looks like these days. She was a real beauty back in the day.

But enough nostalgia. I'm getting all misty over here.

The session breaks up and Leon comes over to me and apologizes for giving me static about the chair. More water under the bridge. In the waiting room he introduces me to Desmond, the lint-picker. Now that he's standing I see Desmond is shorter than I thought, one of those people with compact legs and a long torso. He sports trendy tinted glasses and the likewise trendy habiliment of a club-kid/video game designer. I'm not far off. He proffers an expensive-looking business card with a lenticular photographic image that goes back and forth between his close-lipped smile and then flashing his pointies, like those novelty pictures of Jesus on the cross, eyes closed, then open and cast Heavenward. Blinking Jesus. The card reads, "Desmond Hughes: What You Need, in About an Hour." He grins as I look up, well pleased with his nod to the mortal world.

"Like LensCrafters holds a patent on fast service," he says, a faint British accent lurking beneath his Americanization, picking lint that on closer examination I'm sure exists only in his mind.

"And what would I be needing?" I ask.

"How's your documentation? You all up to date? Or should I say, you up to date in a way that makes sense to outsiders? Let me see your driver's license."

"Don't have one. Don't drive."

"Want one? Okay how's about a passport?"

I hand him mine and he sniggers as he examines it. "Oh dear. Your *real* birthday, I'm guessing?" I nod. "How long is that going to work for you? You're fifty-four, correct? But you had the change of life when? When you were what, maybe twenty-five?" I like this Desmond. He's the first to guess younger. But *change of life*? What is this, menopause?

"Twenty-seven," I say.

"And you pass this to people and they give you the hairy eyeball, correct?"

"Pretty much."

"Not a problem."

Leon and Eddie lean in and confer. Leon hands me his driver's license and passport and Social Security card. All list his birth year as 1964.

"I was born in *eighteen* sixty-four," Leon explains. "But Desmond here, with his computers and shit, he can whip up anything."

"Listen, my man," Desmond says, "I was kicking it with Chas. Babbage, you know? You heard of him? Of course you have, you're an educated man, I can tell. But Babsy? It's all been a piece of piss since old Babsy's Analytical Engine. Then again, Babsy himself was easy to take the piss out of. All you had to do was start humming, maybe a bit of Chopin, whatever, and he was through the roof. 'That bloody row is wrecking my concentration!' Fuck, it was a giggle."

"So you're a hacker and counterfeiter," I say, perhaps unnecessarily.

"To call a spade a spade, yes. And no. I can get in to all the databases, changes records, whatever. But I'm not a counterfeiter. That's the beauty part. I have the real establishments send you your new, totally authentic documentation. So instead of being some young stud with the birth year of a middle-aged geezer . . . "

"I gotcha."

"Yes, you do." Desmond winks.

"And what does this cost?"

"Nothing. Call it community service. I live quite comfortably skimming funds from this institution and that one and so forth. Millionaires and billionaires have unwittingly helped me to be a very prosperous upper tier thousandaire for quite a long while. I do the odd paid commission for the odd member of our kind. But for you, pro bono, baby. You have e-mail?"

"Yeah."

"Send me your particulars and an unflattering current photo and I'll get you sorted."

"Thanks. That's very cool."

And it is. Eddie and I walk to the elevators after exchanging eighty-eights with Leon and Desmond, who stay behind in Dr. Ost's waiting room, still chatting. The others have taken their leave.

"So?" Eddie says.

"So?" I respond, pressing the down button.

"Sorry about the misunderstanding about the thing. I just thought, mistakenly, obviously, that maybe you wanted to talk about it with someone other than me. Not exactly to confess or anything, but . . . " He smiles and shrugs. "You know. I mean, even though it's good ol' what's-his-face's burden now . . . "

"Pyne."

"Right, Pyne. Anyway, I just thought you'd like to maybe get it off your chest and get a little unbiased feather smoothing from a bona fide psychoanalyst."

"No, it's cool. No biggie. I'm trying to take a page from *The Book of Frye* and go with the flow. Plus it was nice to meet a couple of fellow bloodsuckers who seem okay. It's real nice of Desmond to do the ID thing for me. But one thing he said got me thinking. And actually I've been thinking about this a lot since I met you. He said 'community service.' About how many of our kind are there? At least in New York?"

"Obviously the census bureau doesn't account for us. Shit, they don't even know how many humans there are. But the current guesstimate is around two hundred, give or take. So, Friday night. You up for anything?"

"Actually I think I'm gonna call it a night."

"Seriously? What about a little midnight nosh? I think Leon and Desmond might be up for some madcappery."

"Nah, I'm good. Besides, unless we do it in a controlled environment, I think mutual noshing is off limits. At least for the time being. Once bitten, y' know?"

The elevator arrives and I step in, Eddie remaining on the landing.

"I think I'm going to hang out with the boys," Eddie says, jerking his head toward Ost's.

"Okay. I'll call you. Maybe *mañana*, okay?"

The doors slide shut and I ride down to the lobby. A couple of hundred. That sounds like so many. It also sounds like so few. How many millions of people populate this burg? Between eight and eleven? Something like that? And only two hundred of us? That's a lot more than I was aware of, but still. I check my watch. It's nearly three in the morning, so this is an early night. Part of me wants to hang with Eddie and the others, but my mind is racing. Twenty-seven years of being pretty much solitary isn't something you just slough off. I used to be a social animal, somewhat. I went to parties, mixed. But from nothing to all this? It's an adjustment that I'm having trouble adjusting to.

The elevator arrives in the lobby and I get out, slipping on a pair of sleek black leather gloves. When it's humid even I feel a little chill. The doors open from the inside without a key and I step into the cool night air. The sky is that odd brownish orange color you get in winter here when precipitation is on the menu. A light snow is falling and I watch the cascading flakes as they flutter down past the streetlights. The white flakes take on the colors of the neon lights, the street signals, some batches momentarily pink or green or yellow or blue. Snow as it's falling is pretty, even in the city. Before it's had a chance to settle and take on the homelier pigments of soot and piss and shit. That'll come soon enough, but for now it's nice. I turn my face up and like the Peanuts kids in *A Charlie Brown Christmas* I catch flakes on my tongue. There's no traffic on Madison and with the quarter inch of snow on the ground everything looks clean. It's quiet. So quiet I can hear the clickings and whirrings of the timing mechanisms of the stoplights.

So quiet I should be able to hear his approach from behind, but don't.

21

"Philip."

Impossible. Im-fucking-possible. My momentary succor evaporates like snow hitting a hot grill. How? Why?

"Shelley. *Fucking* Shelley."

"That's a l-l-lovely w-w-way to greet an old f-f-friend."

"Are you shadowing me? What possible explanation could you have for being here?"

"It's a sm-m-mall world?"

"Not *that* small. This won't stand, Shelley. I don't know what kind of head-trip you're trying to lay on me, but manifesting yourself everywhere I show up is bad form and plenty fucking creepy to boot, let me tell you."

"I'm s-s-sorry. I had to t-t-talk to you."

"So what, you never heard of the phone? You can't call in advance and make a plan like a normal person?"

"If you had a c-c-cell ph-ph-phone, I . . . "

"I don't need a cell phone. I don't want to be always available. It's nice to be off the grid from time to time. What's the matter, anyway, you belt your gal pal again?" That came out too mean, but fuck it, I'm in a Shelley-induced mean mood.

"Oh, Phil," Shelley says, "you cut too d-d-deep." He pulls a small bottle from his pocket, uncaps it, and has a belt. "No, th-

th-that relationship is over. She won't even t-t-take my c-c-calls."

Smart girl, I think, but out of congenital decency don't say aloud. Why do I protect this clown? He's the thorn in my side that keeps going deeper.

"So then what?"

"I'm w-w-worried about you."

I laugh. I can't help it. I laugh with such pure derision I feel a sympathy pang for Shelley, but only a small one. Mainly I'm thinking *I've got to get out of here. I've got to get away from this specter that haunts me. I've got to get away from the front of this building before the others come down because if Eddie sees Shelley, much as I'd enjoy it on some level, I can't bear the thought of someone killing him.*

Someone other than me, at any rate.

"Why on earth would you say such a weird thing?" I return. "What's to worry about?"

"I've f-f-figured it out and I've f-f-figured *you* out. The secrecy and f-f-furtiveness and the distance that's d-d-developed between us. Y-y-you're having p-p-procedures done. Cosmetic p-p-procedures. Every building I've followed you . . . "

"Whoa, whoa, whoa. Slow it down a little. *Every building*? How long have you been tailing me?" And how long have I not been noticing him? Rule one: no witnesses. Fuck!

"N-n-not long, Phil. J-j-just recently. To b-b-bear out my misgivings. Every b-b-building you've b-b-been to in the company of this mysterious n-n-new friend of yours has a p-p-prominent p-p-plastic surgeon. It's so obvious. You're a late m-m-middle-aged m-m-man and you l-l-look like a kid. No w-w-wonder you live so frugally. You sp-sp-spend every cent on these surgeries. Well, you needn't b-b-be embarrassed. It's m-m-money well spent. You look great."

I let out a huge sigh of relief, which is real. Shelley can be so fucking stupid.

"So," I say, "now you know. You've figured me out."

Shelley smiles like a mother who's coaxed a confession out of her favorite son, tears brimming his bloodshot peepers. No, if anyone's going to kill Shelley it's going to be me. I take him by the elbow and gently lead him away from the building, my anxiety about Eddie and company showing up any second on the rise. I can only imagine what Leon would make of this unflushed turd, this overcooked noodle. Shelley allows himself to be guided away, taking deep, grateful gulps from his bottle. He looks so relieved, so beatific. Ignorance is bliss.

We get to the corner and turn west onto a darker residential side street. Beautiful old townhouses line both sides and I get the momentary stab of jealousy. I've always wanted to live in one of these. Maybe someday. You never know. Once safely off Madison I take Shelley by both arms and give him a shake. I don't want to be talking to the happy Buddha; I want to be eye to eye with Shelley the sneaky souse. I need to get through to his desperate, misguided, tormented brains.

"Shelley," I say, voice now firm, eyes steely and intransigent, "you cannot follow me any more. I don't know how I didn't spot you, but I'm going to be trucking around with eyes in the back of my head from now on. I don't *need* you worrying about me and I don't *need* the added stress of a stalker. I don't *need* . . . " My hands grip his scrawny biceps tight, maybe too tight, and obviously some wires are crossed because he doesn't look at me with comprehension, he looks at me with something entirely different. And before I have a chance to react, before I have a chance to identify this odd look on his puss, before I know what's happening he's on me, planting a big, passionate kiss on my lips, trying to force his tongue into my mouth, pumping his mephitic breath down my throat and into my lungs like bellows stoking the flaming sulfur lakes in Hell.

I'm so stunned I take a moment to react. It's probably no more than a second or two, but try balancing all eleven volumes—in hardcover—of Will and Ariel Durant's *The History of Civilization* for a second or two on your testicles, then get back to me on how long a couple of seconds can feel. I shove as hard as I can, which is pretty hard, and Shelley disengages, stumbling backward onto the stoop of a darkened brownstone, his eyes still closed, his tongue lolling out between his thin lips.

"Oh for fuck's sake, Shel, pull yourself together." I spit on the sidewalk, my gob making a dark crater in the fine layer of new powder, then wipe my mouth on my sleeve. Shelley looks up at me, eyes pleading.

"Don't hate me."

If he only knew.

"I'm drunk," he says, like this explains anything. Like this is news. "I'm lonely."

Shelley. Fucking Shelley.

"Just go home, Shel. Sleep it off. Leave me alone. Just fuck off for a while, okay? Gimme some space."

"I . . ."

"Don't follow me any more, Shel. You follow me and we're quits for good, you savvy? I'm dead fucking serious. If you drove in, get in your fucking car and go back to Connecticut."

He nods and I walk away, not looking back. I'm sickened more by my own compassion than Shelley's sorrowful neediness. He stays put on the stoop, snow gathering on him as he snuffles into his scarf. Maybe he'll stay there all night. Maybe they'll find him the next morning, frozen to death, a mope-sicle. Keep it unrequited, Shelley, just keep it unrequited.

I turn the corner and then, out of Shelley's eyesight, do something I seldom do: I tear ass and run like torch-bearing villagers are chasing me. My mouth tastes like someone took a dump in it. My own eyes begin to well up. I feel sorry for Shelley. I feel sorry for myself. He's lonely? He's got the brass to complain about loneliness? I live alone out of necessity. He could have a relationship, but no, he dangles women along while he tilts with a windmill named Phil Merman. The idiot. After several blocks I stop running and the dam bursts. I don't think I've cried in a couple of decades, but I do now. Maybe it's an after effect of having gone to therapy tonight. So I didn't participate. Not really. Maybe it's some subliminal after-effect. I don't normally feel sorry for myself, but Shelley's pass really fucked me up. It shouldn't have surprised me, but Jesus.

After a few minutes I get my shit together and wipe my face. I spit again on the sidewalk. Normally I find public spitting uncon-scionable, but this is a special occasion. My mouth feels seared, the alcohol, the honeyed rotting meat, drowning in the despairing waters of the Shelley Poole. I spot a twenty-four-hour deli and cross the street. The snow's really beginning to come down and accumulate. I'm sure by morning it'll be a few inches thick.

I step into the deli and make a beeline for the mints, receiving a curt nod from the middle-aged Korean gent at the register. I re-turn the halfhearted greeting and look at the selection. Are Altoids strong enough? Is anything strong enough? Eddie's smart to keep mints on hand. I'm not a fan, but I at the moment I'd gargle Lysol to kill the taste in my mouth. I know half of it is psychological, but mints will have to do. I realize I feel parched, too, so I walk to the refrigerated section to snag a bottle of water. My heart is racing. I'm sweating from emotional tumult—*tsuris*. Shelley really japped me with that sneak attack. As I make for the counter a young black dude dressed in the modern thug idiom—The North Face over-stuffed coat, oversized stiff dark jeans, Timberland boots, do-rag—busts in and stomps right up to the counter, shotgun in hand, demanding cash. I am so not in the mood for this.

"Yo, empty th' regista, bitch!"

He spots me and to underscore his point about fulfilling his demand in a timely manner he pumps one out of his Mossberg Super-Shorty into my abdomen. I stumble backward, feeling like my guts have just had a hole blasted in them. Oh, wait . . .

Do you have any idea how painful it is to get a bellyful of shotgun discharge at close range? Probably not, and I must admit that I'm new to this myself so words fail me. All I can say is it hurts worse than any physical hurt I've ever been hurt by. Ever. Boy, does it hurt. Plus, on top of all this pain I've got to strategize my next move. I can only play dead if the shooter kills the shopkeeper. If he doesn't and I get up and walk away that will cause all kinds of trouble. Can't have that. On the other hand I've got to feed. I've got to have fresh blood if I'm going to heal, and this is a bad one. My worst yet. So bad I'm not even thinking about my clothes. Or maybe I am, because I'm thinking about not thinking about them, which is really a kind of passive-aggressive way of thinking about them anyway. Fuck, I'm rambling. My mind is racing. My heart is thudding. Good, he missed the heart. My ribs feel pretty much intact, but oh mommy, my innards are fast on their way to becoming out-ards. I'm losing lots of blood and my ears are pounding. I can barely hear myself think.

The shooter's got to pay. That's all there is to it. Low rent vigilantism. That's what Eddie called it. But it isn't going to be vigilantism if I have to take out the Korean. I'll feed on him, too, if I have to. That would justify it. Sort of. I've got to adapt my profile of acceptable kills. I'm going to need a lot of blood to patch this sucking crater in my middle. I can't let the culprit get away. Christ, this is agony. I need this like I need a hole in my . . . Oh wait. Again.

Since I'm no longer an object of even passing interest, I lift my head to scope out the action. The shopkeeper is playing ball—duh—and emptying the register.

"You got a safe, bitch?"

"No. No safe. Only register. You go. You take money. Go. Please. No more trouble."

"Gimme yo watch an' yo jewelry!"

As the shopkeeper undoes his watch the gunman empties candy trays into his duffle bag, the greedy prick, but that's fine. It gives me the element of surprise. No one expects a dead man to attack. I lunge at the shooter and twist him away from the Korean, not wanting the counterman to know exactly what I'm doing. This isn't your standard takedown. With my back turned to the Korean, I dig in and suck for all I'm worth, draining this miscreant's lifeblood. The gun drops from his paralyzed fingers as my toxins make him go placid. The shopkeeper is shouting in Korean. I don't know the words but I recognize the spirit in which they're being shouted: basically, "Get that scumbag!" Only too happy to comply. Be happy, Mr. Grocer, *for now*.

The residual pain will linger a while, but I can feel the flesh knitting as I suck.

"You hurt man," the Korean instructs, "I call police!"

I stop what I'm doing and, on the mend, bound over the counter and snatch the phone away from the guy, who now brandishes a .38 snub nose.

"What you do?" he shouts, no longer my pep squad, now frightened as he sees the blood dribbling down my chin. Usually I'm neater, but cut me a wedge. I've got blood everywhere. Mine. The shooter's. Everywhere. "You no come here," the Korean

stammers, trying to aim but too scared. "You no good. You a devil!"
This is gratitude? Oh well, give the devil his due. I sink my fangs
into his throat. I don't feel good about this; honest I don't, but
sometimes you've gotta do what you've gotta do. He struggles for
a nanosecond then slips into blessedly comatose submission.

After I finish him off I look back at the shooter who's stupefied
but not completely sapped. If I leave him like this he might turn. I
don't want to be responsible for creating an immortal scumbag
like him. I don't want to be responsible for creating any more of
my kind, period. I take the grocer's keys and lock the door, turn
off the lights and even though I'm full I drag the stickup thug out
of view and finish every drop. I look through the tattered mess
that was my jacket and shirt and see my solar plexus looking better. Not perfect, but getting there. I might rattle like that maraca
Eddie mentioned when I fished the slug out by the waterfront.
Who can say? Maybe I'll be passing buckshot like gallstones.

I look around to see if there are any recording devices. A video
camera. Of course. Fuck, this just keeps getting better and better. I
go to the office behind the store, a small, cramped space, not very
tidy. There are two VCRs running. I press the stop button, rewind
for a few seconds, hit play looking at the small black and white
monitor. There I am, doing my thing. Okay, I've got the evidence.
I eject both tapes, praying there's no backup, but I doubt it. This
isn't a chain store, just a simple Mom and Pop, minus Pop. I pocket the tapes, take a bulky winter coat from a hanger and put it on.
My pants, being black, mask the saturation of blood.

In the dark I survey the mess. Blood on the floor—mine. Behind
the counter the Korean lays dead. In the aisle by the cookies lies
the shooter. I drag him back to roughly where he was standing
when threatening the Korean, then I go behind the counter and
pry the gun from the Korean's cold dead hands. Sorry, Charlton.

From the cashier's position I shoot the thug in the throat, face and chest. I then prop the Korean up on a stool, take the thug's shotgun—nice heft, a comfortable rubber pistol grip—and blow off the Korean's head.

Gee, maybe I'll get to scan the slides of this crime scene someday. Won't that be fun? Ah, all the crime photographers use digital these days. Just as well. Still, where's Maureen Dooley when you need her?

I contemplate squirting some lighter fluid around and setting the place ablaze, but I don't really want to add arson to my résumé. I've never done arson before to cover my tracks and I guess I don't plan on starting tonight. Gunshots should bring the cops any time so I unlock the door, check the street, which is vacant, and hightail it out of there. I don't feel good about any of this. I'm glad I had gloves on, though. That was fortunate. Who wants to do a wipe down? Clean up in Aisle Three. No thanks.

I speed walk five blocks before I realize I forgot the mints and water.

Do I get points for not shoplifting?

22

"Oh my *God*," Adélaïde gasps as she opens the door and lets me in. "Whatever *happened* to you, Philip? You look a fright."

I must. Not having taken a cab, my jaunt six avenues east and a couple blocks north in the blizzard has left me looking like a dinner theater version of Cesare from *The Cabinet of Dr. Caligari*, my hair plastered to my forehead, the parka dripping melting snow.

"Sorry to show up unannounced like this, but . . . "

"Not at all, not at all. Come in, come in," she says, taking my arm and pulling me into the foyer. A servant appears and coaxes the pilfered coat off, revealing the mess underneath, which elicits another gasp from my twiggy hostess. "Oh, *Philip*, you *have* had a rough night."

I nod, bloodstained water dripping onto her pristine marble floor.

"We have to get you out of those wet, ruined things."

"And into a dry martini," I say, not smiling.

"Well at least you maintain your wit," she says, also not smiling. She takes my hand and leads me into one of her bedrooms and closes the door. "I know you're a bit more modest than some of my regulars, so privacy for *Monsieur* Philip whilst he explains his terrible appearance."

So I tell her as she strips off the bloody remnants of my shirt and undershirt. I go into full confessional mode—maybe it's shock, maybe

I'm traumatized, not by any one thing but the cumulative effect of the night's mercurial dive from pleasant to horrific—but I spill it all. I tell her about Eddie dragging me to group therapy, why he dragged us there in the first place, the whole waterfront incident, Shelley and his disgusting pie-eyed pass, his abject pining, about the grocery store episode, everything. She listens without commentary, slipping off my pants and underwear. I'm so caught up in the recounting of events that I don't even notice that I'm naked until I've finished.

I'm naked.

And so is she.

Maybe it's the light. Maybe it's the trauma. Maybe it's all I've just been through and my vulnerable mood. Maybe it's that she is a she, but in this soft light Adélaïde looks less harsh, less a collection of hard angles and fleshy geometries, and when she drops her robe, drops to her knees and begins licking coagulated blood off my belly I don't protest a jot. Her tongue traces across the raw surface of my abdomen, which still looks like a topographical map of several mountain ranges all lumped together. She purrs and looks up at me.

"*Mmm*," she says, eyes half-mast, "smoky."

Something about the way the word "smoky" rolls off her tongue, something about the way her tongue rolls off the tip of my glans, but Adélaïde is fast on her way to being the hostess with the mostest. She takes the head into her mouth and—*nirvana*—I forget my woes. She eases me back toward the massive bed, my knees buckling as my legs make contact with the mattress. After fellating me for what seems like hours she climbs on top of me and impales herself. I just lie there, not because I'm lazy but because she knows what she wants and is taking it. She grinds her bony mound into me, like pestle to mortar. In this moment she is beautiful. She looks like a sexy Gustav Klimt painting, or, if such a thing is possible, a zesty, healthy Egon Schiele girl, a German expressionist pinup mocking the fullness and curves of Vargas and Petty and Elvgren. I close my eyes and inhale, smelling her softly perfumed femaleness. With the drapes and shutters closed I have no idea how much time passes but it feels like an eternity I might actually find endurable. Enjoyable even.

She begins to grind harder, her noises more feral, and stunningly, we come simultaneously. This gal really knows her stuff. My orgasm is powerful but I don't feel depleted—quite the opposite. I feel invigorated and rapacious. I want more. I want nourishment. Adélaïde dismounts and curls around me, petting me, touching my face and chest. Her hand stops its searching and teasing and becomes still. An almost imperceptible sound of dormancy escapes her small, pursed lips. She's asleep. I want more.

I want this wound all the way healed.

I want a double.

Naked and somewhat dazed I leave the bedroom and walk across the living room to the bartender, who greets me with a raised eyebrow and knowing smile.

"You look a lot more settled in than you did last time."

"Oh Jesus," I say, suddenly feeling embarrassed about my nudeness.

"Nothing I haven't seen before," he says. He nods at my lacerated belly and offers the Ecuadorian, which I accept. In for a penny is my current mood. When in Rome, you know? He fills a snifter Dean Martin would balk at and slides it across the bar. With a wink he offers me a straw and I take the fishbowl and drain it. It's heady and wonderful and I feel the last vestiges of my injury smooth over into seamless perfection. *Mazel tov.* I drum my palms on the bar and grin like a happy pig.

"Phil," I say offering my hand, which he takes and gives a thick, meaty shake.

"Paul."

"Well, Paul, I've had me one helluva roller coaster of a night, my friend."

"Took one in the breadbasket, did you?"

"I cannot tell a lie. I did." I feel drunk, but not sloppy out of control ordinary drunk. Beatified, euphoric drunk. Adélaïde's house blend. *Goddamn*. "If you'll excuse me, Paul, I think I want to mingle. Hey, are um, oh, what's her name? I feel like such a heel. Gimme a sec. Oh, are Sheila and Brianna around?"

"Wow," he says. "Didn't you just exit the Mistress's boudoir?"

"Oh, you're right. That would be uncool, huh? A bit loutish after Adélaïde's hospitality."

"Not at all. As libertines go, she's the libertiniest. She won't mind. Yes, Sheila and Brianna are in one of the bedchambers, but they might not be alone. They might already be engaged. Knock first."

I leave Paul and pad across the cool marble floor, across several expensive rugs and down a hall, where several doors are either closed or slightly ajar. It's got to be past sunrise so maybe Adélaïde's other guests are sleeping. I peek in the first door and the room is empty, save for the posh furnishings. Tonight I don't feel like the covetous Queens-boy who hates the rich. Adélaïde made me feel so welcome—I guess that goes without saying, actually—that I was, *am* one of the club. The inner circle. I guess I have to thank Eddie for that. I have to thank Eddie for a lot of things. I hate to think of myself as the TV movie "gruff but lovable old man who learns the true meaning of Christmas," but it's been so long since I felt fraternity for anyone that friendship is a new and scary concept. Acceptance. Lack of shame. These will take some adjusting to.

I rap gently on the next door and when I get no reply open it a crack. I have to thank Eddie bountifully. Sheila and Brianna are engaged all right, locked in a pornographic *soixante neuf* that would make Bob Guccione blush. Seeing all those curves, all that smooth, undulating flesh, those breasts, those asses. My mind flits back to Shelley's mouth on mine, his yearning, desperate eyes. I deserve this. I deserve immoderation, profligacy. Emboldened by Adélaïde's house blend I enter the room and shut the door behind me. It's only when my engorged dowser enters Sheila's field of vision that my presence is divined. Sheila looks up at my rude protuberance and leers, patting the bed. I join them. The three of us spend the next few hours making the saints cry.

$$\bullet \ \bullet \ \bullet$$

As the steam wafts around the sauna, Sheila and I sit on the hot bench and smile those, "the sex was great, but the sex is over, at least for now, and let's face it, we have nothing to say to each other" smiles. It's true, and it's a little awkward, but sated as we are, it's tolerable. I enjoy her nakedness; she seems to enjoy mine.

"Well," she says.

"Well, indeed."

"You fuck really well," she says.

"You do, too."

"So . . . "

"So, indeed."

"So maybe you'll remember this time."

I laugh. "Yeah, definitely. Definitely."

"Well, I'm going to catch some zees with Brianna. Join us if you like, there's plenty of room in that big ol' bed."

Grabbing a towel, Sheila peels herself off the bench and walks across the room, adorable pink horizontal impressions across her ass from the planks. Before she makes it to the door she fades from sight in the thick fog. I stay put and enjoy my *shvitz*. I'm a middle-aged—at least in human years—Jew from Queens. Okay, so I'm an atheist, but culturally speaking. Sue me. I inhale the hot, moist air. It feels good in my lungs. I close my eyes and just see the orangey redness of the inside of my lids. This is womblike, comforting. I keep telling myself, I deserve this, I deserve this. Shelley's clumsy overture, the Korean, the thug, getting shot in the guts. After all that lousy crap, *I deserve this*. Goddamn right I do.

In this muzzy nebula I lose all track of time, dipping in and out of wakefulness, dozing in the haze. Mixed thoughts and images pass through the murk of my consciousness. I think of my mother, how much I miss her. Maybe it's that womb thing. I think of my father and how maybe bagging three chicks in one night might've impressed him slightly. But then I think of how the whole of this night would nauseate him and the mellow fades. The dull unripe purples and sick yellows of bruises creep into the periphery of the comforting coral hue. Since I'm neither awake nor asleep I can't really control the nature of my thoughts and impressions. I've never mastered lucid dreaming, and I think you have to be fully asleep for that anyway.

The bruise grows and the pulchritudinous images of Sheila and Brianna and Adélaïde, their curves, their suppleness, their inviting clefts and delicate folds, are subsumed by darkness. Their labia metamorphose into my gut wound, which blossoms into a scorched Hiroshima cavity, conflagrant, angry. Rudderless, I sink into that chasm and death surrounds me on all sides, a personal collection of atrocities born of my need. My own private holocaust. Thousands of accusing eyes, my victims. I remember all their faces, and each shimmers into hard focus, their eyes seeming to say, "Sure I was scum, but did you have to kill me?"

Sorry, I'm afraid I did.

I sink deeper and deeper, my psyche culling recent additions from the herd for special consideration: the Korean, the two teens.

Sorry, sorry, sorry. I sink and sink and sink and after an eternity my feet touch ground again. It's pitch-black. Dark so tenebrous even I have trouble seeing. And when my sight returns my gaze is returned by Shelley's and I know I've hit bottom.

23

Saturday, January 27th, 2001

A hand is slapping me hard across the chops, again and again, a muffled voice accompanying each blow. I feel cool air on damp skin and I'm shivering, something I seldom do.

"Wake up, Philbo! Come on, you, wake up!"

My left eye pries itself open and I see Eddie hunched over me. I'm lying on the floor, naked, Eddie straddling my chest. I must've blacked out from the potent combo of steam, Adélaïde's house blend, the tournament of sex, stress, all of it. When I lock peepers with Eddie he grins and gives me a final light slap on the cheek.

"Somebody overdid it."

"Wha'? Stop hitting me, you." My speech is ossified, the insides of my mouth gummous and ucchy. I lift my head off the floor and tom-toms pound behind my eyeballs, trying to evict them. "Jehoshaphat. I feel like shit."

Like Dorothy waking up in Kansas surrounded by those hick farmhands and relatives, I look up and beyond Eddie to see Leon, Desmond, Paul the bartender, and Adélaïde. Adélaïde looks concerned, but the other four grin like idiots. Leon elbows Desmond in the ribs, emitting his tractor pull laugh. Eddie stands up and proffers a hand, which I grab and he eases me to my feet. I'm still in the sauna, only now it's cold, the steam off, the walls sweating condensation.

"Fuck," I burp, fanning the air by my mouth. "'Scuse. I need to use the convenience."

"Nice one hangin'," Leon chuckles, loosening a few tiles.

Mortified, I hasten to the toilet in the adjacent room and empty my bladder. I yearn for clothes, even my bloodied rags. I look in the mirror and my body is impressed with a red grid from the tile floor on which I passed out. On Brianna the stripes looked cute. I look like I've been scored for easy disassembling. When I exit the restroom, Eddie, now alone, offers a slate-colored silk robe that I accept and slip into with abundant gratitude. He pats me on the shoulder and smiles with nothing other than camaraderie. What a *mentsh*.

"Who's got your back?" he says. There's a little pause while I shrug on the robe, then he continues. "Addie told me a truncated version of your little adventure. Made the morning paper."

"Great."

"They're chalking it off as a robbery gone awry. Small column, not exactly front page material."

"So I shouldn't worry."

"You should never worry. Worrying is for the little people. Anyway, Addie bought you a gift."

I follow Eddie to Adélaïde's bedroom and laid out on the bed is a very attractive spread of men's clothes. Being the outer boroughs skinflint that I am I immediately look for the price tags, certain this snazzy ensemble costs more than my monthly paycheck.

"Like Addie buys off the rack. Jesus, you really are a fucking clodhopper sometimes, Philpot. Addie's a classy lady. She'd never leave the price on a gift."

"Was that terribly déclassé?"

"Terribly. It's lucky she wasn't here to witness it. She might've sent you home naked."

"I wouldn't have done it if she was in the room. Still, these boxer briefs probably cost more than I'd spend on a pair of regular pants."

"No comment. You going to dress like a working stiff for the next hundred years or are you going to take a page from the *Book of Frye* and dress a little chic now and again?"

"I *am* a working stiff. But at least I've got me one set of glad rags, yeah?"

"That's just what she laid out for you. There's more in the armoire."

I take a look in the wardrobe and there's a new set of duds for each day of the week. And what's my reaction? Guilt. I feel guilty that Adélaïde felt so bad about my bedraggled appearance that she felt compelled to shower me with gifts. This is nice stuff. I look at the labels and it's all the biggies, the stuff I don't even think about thinking about.

"She bought you a watch, too, you lucky dick," Eddie says. "A TAG Heuer. I've been coming here for years and she's bought me squat."

I stop myself before asking if he ever had sex with her, either, slipping into the clothes. They fit perfectly, like they were made for me. I admire myself in the mirror. Though my hair is a bit of a mess and I could use a shave, I look good. These clothes suit me right to the ground.

"You're a good-looking guy, Philbo. A real heartbreaker. Next time your creepy stalker shows up he's gonna come in his drawers."

"Adélaïde told you about that, too, huh?"

"I asked you if he was going to be a problem."

"He's not. He thinks I'm going in for cosmetic surgery."

"I don't care what he thinks. If he shows up again I'm going to take care of him. Just so you know."

"No, Eddie. *I* will."

"Okay, then."

"What time is it anyway?"

"Your new timepiece is set correctly, genius. Don't make me embarrass myself with the clunky old thing I've got on my wrist."

I check the exquisite piece of machinery on my wrist and it tells me it's seven thirty-two. I don't know when the girls and I stepped into the sauna, so I have no idea how long I was unconscious. To get some idea, I have Eddie confirm that it's the post meridiem, which it is. Much as this stay at Maison Sigismund has been a blast, I think it's time to mosey. I admire my chronograph one more time, turning it this way and that, appreciating the grace of design, the quality of materials, earning me a disapproving sniff from Eddie. I slip into a baby-soft black leather coat and together we leave the boudoir. Even with my tousled hair, I do look good. Really good. I sure don't look like a guy who was shot in the stomach a day earlier.

When Eddie and I enter the living room Leon is going down on Desmond and my entire notion of both of them is knocked on its ear. For a fleeting moment I worry that maybe Desmond expects this from all his clientele. Maybe pro bono is really pro boner. I don't begrudge anyone their proclivities, but I don't need falsified papers *that* bad.

"Gentlemen, gentlemen," Eddie says as we walk past them, "a little decorum, if you please."

Leon removes his mouth from Desmond's business long enough to tell Eddie to get bent.

"Sorry, Leon, but Homie don't play that."

Okay, so I have preconceived notions. Who doesn't? I just don't picture large, brutish sewer workers blowing computer nerds, even if they are groovy, fashionable nerds. Does anyone picture that, for that matter? Eddie and I make our way through the mélange of copulating twosomes and threesomes and so on, some straight, some gay, some mix and match. It's really nonstop, at least when I've been here. Funny how fast one becomes inured to the sight and proximity of this kind of thing. My mind drifts to my recent activities here and I feel a fleeting pulse in my trousers. One could become addicted to this kind of rampant hedonism. I think about how many times I came last night and it hits me.

"I didn't use any protection last night."

"Protection?" Eddie asks. "Whattaya mean protection? Protection from what?"

"Protection from making babies."

"You're a little old to be getting the facts of life chat, but . . . "

"Can we reproduce? I never really thought about it before. Can we, other than by turning humans? Can we make babies?"

"Nope. Sterility is a byproduct. Think about it: we don't age, so how could a baby even develop? It couldn't. Part of our makeup is losing the ability to procreate. The only way we propagate our kind is by conversion. I think that's a blessing. Keeps the numbers low, keeps the standards up. It's like eugenics."

"Hitler would approve, huh?"

"Not of you, Mr. *Merman*, but in theory. And don't forget, eugenics wasn't born in Deutschland. It was a Brit who came up with it. Then America picked up the ball and ran with it. The krauts just brought to the mix that special homegrown malevolence they're so good at."

• • •

As we trudge south on York Avenue I keep thinking about our inability to breed. I'm sterile. Don't get me wrong, I'm happy about that, but the odds of finding a casual hookup who'd let you fuck her without a condom these days are pretty dicey, so chances are I still will have to sport latex if I dabble in human genitalia. Maybe I won't even bother—with humans, I mean. But it's comforting to know I can't impregnate anyone any more. That's a load off, so to speak.

I consider Eddie's comment about eugenics. I think about the origins of eugenics, its original lofty aspirations for bettering humankind, then its bastardization and corruption; what came to be known as "negative eugenics." The Nazis had their "final solution" to the "Jewish question," a racial hygiene program that began with involuntary sterilizations and ended with genocide. Yeah, that's pretty negative, all right. But it gets the gears turning, makes me wonder, so I wonder aloud.

"Why in God's name would anyone do it?"

"Do what?" asks Eddie.

"Turn a mongoloid."

"What?"

"Those mongoloids in that group home. Why would anyone deliberately turn a retard?"

"Oh, that. That was . . . that was *days* ago. Weeks."

"A week."

"That's still stuck in your craw?"

"Yeah, I mean, yeah. It's just so fucking puzzling and weird and counterproductive. Why would you create something you had to keep constant tabs on? Why aren't they just destroyed?"

"Why aren't regular plain old human ones destroyed?"

"I agree."

"No, no. I wasn't asking it for your opinion, I was posing the question, like why do humans let mongoloids live amongst them, too?"

"Exactly, I concur."

"Are you being deliberately obtuse?" Eddie asks, applying some eye drops.

"Only sort of. But with humans it's way different. A human with Down syndrome isn't going to topple a secret society by letting others know it exists. If one of those Downies escaped the home that Deirdre is running it could mean big trouble. Why not just send 'em out for a suntan and get 'em out of the way?"

"Dude, that's harsh."

"I just think they're a liability is all."

Eddie mulls it over and returns an affirmative, but then gives me a funny look.

"Any idea who turned *you*?" he asks. "Was it intentional?"

"No, and I don't think so. The coward bashed me one in the back of the skull, then pulled down my pants and fed from my inner thigh, if you can believe that. Just a few inches below my batch. Twenty-seven years of feeding and I've never once had the urge to feed south of the belt." Eddie laughs. "I don't know. I never saw it coming. At least I don't pull that kind of cowardly shit. I always make eye contact before I do them. It's a point of honor, maybe because I never did see the bullet—or fang—with my name on it. Alls I know is that fucker cost me my life, my marriage, my happiness. If I ever found out who did me I'd hunt the mother-fucker down and make him die slowly."

"Why assume it's a him?"

"Get real."

"Yeah, I suppose."

We head downtown and go to a club. The doorman cards me, looks at my ID, then my face, then my ID, then my face. I can't wait until Desmond comes through. It'll be nice to just get the usual sneer of indifference. We go in. Eddie chats up some girls. Dances. I watch, lose interest, leave without saying goodbye. I have to admit, all this high living takes its toll. I want to sit on my couch in my comfortable but unspectacular apartment with the mediocre views—rutting Latinos notwithstanding—and watch the tube. I want to watch a movie on my not too big, not too small twenty-seven-inch TV. I want to sit there in my fancy new underpants and veg out.

Sounds like fun.

24

Tuesday, January 30th, 2001

I have a new boss, Hugh Lemming—seriously, *Lemming*. To my complete surprise, Kate was axed for sexual harassment. I couldn't be more stunned; she just didn't seem the type. The story goes that she was coming on a little strong with an intern, pitching innuendo. I really can't envisage such a thing. She's such a mouse. Oh well, I'll miss her apology notes.

Lemming comes in and introduces himself. I don't really need the intro since he was promoted from within, but I shake his hand and he gives it three vigorous pumps, each identical, as if measured in advance using the recipe for a good, manly handshake. He's a big black guy, baby-faced, barrel-chested, tall. Between his two front teeth is a gap you could fit an almond in if you were so inclined, and beneath his lower lip is a thick soulpatch.

"So, Phil, I understand you're our resident ghoul," he says, voice deep, with a hint of boss-to-subordinate jocularity.

"Huh?" I manage. "Oh, I gotcha."

"*Yes,*" he says, bulging his eyes, "the splatter guru. It's good that you don't seem to mind this stuff. I, for one, have no problem with it either. Fact is it fascinates me. I could look at this stuff for hours. Mind if I sit in and watch the master at work?"

Red alert. The thing I like about this job is the near isolation. I can't have this jovial gorehound breathing down my neck getting his jollies looking at the nightly panoply of death. How to play this? How expendable am I?

"Gee, Hugh," I say, but he cuts me off.

"I *hate* the name Hugh. Call me Lemmy, like the guy in Motörhead, only *way* better looking." He winks and air-elbows me, pointing at his cheeks. "No mushroom-sized carbuncles on this beautiful mug, right?"

I don't know why, but it surprises me that a fortyish black guy would make a reference to Motörhead. Actually, I guess I do know why.

"Okay, *Lemmy*," I say, voice placatory, robotic smile on lips. "The thing is, I'm kind of a, how to put it, solitary guy. I don't do my best work when I feel distracted or like I'm being scrutinized."

"Lone wolf, huh?"

"Kind of, if that's okay with you."

"There's no 'I' in 'team,' Phil." He stews for a few moments, chewing his lower lip, then breaks out in a fake smile. "Well, I understand. You do good work, so I'm in no position—*other than being your boss who could fire you*! Hey, I'm just joshing." He air-elbows again. "But maybe you could let me sit in from time to time, just for fun. Or at least give me a slideshow at the end of your shift. How's that grab you? A compromise, huh?"

"Sure, *Lemmy*," I say, allowing the muscles in my face to go slack enough to mask any overt dismay. "That would be fine. Shall I buzz you when I finish tonight's cavalcade o' carnage?"

He erupts with heinous laughter, bellowing, "That's *great*! 'Cavalcade o' carnage'! I *love* it! *Har-har-har*! Yeah, that's *great*! Call me when you're through, champ!"

He leaves the office, still guffawing. I already miss Kate and her inability to laugh. I go through the startup ritual, slightly off because of the recent trauma, then open the first box and get down to it.

Label: "Duffy McDevitt. Long Island City, Queens. July 10th, 1996. Dawn. © Duffy McDevitt, Inc."

Murder-suicide. Very bloody. In what appears to be a railroad apartment, one room leading into the next into the next and so on, rooms narrow, windows only at the extreme ends of the apartment, lay the victims and the perpetrator. In the first room is an infant in its bassinet, throat slashed. Amazing how much blood escaped from this tiny baby. The duck and bunny sheets are soaked through, blood dripping and pooled on the linoleum floor beneath. The baby looks placid, peaceful, never saw it coming. I'd guess it's in the same posture it was sleeping in, no change. Bloody tracks leave the room, documented by McDevitt's camera.

In the next room is an older child, a girl, maybe four or five. This one is contorted in a position that to my eyes indicates at least a bit of a struggle. The face is distorted with fear and sorrow; the death-dulled eyes wide open, staring straight into the lens. This one has a slit throat, too, but also multiple puncture wounds in the chest and one through the open palm of the left hand. More blood, some on the wall—arterial spray.

In the kitchen are the mother and oldest child, maybe eleven or twelve, a boy. Stealth was out the window for these two, both blasted open with shotgun discharge. I feel a slight twinge in my belly—sense memory—and sympathize. The mother has passed on with a look of permanent disappointment and disgust, a look I'm guessing dad saw many times. Maybe it contributed to this rampage. The son just looks absent, lights out, nobody home.

In the bedroom dad finishes the business at hand and even leaves a punch line to his sick joke. A cop holds up the neatly printed suicide note for the camera, a quizzical look on his face. He doesn't get it, but I do and for a moment I laugh, almost liking dad, the twisted fuck. The note simply reads, "Because where's the fun in that?" The cop's face is so stupid and uncomprehending, but isn't it obvious? I want to grab this boy in blue, shake him, and ask him, "What's the one question everyone asks when they hear about a murder-suicide? They say, 'why didn't the sonuvabitch just kill himself first?'"

Label: "Frances L. Ross. Morningside Heights. April 11th, 1987. Morning. ©1987 Associated Image Bank Syndicate."

This one's almost cute enough to be a postcard. Stabbing death, old lady. That's not so cute. But the old lady, lying on the floor on an ornately woven rug, has a white Persian kitty-cat on her lap. The kitty is looking right into the camera, its eyes glowing green from the flash. In the next picture the cop shoos away the kitty, but whimsy doesn't often crop up in these sequences. This, other than the opener, is a very routine, very dull set. Unspectacular. Next.

Label: "Charles B. Pierce. Jamaica, Qns. November 3, 1999. ©1999 PPM, LLP."

Drive-by multiple shooting. Some probably intended, some probably not. Kid in stroller. Not. Lady pushing stroller is winged, but her offspring is dead, dead, dead and she mewls inconsolably. Young black thug types, similar to the one who shot me. They might have died differently but the end result is the same. They're just as dead. Lots of onlookers, all jaded, some laughing. It's always the laughers who catch my eye. They're human but inured to death. They lack empathy, I guess. Maybe they knew the victims and are glad they're dead. Maybe they're the killers, come back to gloat, hiding in plain sight. Who knows? Blood, body bags, same old shit. This is as routine for the participants in the images as it is for me. That's kind of sad.

Label: "Sven Lindquist-Gonzalez. Elmhurst, Queens. August 13, 1974. Late night. ©1974 Lindquist-Gonzalez Trust."

Elmhurst, Queens.

August 13th, 1974.

I feel a little chill as the first image, strip by strip, fills my screen. It's the Elmhurst subway station back in the days of Abe Beame's nearly bankrupt New York. There's garbage all over the platform; everything looks filthy and greasy. A couple of cops with bushy mustaches, sideburns, and hair that looks too long to be officially sanctioned stand in the foreground. Beyond them is a body, the head obscured by one of the cop's hands, a blur of motion. The body's legs are parted and bent at the knees, the pants black, the cuffs slightly pegged. Between them is a telltale puddle—the poor slob whizzed himself. One shoe has been kicked off and lies a few feet away, sole up.

Lindquist-Gonzalez moves past the cops and shoots a few atmospherics of the platform. Then he shoots the wall above the victim. A small amount of blood stains the wall, smears down, swiped along a shredded poster for Levy's rye bread, the classic "You don't have to be Jewish to love Levy's" campaign, a smiling Native-American holding a sandwich to his face. Nice. Then comes the victim. His face is surprised, his wide open, very *not* dead. Except for the blood on the poster and tile, there's none elsewhere. Nor are there any visible wounds. Visible. But I know where they are, hidden from plain sight. Just pull down his pants, check his upper thigh. You'll find two bite marks.

I know the victim.

It's me.

25

Tuesday, August 13th, 1974

Hands are poking and prodding me, turning my head this way and that, my head lolling. I can't open my eyes or move. Am I paralyzed? My head is throbbing and I feel a sharp pain in the back of my skull. What happened to me? I was coming home from the city, I got off at my stop, made for the exit, and then the lights went out. Ridiculous thoughts are running through my head, competing for attention. That Vicki Lawrence song, "The Night the Lights Went Out in Georgia," flits into my head like an uninvited guest and refuses to leave. I can't move. I can't open my eyes. I don't know what's happening and those stupid lyrics are flowing through the murk.

"That's the night that the lights went out in Georgia / That's the night that they hung an innocent man . . . "

Shut up! Get out of my head, Vicki!

I hear voices in the dimness. Someone is saying something about someone being dead, no vital signs, the body's cold. Something. It's hard to hear, the external voices being drowned out by Vicki's incessant singing.

"That's the night that the lights went out in Georgia / That's the night that they hung an innocent man . . . "

It's an endless loop. I only know the chorus, so that's all my internal Vicki can sing. Not even the whole chorus. Just that fragment. Please, Vicki, give it a rest. Let me hear what these guys are saying, it might be important. Flashes of light pulse beyond my eyelids, which won't open. Vicki begins to sing more quietly and the external voices have moved on to baseball. Great. Okay, Vicki, you can come back. But, no, Vicki's on break.

"Billy, don't be a hero, don't be a fool with your life / Billy, don't be a hero, come back and make me your wife . . . "

Shit! Shit! Bring back Vicki! Anything but fucking Bo Donaldson. Or is it Paper Lace? It's both! Fuck! I'm trapped in some hellish void and all I've got for company are unseen kibitzers and AM radio hits. Gene Klavin is bellowing in a Yiddish accent, "Mr. Nat is here!" What's next, Hurricane Smith? Shut up. Don't tempt fate. The external voices are still shooting the shit about sports. Something about the Mets. One is for 'em, one's not. This is Queens. Gotta root for the home team. Shut up.

"Billy, don't be a hero, don't be a fool with your life / Billy, don't be a hero, come back and make me your wife . . . "

Why can't I ever retain more than bits of the chorus? It's maddening. I wish I didn't know any of the lyrics to these shitty tunes. Billy, don't be a hero. What do I care? Go get yourself killed, Billy. It's no skin off my ass. The brume is fading. My eyes pop open and I see a bright white light. Which then fades and a stunned looking man with a camera blinks at me, mouth agape.

"Uh, officers," he says. "You might vant to take a look at dis." He has some kind of accent. Can't quite place it. Two TA cops, both young with de rigueur mustaches and chops stand nearby, thumbs hooked in belts, bellies pooched out, hair too long in the back. I cough and the nearer cop whips his head at me and shrieks, "Holy shit, that guy's alive, man!"

"You took his pulse," the second cop says accusingly.

"You guys calt it in," the photographer says, patting a large radio strapped to his shoulder bag. "I don't do injuries. I chust shoot stiffs."

"He was . . . " the first cop says. "Shit. Is EMS coming?"

"I only swung by because I hert on da radio," the photographer says. "You calt in a dead body."

"Shut up," the second cop says. "Don't make me confiscate your rig."

"I'd like to see you try," the photographer says, haughty. "I'll sue for interfering vis my chob."

I can't move anything but my head, which is pounding. Both cops come closer, the one further away shoving the shutterbug to the side, the nearer one kneeling down, his face inches from mine. His breath stinks of coffee and cigarettes and something horrible being digested. He's got b.o., and sweat is dribbling down his face.

"You okay, pal?" he says, voice uncertain. "I mean, uh, you okay?"

"I'm not sure," I croak, not recognizing my own voice.

"Dat man iss not dead," the photographer says, putting away his camera.

"You took some kinda blow to the melon," the second cop says. "We thought you was . . . "

The one kneeling next to me shakes his head and shushes his partner. "You wanna make us sound stoopit?"

In my head the hits keep coming, my skull throbbing in time with the beats.

"I heard my mama cry / I heard her pray the night Chicago died . . . !"

Fucking Paper Lace. Two for two. I begin to feel my extremities and move them. I'm wiggling my toes. My left foot feels funny. I look at it. My shoe is missing. What the hell happened here? One minute I was heading for the exit, the next it was "Goodnight, Irene." I push up on my hands and sit upright, both cops looking a bit jumpy.

"Uh, lemme give you a hand," the kneeling one says, rising, helping me up. I feel lightheaded, woozy. The platform sways, the concrete replaced with oatmeal and foam rubber. I steady myself, and the second cop hands me my shoe. I don't want to bend down, afraid I'll lose my balance. I take the shoe and begin to hobble toward the exit.

"Hey, uh," the first cop says. "You, uh. We need to take a statement. You think you was, uh, attacked or something?"

"I don't know," I say, rubbing my head. "I don't remember."

"You think maybe you slipped?" the second one asks, pointing at a greasy-looking puddle several feet away. My pants feel wet but I think I might be the cause. I feel a flush of embarrassment.

"Yeah. I dunno, maybe. I think maybe I passed out." I don't really think so. I think I was attacked, but I can't remember and don't feel like prolonging this situation by extending my visit with the Thompson twins.

"You wanna go to the hospital? Maybe you oughta do that, buddy. Go to the hospital, get yourself checked out."

"I'd rather just go home if that's okay."

"Zat man is not dead," the photographer sniffs, sounding perturbed.

"Shut up and beat it," the first cop says. "Ya fuckin' vulture."

The photographer mutters as he walks away, pausing to jot something on a poster and take several pictures of it. "Better a vulture den a pig," he whispers to himself.

Neither cop seems to hear the comment or if they do they choose to ignore it. The second cop is yammering into his squawk-box, telling the medical examiner that this was a false alarm.

"You're really pale, buddy," the first cop tells me. "You look like you're down a quart or two, if you get my meaning."

"Plus you're cool to the touch. It's gotta be like a hundred on this platform." To illustrate his point he whips out a hankie and mops it across his glossy brow.

"It's okay," I say, feeling a bit better, feeling logy but wanting away from here. I didn't see whoever it was so I can't give a description of my assailant. I feel my pockets and aside from the unfortunate dampness all is as it should be. I wasn't robbed. I have my cash—what little there is—my wallet, my keys. My watch. "Seriously, officers, I think I must've blacked out and conked my head or something. Maybe heat prostration or something."

"Well," the first cop hems and haws. "We can't hold you if you wanna split of your own will."

"I do."

"And you're awright to get home? You live nearby?"

"Just a couple blocks away, on Judge Street. I just need to get home, shower. My wife'll tend my wounds." I manage a smile. "Mostly wounded pride."

They both chuckle with relief.

"If it's all a same to you, this never happened, okay, pal? We don't wanna look stoopit." He waggles his big official police pad, tears out a page, and crumples it up, tossing it onto the tracks. Litterbug. I nod my head and he grins. "T'anks. You just get home an' take care a that head."

I leave the two of them on the platform. I look at my watch. It's five sixteen. Shit, Monica is gonna kill me. She must be worried sick. I was supposed to be home hours ago. When did I leave the city? Like elevenish? Oy, this is bad. Maybe I did slip. It's hot down here but I'm shivering. I feel feverish all of a sudden. When I hit street level I feel woozy. It's cooler up here but I break out in a sweat. My eyes hurt. It's still pretty dark, so maybe I can sneak in without waking her. But do I want to wake her? To be taken care of? I feel the front of my pants and can't believe I pissed myself. Jesus, maybe I did blackout. I don't often drink but I had a few belts last night. The heat, the humidity. The train with no air conditioning. Maybe I really did blackout. It sounds more and more plausible. I feel like a complete idiot.

I walk up Elmhurst toward Judge, the only schmuck on the street at this ungodly hour. I turn on Judge, enter the vestibule, let myself into the lobby. A short elevator ride later I arrive on the fourth floor. I clutch my keys so they don't jingle as I let myself in. The apartment is dark, warm. The ceiling fan in the living room is on, pushing warm air around, not really cooling anything. Thank God she's a sound sleeper. She'll probably be pissed when she wakes up in a couple hours to get ready for work.

In the bathroom I close the door and switch on the light. It seems way too bright. I remove my pants and throw them in the hamper, then fish them out realizing the urine smell will get worse when they dry. I turn on the faucet in the tub, cursing under my breath when it squeaks, and run hot water on the soiled pants, squirting some shampoo on them. No way am I leaving the room to get detergent from the kitchen. I sit on the toilet and lean my head under the spigot in the sink, running the water, cooling my head. I'm still shivering, but now I have a reason. The water feels good, even though as it circles the drain it's tinged rusty red from my head wound. I turn off the tap and notice my thigh.

Wait a minute.

I didn't slip and do *that*.

There are two puncture wounds on my left upper thigh, just below the balls. What the fuck? I touch the wound and a small rivulet of blood oozes out. I notice that my legs look really pale. Maybe it's the light in here, but then again, maybe not. I get up and look in the mirror. *Eww.* I don't look so hot. I look really sallow and drawn. Yuck. I join my pants in the tub and turn on the shower. The water feels good. I adjust the temperature and let it wash over me. I close my eyes and luxuriate in the pressurized spray. After a few minutes the shower curtain whisks open, cool air hitting me and I see Monica, smiling, naked, stepping in to join me. She doesn't look mad, quite the opposite. With sleepy, horny eyes, she tilts her head at that angle that says, *kiss me*, and I do.

"I should be mad at you," she says.

"You should be."

"You're going to have to make it up to me," she says.

"I will."

Her hand travels south from my chest along my stomach and to my cock. She takes it in her hand, gives it a tentative yank.

And I vomit on her.

26

Lindquist-Gonzalez's graffito message to the cops was "THANKS FOR WASTING MY FUCKING TIME!" That's what he boiled my death and resurrection down to. I imagine if he'd been around to see Jesus emerge from the cave he'd have scrawled the same thing. The gospel according to Sven Lindquist-Gonzalez. There's just no impressing some people. Of course he didn't know I'd just come back from the dead, but then again neither did I.

Out of curiosity I look at the next few slides, all of which are shots of Sven's angry epistle. Right, he killed the roll. I put the slides away, pocket the box, and sit still for a few minutes. On the heels of Kate's dismissal I feel a little shaky about stealing from work, but these slides have got to go. I don't need these being archived for posterity in some accessible database. I can't worry about getting canned. Every job I've taken since I was turned has had a shelf life. You can only stay someplace without aging for so long before becoming the object of unwanted scrutiny. I've been with Güdegast for nearly seven years. The time to move on may be upon me.

For a couple of minutes I stare into my own startled eyes on the monitor. Sven caught a real Kodak Moment. How many people have pictures of themselves coming back from the Land of the Dead? That tops any holiday snap. This picture is twenty-seven years old. I'm twenty-seven years old in it. I still look the same. Maybe a little better, actually. People mark the passage of time with pictures. They look at them and think, *look how young we were. Look how thin, how in love, how whatever*.

I delete the digital files of the scanned images from this set and get on to the next batch. Asshole Lemmy will be stopping by later to see what I've done. I can't stomach people like Lemmy, callow cowardly thrill seekers who treat death as a spectator sport. I get no thrill from any of this. Sure, maybe my taste buds get activated from time to time, Pavlovian pooch-style, but if you were afflicted with a sweet tooth and processed pix of cakes and candy all day you'd drool a little, too. I whip through the next couple of boxes, not taking my usual care. It's okay; they're well preserved and need little correction. Certainly an oaf like Lemmy won't notice any flecks or scratches. He'll be too busy getting his jollies. There's plenty of gore, plenty of man's inhumanity to man. It's funny how one person's archive of clinical recordings of death is another's snuff porn. I wonder if Lemmy gets a boner looking at these images. I guess I'll find out soon enough.

• • •

Sure enough, near the end of my shift Lemmy saunters in and settles down on the chair next to mine.

"Okay, maestro," he says, eyes trained on the screen.

"You want a tub of popcorn, or maybe some Kleenex?" I say. Fuck it, let him fire me.

He laughs, slapping his knees. He actually slaps his knees. What a goon.

"Let 'er rip," he says. He's bouncing in his seat.

I click the slideshow icon and the images flicker by in five-second intervals. A couple of times he asks me to go back so he can really soak it in. He makes titillated giggles and hilarious and original asides like, "Ooh, that's *gotta* hurt," and "Save me the drumstick." What a card. I watch him watch the screen. I'd love to drain him like the fleshy cocktail he is. I keep my eyes on his puffy face. I refuse to look at his crotch to see if that boner showed up. That would be too much. Though his hair is thinning he wears it in graying cornrows, making the patchy top of his head look like a failed crop. *You're not fooling anyone*, I think. *You're going bald. Embrace it.*

A sequence of a nude, butchered young woman cycles through and he sits upright, fingers digging into his chunky knees.

"Holy crow," he says, awed. "Holy freakin' crow."

"Find the girl of your dreams?"

"I. It's just. Wow. How do you think someone could do that to someone? Can you imagine?"

"Like Bryon Gysin said, 'Man is a bad animal.' Nuff said."

"Who?"

"Just some guy."

"Wow. I can't even imagine." Lemmy says this with awe and what appears to be reverence. I feel a creepy shiver in my spine and the hairs stand up on my neck.

"What's your whole name, Lemmy?"

"Huh? Oh, Hugh Thomas Lemming. Why?"

"Just curious." Three names or not, it's a lousy handle for a serial killer.

"What's yours?"

"Philip Arthur Merman."

"Pam. That's your anagram. Pam."

"Acronym."

"Yeah, yeah. Well, Pam, thanks for the slideshow. I guess it's against company policy to run off copies, huh?"

"I guess it is."

"Even if I'm your boss, right?"

"I believe so, yeah. Why, anything in particular catch your fancy?"

"Yeah. I don't know. No, I guess. Yeah. I don't know. It's just kind of fascinating is all. I bet this stuff would go for big bucks on eBay."

"Or alert the authorities, or just end up on any number of gross-out sites. These kind of pix aren't the rarity they once were, you know?"

"Yeah. Yeah. Anyway, just thinking out loud. See you tomorrow, Pam." He chuckles. "Just joshing. Phil."

"Can't wait."

Lemmy stands up, smoothes his pants as if brushing off crumbs, and departs. I switch off my equipment and as I make for the door my extension rings. I wish we had caller ID, I really do, but this cheapskate outfit won't spring for it. It's an outside line so I pick up.

"Y-y-you said I should t-t-try calling, so here I am."

"Hey, Shel, I was wondering when I'd hear from you."

"I'm at the p-p-payphone around the c-c-corner. You think maybe we c-c-could get together for a d-d-drink?"

"Yeah, why not?"

I tell him to meet me outside in five minutes, which he does. When I emerge from the building there he sits, on *my* standpipe. Ugh, I'll never sit on it again. It's snowing and I'm jolted back to when I left him on the stoop. So much for him freezing to death. Maybe he did. Maybe he's a ghost, my own Jacob Marley. Nah.

"I w-w-wanted to t-t-talk to you about the other n-n-night."

"I'd just as soon forget the other night if it's all the same to you."

"It isn't. I n-n-need to talk about it."

"What about what I need, Shel? That ever occur to you? What does Phil need? Maybe Phil—I'm talking about myself in third person! You see how crazy you make me? Maybe what I need is to not dwell on your hamfisted attempt to french me. Maybe that's what I need."

Shelley's head droops, snow collecting on his bald head like a powdery toupee.

"I can't believe you're going to guilt me about *your* offense," I scold. "You fess up to stalking me and then you try jamming your tongue in my mouth."

"It wasn't l-l-like that!" Shelley shrieks. I'm taken aback. Shelley's not one for raising his voice. Okay, he's got the floor. "I wasn't just trying to m-m-molest you, Philip! I c-c-can't hide my feelings for you anym-m-more."

"*Oy gevalt*, Shel. Stop shitting in my brain, *please!*" I begin pacing back and forth, creating a rut in the fresh snow. "Okay, get up. We can't have this conversation here. I can't do this in front of my office. I don't need to compound this cockamamie *chozzerai* by having my asshole boss show up. That would be too much!"

"S-s-so where are we g-g-going? To th-th-that bar on . . . "

"Nowhere. We're just walking. Two old chums taking a nice midnight stroll in the snow. Up. Let's go. Come on, up, up!"

Like a dutiful little bitch he gets off the standpipe and we walk north along Hudson. No bars. No audience. He either gets the picture or gets the chop, one or the other. Several blocks of silence is broken by Shelley.

"Wh-why the surgery, Phil?"

"What?"

"The cosmetic s-s-surgery? Are your l-l-looks that imp-p-portant? Since your m-m-marriage ended I've never seen you w-w-with a woman. Who's it f-f-for?"

"*What?*" Oh, right, his *fakakta* theory. "Listen, what I do is my own business. And don't talk about my marriage. That's ancient history but it still bothers me."

"Do you know whatever b-b-became of . . . ?"

"You're already on thin ice, Shel. The thinnest. Let's just pretend this is *Who's Afraid of Virginia Woolf?*, okay? Only substitute the word 'wife' for 'baby.' 'Don't talk about the *wife*, Martha.' Okay?"

"What kind of st-st-straight man would make a r-r-reference like that?"

"One who likes movies? What kind of stupid . . . ? What is it with you, Shel? Do you enjoy pushing my buttons? It's like you're trying to drive in a wedge with a fuckin' mallet."

"I'm s-s-sorry. It's j-j-just that you're obviously qu-qu-quite vain, Phil. The cosmetic s-s-surgery b-b-bears that out. B-b-but only ever since Monica l-l-left you . . . "

I don't like to think of her by name. I do, and often, but it always pains me. And I especially don't like hearing her name from *his* mouth. I pick Shelley up by the lapels and slam him into a wall as hard as I can. I'm actually holding him a few inches off the ground. He's gotten my blood up, riled me. I'm not *that* strong, especially between feedings, but he's a flyweight. He looks down at me, eyes wide, imploring. That's right. Maybe now you get it, Shelley. Maybe now you see why you shouldn't keep ticking me off. See how much trouble it could get you in?

"*I could kill you so easily,*" I hiss.

"I w-w-wish you w-w-would," he whimpers. "Oh *God*, I w-w-wish you w-w-would."

Fucking Shelley.

He ruins everything.

I let him go, easing him to the ground. I refuse to martyr him to the cause of I don't know what. I shake my head and a poor imitation of a laugh escapes my mouth. I crane my head back, tilting my face toward the sky, letting the snow fall on it. Shelley's an orphan. Maybe he's got some uncles and cousins, but is that enough of a reason to spare him? Would anyone really miss him? He doesn't work, which as far as I'm concerned is part of his problem. A man needs to work, or least have purpose, direction. What the hell does he do with his time? Indolent Shelley. Inebriate Shelley. Between family investments and the insurance, Shelley was left pretty well off after his family was barbecued. They never did solve the case. I'm tempted to mention the slides of his kin's broiled look-alikes. Ask him if he wants a set for the family album.

He looks at me with eyes that say, *Put me out of my misery*. Is his wanting me to do it enough of a deterrent? Yeah, it is. I refuse to accommodate him. If he's so fucking sad and lovelorn, let him kill himself. I won't oblige. Sorry, Charlie.

"Aren't you g-g-going to k-k-kill me?" he stammers.

"What am I, a fucking killer? You've got some funny notions about your friend Phil, let me tell you."

"B-b-but you s-s-said you were."

"People say a lot of things. You wanna die, there's some things you've gotta do for yourself. Do you really want to die?"

"No, I suppose not."

"Get help, Shel. Take some of that money of yours and get some serious fucking help. Get in a program. Dry out. Switch from self-medicating with booze to drugs. Serious prescription behavior-mod drugs. I can't be your shrink. I got problems of my own, but they pale by comparison to yours. I'm not the Grim Reaper. I'm just a guy. Seriously, Shel, as a *friend*, get yourself straightened out."

"I will. I'll get help. I promise."

He's promised before. He's even gotten help and gone through periods of sobriety. I'm not a fucking martyr, myself. Shelley, hard as it is to remember, has been decent company on and off, from time to time. He's smart, witty, well read. In the past I've found his company pleasant, desirable, even. When he puts his mind to it he can be a great one for conversation. But not in such a long time. Shelley slides down the wall and squats, holding his bony knees to his bony chest, all wrapped up in the bony ribbons he calls arms. What a rotten package. I hunker down in front of him and say, with all the empathy I can muster, "Get yourself straight, Shel. You even make an effort and it'll make all the difference." He nods. I get up and leave him there.

Seems like I've been leaving him in the snow a lot lately.

• • •

When I arrive at my stop I feel restless. Not hungry, exactly, but not ready to call it a night. I wasn't in the right head to call Eddie when I left the city and I'm not keen to go back tonight. It's only two thirty. On autopilot I make towards the end of the platform, pass through the gate bearing the admonition, DO NOT ENTER OR CROSS TRACKS, and wander into the tunnel, walking along the catwalk. It's comfortingly dark, the jaundiced bare bulbs spread far apart, dulled by layers of amber grime and black soot. It's nice that some things never change. No matter how many cosmetic "improvements" get made to the stations, these inky expanses of no-man's land remain unaltered. Maybe the surfaces gain girth from accrued sediment—or lose it from erosion—but that's about it. Who needs a trip to the touristy Carlsbad Caverns when you can go spelunking courtesy of the MTA? There are even stalactites of calcified *yecch* hanging down from the ceiling. I imagine people would pay good money to go on tours down here, like they do in the sewers in Paris. But I'm glad they don't. At least not in Queens.

About midway between stations a train roars by, the windows a blindingly white blur. I keep walking, unnoticed. I've tucked away so many bodies in these tunnels—maybe not these specifically, but subway tunnels. (Rule two: don't feed where you sleep.) I've descended into hollowed-out burrows, spaces between the supports, gone deep under the actual tracks. I've climbed up into the rafters. There are warrens all over the place stuffed with the bones of my victims. I drained them, the rats no doubt polished off the meat. It's pretty revolting when you think about it.

I arrive at the next station, Grand Avenue, which is empty save for a homeless guy sleeping on a bench. I walk to the far end and enter the next tunnel. Maybe I'll just keep going until the end of the line. When the trains are absent the tunnels are remarkably peaceful. So quiet you can hear all the tiny sounds. Water running down the walls. The skittering of rodents. I'm not saying these are good sounds, but you can hear them echoing in the chasmal space. You can hear yourself breathe and if you stand very still you can hear your pulse. Then a train thunders by. I enjoy the contrast.

I reach the next station and keep going. Woodhaven Boulevard. 63rd Drive. 67th Avenue. The local line ends at the next station, Continental Avenue, so my constitutional will end there. Onward. As I reach the middle of the tunnel I hear the metallic groan of a door opening: the emergency exit. I freeze and press myself against the wall, watching. A lone figure steps onto the catwalk, a spindly teenage boy.

"But what if we get caught?" he says, voice thin, uneasy. He's not alone.

"Don't worry about it," says another voice, also young, but deeper, more self-assured. "You worry too much."

A thickset teen joins his scrawny compatriot. I wait to see which way they're going. If they come my way I'll wing it; if they go the other way I'll be relieved. I don't want to get into it with these two. I don't look like I belong down here any more than they do. The good thing about being someplace you don't belong and having someone else show up—someone unauthorized, that is— is that there's a bond of wrongness. No one's going to narc.

"So, whattaya wanna do?" asks Skinny.

"Just check it out. It's cool down here. I've been down here like a zillion times. Come on, this'll take the edge off." Fatty reaches into his puffy army surplus coat and produces a joint. He sparks it and takes a deep drag, holds it, lets it out real slow.

"I dunno," Skinny says. "I don't think I should."

I'm stuck here watching a live-action PSA.

"Come on," Fatty says, half chum, half bully.

"Nah, I don't want to. If I get high I might lose my balance and fall in front of a train."

"Pussy."

"Am not, I just don't want to is all. Maybe later."

"Suit yourself."

Fatty takes another deep hit, then stubs it out on the moist wall and pockets it. They deliberate for a moment or two and then head the other way. I'm grateful for the anticlimax. It's not like I would have killed them, but who needs the hassle of confronting trespassing teens, especially a chunky one emboldened by weed? After they put a goodly amount of yardage between themselves and myself, I decide to go out the exit they so carelessly left open. Being the good citizen I am I close it behind me, finding myself on the middle traffic island on Queens Boulevard. East and westbound traffic whizzes by, as it always does on The Boulevard of Death. Actually, I'm right near one of the most treacherous intersections, where Queens and

Yellowstone Boulevards crisscross. Lots of pedestrians get nailed there. Lots of fender-benders, too. Because people love to commemorate death there are snow-covered wreaths and dead loose flowers affixed to and scattered around the base of one of the streetlights. Black petals on white snow forming a macabre smiley face.

It's stopped snowing, which is kind of a relief. I stand on the island and scope out the terrain. There's a large apartment complex on the south side of the boulevard, some small stores on the north, several of which are vacant. Times are tough. There's a small gallery so I jaywalk over to look in the window. *Oy*. I think about the stuff in that gallery on Madison, those nice beach scenes. This is *drek*. Sad clowns, graceless ballerinas that would make Degas hurl, lopsided galleons, half-assed nudes, still lifes you know were not done from life, still or otherwise. This is the Bob Ross crap. Not even that good. How do places like this get by? Are they fronts? This neighborhood has become home to a huge influx of Uzbekistanis and Tajikistanis. I can't imagine they're keeping this gallery afloat. I really wonder about this stuff. And then I wonder about wondering about this stuff. Living a life of perpetual night can do strange things to your head.

With hours to go before sunrise I decide to trudge home topside. The snow is fresh and clean and not too deep. I'm not really wearing the right footwear for it, but fuck it, it's not like I'm going to catch cold. As I pass the 67th Avenue station Fatty and Skinny emerge from the entrance, led away in cuffs by a stern-looking transit cop. I grin as they're escorted past me. I dodged that bullet. I wonder if it was the dope or the trespassing that got them in trouble. Maybe both. Who cares? The fat one sees me grinning and gives me a belligerent look.

"Th' fuck are you lookin' at?" he says in his best attempt at a hardened perp-walk snarl. It doesn't mask his fear at all—I can smell it on him. I'm intimately acquainted with the scent of fear.

The skinny one radiates candid terror, eyes cast down at his shuffling feet. He's dreading *The Call* to his folks.

"Shut up," the cop says, shoving Fatty into a waiting squad car.

On the way home, walking past all the uninteresting stores selling crappy merchandise, I pause for a minute to admire a living room set displayed in the window of a furniture showroom. Sometimes you encounter something so breathtakingly wrongheaded you gape in awe, tackiness on an epic scale. A sofa and a loveseat, both upholstered in clashing patterns, little bits of ancient Egyptian fighting with Greek and something else. Mayan? Aztec? Mesopotamian? I'm not sure. Embroidered Louis XIV suns, one smiling on each backrest. But the *piece de resistance* is the sculptural detailing. The feet are burnished gold-plated monstrosities; gnarled dragon claws—or chicken feet—clutching orbs. But even they pale before the majesty of the gleaming griffins that support the armrests. I want this set, but I'm sure it's thousands of dollars. That's a lot to pay for kitsch.

• • •

In my lobby, as I stomp the melting snow off my shoes, I check the mail and am amazed to see an envelope from the DMV. When I open it, sure enough there's an official non-driver New York State ID card, my birth date listed as 8/25/74. That was fast. Like, crazy fast. Desmond came through like a champ. I'll have to do something nice for him, though I'm not sure what. Something. This is very cool. I admire it all the way up to my floor and even as I unlock my door and step into my apartment. Once inside, I look at my prosaic Danish Modern couch and feel disappointed that my setup isn't more outré. It must be the company I'm keeping. What would Adélaïde make of that hideous living room set? I think my liking it, even ironically, would revoke my visiting privileges.

27

I arrive at work and the first thing I see is a Post-It note stuck to my monitor from Lemmy suggesting I come see him when I get in. My first thought is that somehow someone discovered I'd pinched that set of slides and I'm getting shit-canned. If that's the case, so be it. I hang up my coat and head up the hall to Lemmy's office. It is what it is, whatever it is.

"Lemmy?"

"*The Ghoul*," he says, making Fifties monster hands and chuckling. "Just joshing, Phil, come on in and grab a chair."

I look around and see there's only one chair besides his, so I plant my *tuchis* and put on a placid expression.

"You going for the grunge look, Phil? I thought you were more into the Goth-Metal thing." He chuckles at his boffo observational jibe at my garb. I'm wearing the same shit I usually wear, only maybe a little more worn. "It's okay, Phil. Consider this Casual Friday. Oh, wait, you consider *every* day Casual Friday." He chuckles again, adjusting his wide paisley tie. I'm not dressed *that* bad. More Old Navy than Banana, but jeez. Eddie and I have something going after work.

"Okay, Phil, here's the thing," Lemmy says, assuming his serious mien. Wait for it. "I wanted to let you know that our parent company,

Allied Fotek Corporation, is consolidating their operation. They, as you know, acquired Güdegast Photo Archives last year, as they did many of our former competitors." He rattles off a list of other photo archives, stock photography houses, film and video archives, all located throughout the lower forty-eight. I smile and nod like I give a shit. "Anyhoo, Phil, Allied Fotek wants to tighten up their outfit since we're all one big happy now. So, the thing of it is, Phil," in the span of his dramatic pause the word "downsized" pops into my head only to be replaced with his next two words, "we're moving."

"Moving."

"That's right."

"And where might we be moving to?"

"Knoxville."

"As in Tennessee."

"Exactamundo. New York is just too expensive and this is all about economics. Knoxville is way cheaper to operate from."

Okay, so this isn't getting fired, but it's close. No way in hell am I relocating to cracker central. Even if this was feasible, which it isn't, I can't see myself ever living down south. Even in my human days I would've gotten run out on a rail. But now? Please. I'd much rather have been downsized; then I could collect unemployment. Do you collect unemployment if you're forced to resign? Because that's what this bastard is doing.

"And when is this going down?" I ask.

"Not for another couple of few months, but I wanted to let you know in person. I figured better you hear it from me direct than through some memo. That's cold."

"Yeah, this was *so* much better."

Lemmy makes with his basso profundo chuckle and winks at me.

"So, do I give notice now or what?"

He looks at me uncomprehending.

"Do I pack up my things now? What gives, Lemming?"

"You won't even consider relocation?"

Lemmy's smile fades as I explain that The South is not for me. He leans back in his chair, which creaks in protest, and frowns deeply. What was he expecting? That I'd blithely accept this miserable news and do a little jig singing, "*O, I wish I was in the land of cotton, Old times there are not forgotten! Look away! Look away! Look away! Dixie Land!*" Why the hell is a northern black man so keen on moving down south? Lemmy assumes his version of a compassionate demeanor and leans forward, making lots of gooey eye contact, and tells me I'm just being emotional. He suggests I take some time to think about any rash decisions like leaving the company. I pretend to agree to this strategy and he pretends to believe me.

Back at my workstation I glower at my CRT. Tennessee? Jesus, even Jersey would be better than that. I might even consider that, if it were on the PATH line. Hoboken I could manage. Maybe even Westchester or Yonkers or White Plains, but Knoxville? *Knoxville*? I'm really tired of having to switch jobs, and unfortunately my résumé at this point only qualifies me for jobs like this one, and fucking Allied Fotek Corporation has bought up all the other joints in town that do this kind of thing. And is moving them to fucking Tennessee. I'm too old for entry-level bullshit jobs. I've got to start picking Eddie's brains about how to scam loot and not have to work so hard. Maybe I'll join Leon in the sewers.

I sit and stew for a while, my gaze drifting around the room. This job wasn't much, and I was going to have to move on soon anyway, but I wasn't prepared for this. Plus I wanted to be the one to decide when I was going. They say it's easier to get a job when you have one, but interviewing is always a tricky endeavor when you can't come during the day. Fortunately it's still winter so I can always set up interviews after five. But if I don't get a job by spring . . . *Que sera, sera.*

I do tonight's bundle of atrocities—the usual mélange of suicides, murders, and accidents—but am not paid a visit by Lemmy. I think my disinclination to sashay south dampened his esprit de corps, which suits me fine. I wasn't too stoked about my new role as his provider of cheap thrills.

TGIF is all I'm saying, you know?

28

Against my better judgment Eddie's convinced me to go hunting with him again. Other than the catastrophe with the runaways, he enjoyed our waterfront expedition and wants to "rough it" again. He's apparently burned through too many clubs to keep supping on sparkly perfumed necks, at least for the time being. The great thing, he informs me, about the club set is that they're all so superficial they never notice when one of the herd vanishes. Most don't even maintain contact with the non-clubbing world, i.e., family, so they seldom get reported as missing. Still, one must try new things. One tires of Ecstasy-glazed eyes.

Instead of in front of my office I've agreed to meet him at West 72nd and Riverside, just east of the entrance to the railroad yards. Eddie says he's done a cursory investigation into the subterranean community, a little reading and poking around. I'm not very comfortable with the idea of invading a community, however makeshift and secretive. I'm aware of the folks who live in those tunnels, near the Amtrak lines, way below. I've never fed on one of them. They've got a sense of unity that I don't want to disrupt. I kind of admire their tenacity and gumption. It takes real balls to say, "Fuck the system, I'm going my own route," even if the system's given no other tenable option. Eddie assures me they're not all innocent victims of circumstance. Some are bad and crazy and dangerous. Those will be our prey.

At a quarter to two I arrive and Eddie and I hop the chain link fence and head down several flights of metal stairs, arriving on the surface of the yard. Plentiful weeds poke up through the snow, which by and large remains unspoiled. There are seemingly dozens of tracks leading into the massive maw of the northbound tunnel that runs from here up under Riverside Park and beyond. There are freight cars scattered about, but all look forsaken. By the waterfront are the rusted skeletal remains of long abandoned loading winches and other industrial machinery, the jagged corrugated housings corroded like mouths of rotting teeth. Rot is the dominant theme here. Looking south there seems to be some vitality, some warehouse type buildings. There are lights on in that direction. We go the opposite way, into the tunnel, black, sepulchral, and seemingly infinite. Even with perfect night vision the bowels recede into nothingness. Eddie grins and in passable Fudd-ese says, "Be vewy, vewy quiet, I'm hunting homewess people, *Huh-huh-huh-huh-huh*."

"Cute."

"I know."

The snow only reaches about twenty feet into the tunnel and soon we crunch along the bare tracks, the ties long ago submerged in a dense layer of crag. The deeper we get, the louder the echo of our footfalls becomes. There's something almost religious to a place this massive. I've been in cathedrals that weren't half as awe-inspiring. True there aren't dazzling frescos on the ceiling, but there's plentiful graffiti and some of it isn't half bad artistically. Most is crap, but still. After trudging for about half a mile I ask Eddie if he has any idea where we're going. I'll admit it. I'm hungry and getting cranky. I put off feeding yesterday expressly because of this hunting jaunt and now I'm feeling a bit testy. This isn't a stomach thing. Hunger doesn't affect me there any more.

It's a system wide buzz, like my veins are expanding and contracting. It hurts and the longer I deny myself sustenance the worse it gets.

Eddie points at an upper tier than runs parallel to the outmost tracks and says we should get up there. You've got to go up to go down, he explains. We find a ladder embedded in the wall and climb to this level, some ten feet above the tracks, and Eddie points to a partly covered hole in the ground. He *has* done some homework. We go over to the opening and push aside the slabs of splintered plywood and bits of cardboard that mask it. Eddie points to the hole, which is darker than Satan's asshole.

"Ladies first," he says.

"How gallant."

I test the open space below with my toe, which makes no contact with anything for the first few wiggles, then finds purchase on a diagonal slope of indeterminate solidity. I hear the cascade of fragments coming loose from contact with my foot. I look up at Eddie who makes the chicken gesture with his hands tucked into his pits, but spares me the vocalized impersonation. I lower myself in and my eyes adjust to this even darker space. I crabwalk down the decline and find myself on level ground after several feet. I wait a moment or two and then Eddie crashes into me, taking the hill faster than I did. To call this cavity decayed would be the understatement to end all understatements. The floor, itself spider-webbed with concentric cracks and spokes of deep fissures, is host to all manner of particulate debris and filth. I thought I knew dirty but I find I knew nothing. Compared to this space the subway tunnels are antiseptic. I might have to rethink joining Leon as a career move.

"Christ, it's disgusting down here," I say.

"I'd say we got down here just in time, then."

"Huh?"

"You're getting too accustomed to the good life. These, my boy," Eddie says, arms outstretched, "*these* are your roots. This is good, honest land."

"You gonna burst into song?"

"Maybe. Listen, I'm wearing my bum rags, so I'm down for anything."

I look over at what he's wearing and excepting my wardrobe windfall from Adélaïde it's still a pricier ensemble than anything I own. Leon and me, that's it for bloodsuckers that know the value of a buck. Maybe Deirdre, the chick who runs the halfway house, but that's it. Eddie is beaming, so happy to be on this little adventure.

"You ever see that flick, *The Goonies*?" he asks.

"You are such a fucking retard," I say.

"We're on an adventure, just like them. We're a lot like Spielberg kids. Like the Lost Boys in *Hook*, we never grow old. Like *The Goonies*, going down into the caves."

"How old are you, again?"

"Younger than springtime."

"Wait. *Sssh*."

There's a small, almost undetectable sound in the near distance. We freeze, listening, both attuned to movement. We can see well and hear better than any human down here. We have no flashlights, our sight not impaired by darkness. A stream of focused light comes into view, cutting a fanned out stripe of illumination across the tenebrous expanse of manmade catacomb. It bobs with each step. I whisper, "So how do we know who from who down here, the ones that don't meet my criteria versus some scumbag who needs to get expired?"

"Oh, come on," Eddie says, plaintively. "You can't be serious. These are the most disposable cattle you're ever going to find. You want folks who no one's going to miss, these are them."

"Just 'cause someone's unfortunate enough to find himself residing down here doesn't mean he's . . . "

The beam of light hits us square in the mush and we squint into the light.

"Debate's over," Eddie says.

"Dag!" comes the voice attached to the light, a middle-aged black guy with a soup-strainer beard. "Di'n't speck to fin' nobody lurkin' aroun' in the dark 'roun' here! Y'all lost or some shit? 'Cause y'all don' look like y'all belong down here. Y'all social workers an' shit? 'Cause if yo is, y'all can turn right aroun' an' fuck da hell off."

"No, we're not social workers," Eddie says, smiling with his lips tight, hiding his fangs.

"If y'all are fumma railroad y'all mus' be onna suicide kick."

"Not from the railroad."

"Y'all ain' cops. Cops don' come down here 'less they got a damn good reason."

"No, we're not cops."

"Damn, Wall Street mussa been fuckin' yo shit up good, 'en. Y'all some dot-com boys done lost yo potta gold?"

Eddie laughs and says, "You know about dot-commers going belly up?"

"Jus' 'cause a man lives in th' dark don' mean he's inna dark about the worl', son."

Eddie and I both smile at the guy and then at each other.

"So what's a well informed individual like yourself doing in a place like this?" Eddie says.

"Y'all want my life story? Y'all newspaper re-porters fumma *Daily News*? Shit, hunker down, bitches, an' I'll tell you my tale o' woe. Crack ruineded my life, yo. Fings was much, much betta befaw I evah took up wif da pipe, but now? Gott-dayum, it's got me. I try an' I try to get loose but th' bitch's got me. I feel so bad, it's like I losted evythang but I still keep comin' back f' mo. It's a sickness, yo. For real. A sickness an' damn I'd like to catch da cure."

"Ever consider rehab?" Eddie asks. I'm just observing, not ready to jump in.

"Rehab don' do shit. I been in an' outta programs mo' times 'en you had hot dinnuhs, I mean it." He pauses and rubs his chapped, filthy hands together for warmth. "So for serious, whattaya you boys doin' down here?"

"We wanted to try the local cuisine," Eddie says, the downcast beam of the flashlight briefly glinting off his teeth.

"Local coo-zeen? Damn, y'all niggas are *way* losted. Y'all mus' be all fucked up. Ain' no coo-zeen down here 'less y'all inna mood fo' rat tar-tar." He chuckles at his bon mot.

"That, my friend, is where you're wrong."

And Eddie's on this guy in a trice, the flashlight flying out of the poor bastard's hand and clattering along the craggy ground, the beam of light strobing across all surfaces. The poor slob barely gets out the word, "No," before going limp in Eddie's arms. Eddie feeds noisily, his slurping and sucking amplified by the quietude. The horizontal beam of the flashlight illuminates countless motes of dust kicked up by the fleeting struggle. I stand there, veins burning, hungry and feeling some remorse. The dude was kind of funny and seemed bright in a streetwise, drug-addicted kind of way.

Jesus, I'm getting soft. This guy was *exactly* my kind of victim, fitting my bill to a T. After watching Eddie feed for a couple of minutes I ask, "You gonna keep all that to yourself?"

"Now he speaks," Eddie says, letting some blood dribble out of his mouth. "I'm almost finished for Pete's sake."

"I'm feeling the burn."

"There's just the dregs, Phil, but if you want to finish him off, I'll let you. It's just the kind of guy I am."

"What a prince."

In the distance a train rumbles through the tunnel, disturbing the near silence. I stoop down and begin to polish the guy off when the flashlight beam pitches up and I see Eddie's head fly right off at the neck, bisected by a metallic blur of motion. A small sound, like *kah-ting*, accompanies the action, slightly out of sync like the Doppler effect.

"Fuck me," I croak, sputtering my first mouthful of blood.

Standing behind Eddie's collapsing decapitated body is a rat-faced young white dude with a sharpened shovel, holding it like the axe it's just doubled as.

"Yeah, *muthafucka*, you in th' shit now, *bitch*!" he shouts.

The flashlight beam comes at me from behind and I realize I'm hemmed in by at least two cave dwellers. Eddie's head is off. Fuck. Can we heal from that? That seems . . .

One thing at a time. No time for pondering, no time for panic. I've got to deal with this worsening scenario. But new rule: No more hunting trips with anyone else. *Hunting is a solitary activity.* The ratty teen with the shovel blunders down the incline that leads back in the direction we came from. I need to make mental notes about points of egress. This place is huge, unfamiliar, and labyrinthine. So, behind Rat-face lies the exit point. Noted. The one bearing the flashlight is flanking me, coming at me from behind. I think it's just the two of them. I'm glad I dressed down. What am I thinking?

"Oh, *yeah*, he's *scared. You should be scared, muthafucka*!" shouts Ratty, a pubescent lint-like mustache above his upper lip. His head is shaved, probably because of lice. Ecch. "You *should* be *real* scared! You fucked with *Chedrick*? He *betta* not be *dead*, bitch! I'll cut yo fuckin' nuts off if you killeded Chedrick. Yeah, lookit yo friend, now!"

Chedrick?

He lifts the shovel and I have no choice. I'm hungry and this is another great hunting trip fucked right in the ass. The shovel reaches its zenith and I, lower on the incline than I'm happy about, lunge up and sink my teeth into his—I can't fucking believe this—upper thigh, just below the crotch. It's come to this. He sputters a disbelieving cuss word, and then drops the shovel, toppling backwards, my narcotizing juices flooring him. The torchbearer behind me stops in his or her tracks and then peeps, "Mikey?" Female. Shit, shit, and double-shit. I really hate taking down womenfolk.

While Mikey the Rat-faced Boy lies on the ground, twitching and temporarily out of commission, I pounce from the higher ground and tackle the female. She drops the flashlight, which spirals offside and goes out, thrusting us into pitch darkness. Well, thrusting *her* into pitch darkness, which might be a mercy. I embed my teeth in her throat and clamp down hard. She gets in one weak punch in self-defense and then succumbs. Five liters later I let her drop away. Though sated, I still have to deal with Ratboy, who, in the gloom is trying to crawl away, semi-paralyzed by my toxins. I look over at Eddie's head, which lies face up, his expression one of utter astonishment. A few feet away is his body, the ground by the neck and shoulders tacky with blood.

Over the years I've shed many things in the name of survival, most notably the need and desire for family and friends. In that time I lost all contact with anyone I ever knew and cared about besides Shelley. I learned to live and embrace—to some degree—a monastic, solitary existence. No work friends, nothing. I flattened out, jettisoning strong emotion along the way. When you're all alone, why get worked up? What need for extreme highs or lows? That much solitude with lots of emotion could equal going bonkers, falling victim to despair, whatever. I chose quiescence and it worked out pretty well. So what is this? My veins no longer burn but my face is flushed, febrile.

This?

This is rage.

I'm out of practice. Back in the day I could be quite the hothead. Welcome back, old friend. I stalk over to Ratboy and plant my foot on the base of his spine, grinding the heel into his coccyx. He lets out a small piteous sound, his jaw locked from the partial paralysis. I drop to one knee, which comes down with a faint thud on the small of his back, pushing air from his lungs. I press down on him, bringing my face mere inches from the nape of his neck. He reeks, leaking raunchy breath in fitful spurts. Up close he's hideous.

"Your friend the crackhead, maybe he didn't deserve what he got. Your girlfriend, maybe the same goes for her. Life isn't fair. But you? You deserve whatever I'm going to give you. Oh, *yeah*, you're *scared. You should be scared, muthafucka*."

I already bit him and I'm not sure how this works. I'm sated, but he can't be left to turn. No way. I bite down into his neck and suck a while, but then stop and stand over him. I wish I had lighter fluid. I'd set him ablaze and watch him burn. But I don't, so I kick him as hard as I can, over and over again until I can hear his bones cracking with each blow. I destroy his ribcage, savoring each thick gurgle. *Thanks, asshole*, I think. *Thanks for turning me into a despicable sadist. Thanks.* Kick, kick, *crack*. Don't die, though. Not yet.

I drop back down and press my ear to his back, listening to his laboring heart.

"It's okay," I whisper in the most soothing tone I can manage. Tears leak from my eyes and drip onto his patchy scalp. "It's okay. Relief is on the way." I put my lips on his neck and insert my teeth back in the holes I made previously. I drink and drink and drink until I feel like I'm going to burst. I wretch and vomit up some of his girlfriend's blood—*Today on* Sally Jessy Raphaël: *bulimic bloodsuckers*—then resume draining him. When he's empty I get up and assay the carnage.

Score: three to one, bloodsuckers.

So why do I feel like I've lost?

29

It's been a while since I've experienced genuine loss or grief. Grief? Yeah, that's what this is. Like some bargain basement Hamlet I cradle Eddie's noggin in my lap, looking down at that dumbstruck expression on his *punim*.

"Alas, poor Yorick! I knew him, Horatio; a fellow of infinite jest, of most excellent fancy . . . "

That's all I can remember, grief doing a number on the literary trivia sector of my brain. Eddie was most definitely a fellow of infinite jest, of most excellent fancy. And now he's dead. See what happens when you make friends? Like I needed to re-experience loss. I went through that shit with my folks and my wife. Okay, she didn't die—at least not to my knowledge—but I lost her. Love and loss, love and loss. That's the cycle for mere mortals. Loss, at any rate. I thought I was beyond that. As bad days go, this is one for the books.

I take Ratboy's shovel-axe and hack him and his girlfriend to chunks, then bury the two of them and Chedrick the crackhead in the abundant debris down here. More food for the rodents. Once finished I sling Eddie's headless body over my shoulder and toss his head into a Duane Reade shopping bag found nearby. Gorged with blood and energized by manic emotion I have no trouble hoisting Eddie up through the hole we entered. When we near the exit of the tunnel I fish Eddie's cell phone out of his pocket and go through his preset numbers, finding Adélaïde's, which I dial.

"Hello?" comes a smooth, slightly accented male voice.

"Yeah, hi. Uh, is Adélaïde there?"

"Whom may I say is calling? She's . . . " a smutty chuckle, "*indisposed* at the moment." Another wry, salacious titter follows.

"Whatever she's doing can wait. Put her on."

"My dear boy, one doesn't just *barge in* on Madame Sigismund whenever the fancy takes one. One must have due cause to . . . "

"Shut up and listen to me. Just tell her Phil's on the line and that Eddie is dead."

"Eddie? Eddie Frye?"

"The same. Put her on."

"Eddie's *dead*? Who is this? Is this some kind of joke?"

"Put Adélaïde on, motherfucker! Now! *Now!*"

The line goes quiet for a few moments and I wonder if I lost the signal, but then in the background I hear some hubbub and a second later Adélaïde's velvet voice comes on, stern, apprehensive. "Hello?" she says. "Who is this?"

"It's Phil. Eddie's dead. I *think* he's dead. I mean, I don't think he's going to come back from this kind of damage."

"Slow down, Phil. What damage? Where are you? What's happened?"

I give her the short version and my location and she says she'll send a vehicle to pick us up. I disconnect and put the phone in my pocket, then climb the metal stairs to make sure the coast is clear, leaving Eddie on the landing. Last things I need after a mess like this are witnesses, especially the kind in uniform. It's nearly four in the morning. Traffic at this hour is light, but never nonexistent coming off the highway, so I hunker down and wait behind the fence for whatever vehicle

Adélaïde has sent to show up. After half an hour a black van pulls over to the side of the road and Leon steps out, furrowed and edgy, looking left and right before seeing me on the other side of the fence.

"What the fuck is going on, Phil?"

"I got Eddie on the landing out of sight."

"And?"

"And he's got no fucking head."

Pause.

"I'll get the clippers."

Leon turns back to the van and retrieves a large pair of bolt cutters, then clips the padlocked chain keeping the gate shut. I go down the steps and bung Eddie over my shoulder again, grabbing the shopping bag.

"Is the coast clear?" I shout.

"Yeah, we got a lull."

I exit the stairwell and Leon gasps.

"Holy jeez, I thought maybe you were fuckin' around," Leon says. "Holy jeez. There's a steamer trunk in the back. Put him in that, okay?"

I comply, and then get in the passenger seat and we speed off without incident. I've had enough incidents for a lifetime tonight. We drive in silence all the way to the Upper East Side, Leon breaking it as we enter the underground garage of Adélaïde's building.

"How did this happen?" Leon says, voice choked.

"Let me tell you upstairs. Then I only have to tell it once. I don't think I'm up to multiple retellings."

"Jeez," Leon says. "You'd think with all the shit I've seen I'd be numb, but it's different when it's one of your own."

We leave Eddie's remains in the van and catch the elevator from the garage up. When we reach the landing prior to Adélaïde's,

Raul sees me and nearly falls out of his chair. I'm filthy and drenched in clotting blood.

"M-mister Phil, what *happened* to you? Are you okay?"

"I'm okay," I lie. "I had an accident. But I'm okay."

"He's okay, Raul," Leon affirms.

Raul looks worried and a bit dubious, but scuttles into the lift and brings us up to Maison Sigismund, where Adélaïde waits by the open door dressed in an ornately decorated Oriental robe. Her expression is grave with concern. We disembark and the lift door slides shut and Raul descends, allowing her to speak candidly.

"My God, Phil, what on earth happened to you? I need details. Where is Eddie?"

"In the trunk in the van," Leon says. "Should we bring it up?"

We enter the penthouse and shut the door. The living room, normally rife with debauchery, is empty. Without the rutting visitors it looks larger, more like a spread from *Architectural Digest*. Forgetting my grotty condition, I collapse onto one of Adélaïde's recherché divans and, not noticing it's backless, lean back and do a pratfall onto the floor. No one is in the right mood for slapstick, especially me, and I pick myself up, cursing. Reseating myself, I set about recapping the evening's events, finding myself becoming overwrought, pounding the cushions, wiping my eyes. This high emotionality is for the birds; it's so taxing. As I do the play-by-play Adélaïde paces back and forth like a ferret on crystal meth. When I finish she stops dead in her tracks and glares at me.

"This is a *disaster*. My God, Phil, this is all *your* fault."

"It was *Eddie's* idea," I say, sounding like a defensive child.

"Before you came along Eddie was perfectly content to while away his time here in the safe comfort of my home. He hadn't gone out to forage in the rough for years. Then *you* came along and suddenly his taste for adventure returned. My *God*!"

"I'm sorry."

On a dime she switches gears and looks at me with tenderness. I think we're all on an emotional roller coaster that's just vaulted the tracks and is in freefall. "It's not your fault, Phil," she says, eyes brimming with tears. She wipes them, smearing black mascara. She looks like a composite of Tammy Faye Bakker, Nora Desmond, and some interchangeable contemporary European fashion model. "It's not your fault. Eddie was a very persuasive adult man with the maturity and self-discipline of a three-year-old child. *Oh la-la*, what to do?"

She takes a seat and curls around me, then catches a whiff and scoots away.

"Go bathe and change, Phil," she sniffs, covering her nose with a scented handkerchief. "Eddie won't be any more dead if you attend to your hygiene. And we need a moment to discuss what to do next."

I shed my clothes and discard them in a black garbage bag provided by my hostess. I keep bringing her misery. What kind of lousy guest am I? I turn on the faucets and let the massaging jets pummel me clean. The hot water feels good, lessens the stinging in my eyes. In this genteel setting the events of the night seem unreal, like when I emerge they'll have all been erased and Eddie will be there full of puckish good cheer. I stay under for maybe half an hour and then reconvene with the others, dressed in some of my new finery. Adélaïde smiles and pays me a compliment. She's one gracious lady, that's for damn certain.

"We're going to go down to Leon's van to determine the next course of action," Adélaïde informs me. "I'm afraid I have no idea what the situation is regarding the decapitation of one of our kind. If he lost an arm, we know he'd be fine in due time. But this . . . " She trails off. "This is a horse of a different color. To make matters worse, the coffers are bare." She points to the bar where the curtain is open. Behind it are no exotic spaced-out teens, just the tapping rigs hung on chrome hooks. "We had a few guests earlier, but I sent them home when you called. This is a solemn circumstance. I sent Paul home, too. What's a bartender to do when the casks run dry? Just Leon remained."

"The van comes in useful. Even a la-di-da lady like Ms. Adélaïde has use for blue collar associates, right?"

"Don't make fun at a time like this, Leon."

"Sorry," Leon says, looking out of his depth. "I'm just coping. Dr. Ost says humor is a way of coping so I'm making the best of a bad situation, okay?"

"Of course. Any chance Eddie has involves a great quantity of blood," Adélaïde says, beginning to pace again. "And the next consignment of livestock isn't due until Monday. I don't know. I think it's hopeless. What does one do? Do you soak the head in blood hoping to grow a new body? Do you soak both parts? What happens then? Do you get two Eddies? Do you reattach the head surgically and then add blood? I'm just thinking aloud and to be frank I think this is beyond fixing. I don't think all the transfusing in the world can remedy this."

"So what do I do?" I ask.

"Just wait here. Leon and I will go down to the garage. I need to see Eddie myself. Maybe seeing him will clarify my thinking. In all my years, my nearly three centuries on this planet, I've not encountered a beheading of one of our kind. You'd think I would have, but no. Just incineration. Just the effects of the sun. *Oh la-la*, my dear Eddie." She touches my cheek. "My dear Phil."

She pulls on a sleek pair of knee-high boots, slips a black suede coat over her robe and heads out the door with Leon, who wears the befuddled expression of a dog attempting algebra. "See ya in a few," he says as the door hushes shut with a faint click. Immobile, I look around the empty dwelling. Unoccupied by reveling guests it seems obscenely large but at the same time claustrophobic. I feel tiny, but the walls press down on me. I've never really looked at this place. For all its opulent impedimenta it's bereft of hominess. Maybe it's just my mood, but the décor is inhospitable, surgical, arctic. My covetousness for this Phillipe Starck mausoleum is kaput.

Suddenly my homely little outer borough apartment seems like the snuggest, securest, most comforting place on Earth.

30

Though my feet seem to have plunged roots into the marble I manage to lift them from the floor and walk across the room to one of the couches, making sure it has a backrest before seating myself. The ceiling is higher than I thought, maybe twenty or so feet up, with brushed steel beams from which mod chandeliers are suspended. Sitting on the sofa I stare up at the wide expanse of ceiling, the muted lighting, the roof supports. I lie on my back and just keep staring. I feel like I'm in an operating theater. I close my eyes and the ghost image of the room stays burnt on my retinas, crisp outlines of the geometry of the space. I mentally paint in medical students garbed in crisp lab coats peering down at me, their faces serious, eager to learn.

Maybe I begin to drift off, but the scene sharpens, the brightness boosted, as is the contrast. The students, high in the mezzanine lean forward to look at me on the operating table. My limbs are strapped into place; I'm immobilized, powerless. A figure in blindingly white medical scrubs steps into my field of vision, clear plastic visor over his eyes, surgical mask over his nose and mouth, head encased in a sterile cowl. He begins speaking but unlike the crisply delineated setting, his words are mud; sluggish sounds I can't understand. His mush-mouthed preamble goes on for quite a while as he roves about the theater, gesticulating, pointing at me. He approaches me, noiselessly gliding a chrome trolley loaded with various operating tools into view. He gently runs his gloved fingertips over each instrument before selecting one with a long gleaming blade.

He turns away from me and addresses the students, who all lean forward with bestial countenances, some drooling in anticipation. They don't look studious now; they look like ravenous Biafrans who've seen their first all-you-can-eat buffet wheeled into view. My stomach clenches as the instructor pivots to face me, glittering implement in hand. We lock eyes and his look familiar but I can't place them. They're drilling holes into mine, not the eyes of a surgeon. These orbits are vengeful, bright with animal cunning.

He raises the knife and plunges it into my abdomen, cutting and cutting and I can't move. He begins fishing out my entrails and I crane my neck to take in the damage. Mixed in with the loops of viscera are miniature people, monochromatic, stained and lacquered with my dark blood. The tiny figures struggle with the bowels, trying to free themselves. One tiny face, female, opens its tiny eyes and stares into mine. We just look into each other's eyes, hers the size of pin pricks. Who is this teensy girl? It's the girl from the tunnel. With recognition comes her scream, high-pitched and thin, as knifelike as the surgeon's blade. They all begin screaming. I join them.

"Aaaaggh!"

I need nightmares like I need a dead best friend. Oh wait.

Lying on this sofa isn't settling my anxiety one bit. Feeling disoriented, I get up, do some knee bends and light toe-touchy stretching exercises, and then wander from room to room, flapping my stiff arms against my sides like a bored preschooler. What's taking them so long? I don't even know how long it's been.

Maybe only a few minutes. Maybe an hour. I don't know how long I was asleep. I'm an idiot. I look at my watch. It's five twenty-three; sun's up at seven-oh-four. Maybe they're racing around town in search of massive quantities of blood.

Maybe there is hope for Eddie.

It all begins to hit me how ignorant I am about what I am. There aren't any books about this. Or websites. At least none that I'm aware of. Okay, there are support groups, therapy, but is there any hard data on what makes us tick, or more to the point stop ticking? Besides the sun? I know all that crap about crosses and garlic is bunkum, but what else? Silver? I don't know. Aren't any of us scientists? Does anyone know the answers or are we all a bunch of ignorant ninnies running around hoping for the best? That wouldn't make us any different than the rest of the slobs who populate this planet, but even human beings have some idea of what they're all about, at least biologically speaking. Inquiring minds want to know.

Up until a couple of weeks ago I'd been trucking around for nearly thirty years thinking I was alone in my plight and then I fell pell-mell into Eddie's world. The circle grew larger and larger. If I wanted, I could exchange phone numbers with my kind. But I know dick about my kind. *Dick*, I tell you!

Let's face reality: Eddie is fucked. Maybe Adélaïde and Leon are conferring on how to dispose of the liability known as Philip Arthur Merman. Maybe that's the delay. They've seen what a menace I am to their cozy purlieu and are working up my permanent eviction notice. Maybe they're plotting a little payback, which, from what I've gathered, is a bitch. Eddie was their boy. Me? Some Johnny-come-lately freeloader who was along for the ride. I manifested myself at Maison Sigismund, drank greedily from the house teat, fornicated and fraternized with the house

lovelies, but did I ever bring anything to the mix? I've brought
nothing but contretemps into this welcoming little slice o' hebben,
that's for sure. And I have the stones to scoff at Shelley? He's just
the sniffles. Me? I'm the fucking Bubonic Plague.

That trunk in Leon's van was plenty big enough to house two
dead bloodsuckers. So, leave or stay? Leave or stay? Nah, I'm not
lamming out of here. I'll stay and face the consequences, if there
are any. If this is about accountability I'll plead my case. Shit, I
didn't kill Eddie. I didn't even want to go into that stupid tunnel.
Am I just equivocating? This suspense is driving me bonkers. It's
not suspense. This is something else. Adélaïde doesn't want me
dead. I'm crazy. When I think of the unkind judgmental things I
thought about her when we first met I'm filled with shame and remorse. What a dope I am. What a shitheel. I strutted in here and
looked at all the debauching and salaciousness and got on my
high horse like I'm anyone to cast a first stone. Me and my working class prejudices. Phil the socialist. Down with the rich. Yeah,
in a pig's eye. Adélaïde took me in like long lost kin with open
arms and overflowing generosity.

This is counterproductive. I should be thinking about something constructive, like what I'm going to do to rectify this. But
there isn't anything. If Eddie's dead for good, I've got to move on
and chalk it up to misfortune. The tears begin leaking out again. I
liked Eddie, I really did. It was nice to kibitz with someone again.
I'd forgotten how much I enjoyed tossing them back and forth,
verbal sparring, camaraderie. I'm wondering if I should just go
back to my old ways. Say goodbye to Adélaïde and Leon and give
my regards to the others. Back to my nest in Elmhurst, a menace
only to my meals and myself.

The cheese standing alone.

I slide open the glass door and step onto the terrace, the frigid night air bracing against my sweaty face, and walk east to look at my borough from this privileged vantage point. At Adélaïde's behest the snow has been cleared, leaving the flagstone and furnishings bare. I drift over to the railing, the same one I leant on my first night here, and gaze across the East River, which sparkles under the quarter moon. The sky is clear, filled with stars. The perspiration on my face evaporates, leaving behind a filmy residue. I think about Eddie and a fresh tear cuts a salty path through the salty membrane. Most of the windows nearby are dark, thousands of apartments housing millions of people slumbering, waiting for the break of day.

I used to be one of you regular Joes.

"I don't recall you ever shedding any tears over me, Philip."

A voice from behind me, tinged with sardonicism, inflected with faux British timbre, followed by the smooth click of the terrace door. Impossible. Will I ever be free from this bathetic spook? Without even turning to face him I answer.

"Maybe if you dropped dead I could manage to squeeze out a couple."

I can't bear to look at him. I can't bear to know the how, the why, the what. He's here, that's all that matters. I'm alone on the terrace of a home that he shouldn't know about while the mistress of the house is out trying to score blood for my headless friend that I actually like and care about. Shelley the phantom. My mind fucks off for a moment to Trivia-Land and I recall the comic strip, *The Phantom*, the slogan of which was, "The Ghost Who Walks." Fits Shelley to a T.

"You're so cruel, sometimes, Phil." No stutter at all. Must be soused to the gills.

I refuse to turn and face him. Maybe I'm still dreaming. Maybe this is still my nightmare. The eyes behind the plastic visor; they might have been Shelley's. I'd allow myself to indulge that fantasy if it wasn't cold. No matter how insane my dreams get the climate is always perfect. Maybe it's the result of sleeping in comfortable environs. Maybe if I were some homeless guy, like those tunnel rats, maybe then my dreams would be influenced by outside forces. If I were shivering in my sleep I'd be dreaming I was set adrift on an ice floe. Compared to this reality, the ice floe doesn't sound half bad.

"You're not here," I say to the city beneath me. "You couldn't possibly be here."

"But I am here."

Shelley takes his place beside me, resting his long arms on the railing, drooping his head into my peripheral vision. He's here. I know he's here. And in spite of myself I am curious as to the how, the why, the what. Years ago I was on the roof of a building I was working in, just minding my own business with a coworker, and I thought about Shelley. This was back when we were still chummy. Next thing I knew he was there, coat flapping in the breeze, as if I'd conjured him. This isn't like that. That was just one of those things—weird, but explicable. Everything is explicable, only I'm not so certain I want to hear it.

"So, you wanna tell me about it, Shel? You wanna blow my mind? Go ahead. Thrill me."

"It's so distressing the way you talk to me, Phil. On the one hand you tell me everything's going to be all right, and then you treat me like this. What's a boy to do with mixed signals like these?"

"You're no boy, Shel. Catch a look in the mirror lately? You're looking pretty decent for a middle-aged man," a bald-faced lie for a baldheaded freak, "but that's what you are."

"But you, Phil. You're still a boy. Why is that?"

"You asking? I thought you had all the answers. I thought you had me all figured out."

"More than you ever knew, Phil. And that's the heartbreak of the whole thing."

"Yeah, I know, the cosmetic surgery. I'm so vain I probably think this song is about me. Yadda, yadda." In contemptuously bad Cockney dialect I singsong, "You got me all sussed out, guv'. An' tha's th' truth, innit." I wrap up with an Edith Ann Bronx cheer.

"No, Phil, that's not the truth."

"Oh, it isn't, is it? So go ahead, blow my mind. Make with the revelation."

"The vampirism."

Okay, he's got my attention.

31

Shelley's looking at me and that long lost emotion I once lamented missing has come home to roost: fear. I'm afraid to look at him. I've got this Van Helsing horripilation all over my body. With effort I look away from the sprawl below me and look into Shelley's eyes. It makes sense, doesn't it? The stalking and so forth; his dogged commitment to this waned friendship. Do I find out if the stake through the heart is mere myth, too? Hard data! I look at my watch—anything but his face—and see it's five thirty-two. What's taking Leon and Adélaïde so long? Don't leave me alone with this guy. It's not like I'm *afraid*, afraid. I mean, I can take this guy down if need be. I've considered it many times, but I'm worn out. I'm feeling a bit fragile after all that's transpired in the last few hours.

"So, *vampirism*, you say." I try to sound casual, dismissive.

"Yes."

"You're a funny guy, Shel. You don't show that side of your personality much these days, but you're a funny, funny guy."

"There's nothing funny about vampirism."

"Well, not the way *you* say it. You say it like it's real."

Shelley sighs theatrically and looks at me like the patient parent waiting for the child's confession, but I'm not going to budge. He's the one that owes me the explanation.

"Let's both abandon the pretense, shall we, Phil? I *know* you're a vampire. I've *always* known. How could I not? I've had your lines tapped for years. How do you think I knew you'd be here? I'm not psychic, you know. There's no such thing."

He lets out a smug chuckle, like, *Isn't that cute? Psychics aren't real but vampires are. Tee-hee*. My mind is racing like something that's racing too fast to come up with a clever analogy. How do I play this? Let's go with indignation. Yeah, for starters that will do nicely.

"*You've what*? Whattaya mean you've been tapping my line? What kinda sick twist taps his friend's phone line?"

"Phone lines. *Plural*. The kind who wants to know his secretive best friend's whereabouts. The kind who cares."

"*Ai-yi-yi*. You're crazy. You know that? C-R-A-Z-Y. Plural? What's that mean, my work line, too? And you wanted me to get a cell phone? Jesus, no wonder. I really would be on the grid. But you're not some techie kind of guy, though."

"We have a technically oriented mutual acquaintance who can work wonders. Want the layman's version, which is all I can offer, anyway? Well, then. You place a call, and the call is logged, as is the recipient's number. All the numbers you deal with are logged and cross-referenced. Numbers you call more often than others are flagged for closer scrutiny, so if oft-logged number 'A' calls oft-logged number 'B,' that call is logged, too. Then there's the recent advent of voice recognition software. Anytime your voice is captured it's logged. It's all very complicated, but it works. It's very wizard. Your call from Eddie's cell phone brought me here. This seemed like the perfect occasion."

Okay, my mind is officially blown.

"What perfect occasion? Occasion for what?" All that's keeping me from collapsing on the flagstone is my rigor mortis–like grip on the railing. I'm petrified. I take it back; I'm the sniffles, Shelley is the Bubonic Plague times infinity squared.

"I could deal with you snubbing me all those years, if the snubbing just meant you keeping to yourself, being solitary. You've been a loner for so many years. I knew if I was patient you'd tire of that lifestyle and seek companionship, but I assumed that you'd come back to me, your most loyal friend—your *only* friend. But then Eddie Frye came along and suddenly, it seems, you were of a mind to socialize. And where does that leave your most devoted friend? Out in the snow."

"So *what*, you killed Eddie?"

"Don't be ridiculous."

"Oh yeah, stupid me. I'm yakking with J. Edgar Hoover over here but it's ridiculous to think you'd hire some skells to whack my new buddy. My bad. You go off like some jilted lover and *I'm* the stupid."

"It's just not fair. I blame myself, partly. I should have opened up to you sooner. I should have told you the truth sooner. Years ago I was approached by a man with a tempting proposition. I accepted his proposal but told him I had a few things to attend to before accepting his *très généreux* offer. You knew my family. They'd never understand. So, with some regret I disposed of them. It was easier to eliminate them than have to explain my decision. They were very religious, you'll recall. Try telling your church-going mater and pater that you've decided to abandon the Holy Writ of the Roman Catholic Church to pursue secular immortality. It's still difficult to think about. I suppose I thought it would be easier to live with than it was. I cozied up to spirits to assuage the guilt. But that was then. Lo these many years I've mainly imbibed because of you."

The shoe has dropped. The tight-lipped, tooth-hiding smile. The alcohol-fueled diarrhea. Jesus Christ, he's not a Van Helsing. It's so much worse than that.

"*You're* a vampire."

"Bingo," Shelley says, cocksure.

"You're *the* vampire. *The* one. How could I have not seen it?"

I swoon a little, my grip on the balustrade coming loose, my knees softening into flesh and bone *ficus elastica*. Twenty-seven years of not knowing and then it all hits me like a ton of bricks. Bricks made of shit. Aren't adobe bricks made of shit? No, not shit; sun-dried, unburned brick of clay and straw. I'm reeling from revelations and thinking about Mexican masonry. It's nicer to think about those terracotta-colored bricks in sweet little south-of-the-border huts than this stinky reality sandwich. Some nice cactus. Maybe a lizard or two. I think of El Santo battling all the creatures of the night: the mummy, the werewolf, Frankenstein's monster, and, of course, vampires. He kicked vampire ass all the time. Normally I'd be rooting for the vampires, but right now I'd give my left nut to see El Santo tossing this scrawny flagpole of a bloodsucker over the edge. Only a freak like Shelley would turn someone by feeding below the belt. Oh golly, what else did he nibble on?

"Why'd you do it, Shel? Why'd you ruin my life? Of all the selfish things to do . . . " I can't even finish my thought.

"Ruin your life? I don't think so. I wanted you to be like me because I knew in my heart of hearts that given time you'd come around and we'd be together as we should be. One normal lifetime might not be enough for you to see the light, but eternity. Immortality. It might take time, but time is something we have in abundance. You'll see. Eventually you'll understand my gift. Eventually you will. I know it. Because I truly believe that love will prevail, and I love you. I've always loved you."

The mother of all his confessions.

Jesus H. Christ. Where the fuck are Leon and Adélaïde? I look at Shelley, his bald noggin, the parchment-like skin, sallow complexion, deep-set eyes. His long black trench coat flapping in the winter breeze. Yup. *Nosferatu*.

"But I don't get it," I say in almost a whisper. "You've aged."

"There's the rub. I know about those plastic surgeons because I looked into it. There are top-drawer cosmetic surgeons in every luxury building in the city, so it was a ruse I thought I could use to coax a confession from you. I'd press you about the plastic surgery and you'd laugh and tell me the deep, dark secret of your true identity. Then I'd tell you mine and we'd be one, at last. Twenty-seven years is nothing when eternity stretches out before us. But you didn't crack. You confessed to my fabrication. You humored me."

"That still doesn't explain why you've aged."

As Shelley roves about the terrace he becomes very animated, throwing a near tantrum. I lean against the railing and watch, transfixed. He's not one for big scenes. Neither of us are.

"I don't know!" he shrills. "I was gypped! I fed that Euro-swine my entire family before I torched them. He promised me *life eternal*!" From Shelley's mouth that phrase sounds *much* more natural. "But how great is life eternal if I age? Will I look like a dehydrated scrotum when I turn one hundred? Where's the fun in that? I turn you and you luck out. I don't know how old Eddie was but I bet he lucked out, too. The tech nerd I know who bugged your phones, he's almost two centuries old and looks great!"

"Desmond," I sigh.

"The same. He looks *fantastic* and he's *two hundred years old*. But *me*? I look like . . . " His voice catches, barely choking back the tears. "I look like a middle-aged man. It's not fair! What is it? Some kind of recessive gene? So I only feed twice a month, but can that explain it?"

Twice a month? I think. That's will power. Gotta hand it to him on that one, but what's he looking for? Sympathy? Talk about barking up the wrong tree. The only reason I'm not tenderizing his face with my fist is because I'm temporarily out of order, paralyzed by this tsunami of information.

"How could I ever go to a mortal doctor and expect confidentiality?" Shelley wails. "Who knows if I'm even a candidate for such surgery? Vampires must have unique genotypes and phenotypes. One tissue sample and the jig would be up. You can't trust a human being with such privileged knowledge. I'm so screwed."

And I begin to laugh which is exactly the wrong thing to do, but the laughter comes as unbidden as all my previous tears. It's a belly laugh. I double over, slapping my knees like my idiot boss. Shelley is a fucking bloodsucker and he's still getting old! The selfish prick ambushed me twenty-seven years ago, knocked me out cold, sank his teeth into my thigh—the loon—and arrested my aging process for good, costing me only my marriage, my good relationship with my parents, and every mortal friend I ever had. But *he's* getting *old*! Ha-ha-ha-ha-ha! Am I being insensitive to his plight? Ha-ha-ha-ha-ha!

New tears spill onto my cheeks, but they're the good kind. I don't mind blowing salty if it's from hilarity—especially at Shelley's expense. The guy's a fucking murderer. He killed his own family so he could be a vampire! What a swinish asshole! I managed to just creep mine out and alienate them, but they lived to their own natural bitter ends.

As I wipe the tears from my eyes I lock peepers with Shelley and he's aghast, jaw hanging, eyes wide. I don't think this played out exactly the way he expected. Maybe I was supposed to throw my arms around him and comfort him. I'd comfort him, he'd comfort me—one big happy. Hugs all around. I'd finally abandon this silly little heterosexual phase and we'd be together like he's apparently been deluding himself into believing would happen all these years. Even if I could shrug off my hardwired yen for female, like I'd ever in a million lifetimes be with a yutz who'd massacre his kin and bushwhack his so-called best friend to achieve his own self-centered ends. Yeah, my marriage was just some kooky experiment. I think about how chummy he was with Monica and I want to vomit. Laugh and vomit. Is that possible? You can't sneeze with your eyes open. I've tried.

"What are you laughing at?" Shelley says, his voice taut with emotion.

"What am I laughing at? I'm laughing at you, sunshine. You're the most selfish, self-important, sinister, treacherous, sonuvabitch I've ever encountered. And in spite of all that, you're still a big fucking loser. How is that possible?"

Shelley begins stalking back and forth across the terrace, mute. His arms are rigid at his sides, his hands folded into fists, the knuckles so white, the skin so tightly drawn that the bone might poke through. He keeps pausing to look in my direction, his eyes cycling through every dark emotion: betrayal, disbelief, disgust, anguish. And I keep laughing because if I stop I don't know what I'll do. If I stop I'll really think about what this all boils down to. The mystery of my attacker has been solved. I have the bastard responsible for my fucked-up life within arm's reach. So, I'll laugh.

"Stop laughing!" Shelley shrieks.

I don't comply.

"How can you laugh? *How can you laugh*? I love you! I did it all for you! I sacrificed my family for you! I made my deal with the devil and this is how you repay me?"

I keep laughing.

"I declare my eternal love for you and this is how you respond? This isn't some silly infatuation! This is true love! How can you laugh at true love?"

"Because it's retarded," I gasp. "Because you're one sick puppy and you don't even know it. Because you're Shelley Poole, the biggest fool on Earth."

I tilt my head back and close my eyes, laughing, gulping air. It's too much. It's all too much. I laugh and then feel a sudden thud against my shoulders and chest and the sky tilts in an unnatural direction and is replaced by dark rectangles and lines and geometric shapes rushing at me, wind ripping at my face. My feet above my head, my head above my feet, the sky and the rectilinear shapes trading places at infinitesimal intervals. Another shape is mixed in with all this, dark and inchoate. Falling, both the other shape and myself. I briefly make out something else as I tumble and somersault downwards: the railing of Adélaïde's penthouse, high above and getting further and further away. Smaller and smaller.

And then I hit something hard.

Harder than anything I could ever imagine hitting.

• • •

So here I lie, broken and splayed like the centerfold from *Broken and Splayed Monthly*. That's not very clever, but what do you want? Every bone in my body is shattered and I'm leaking fluids like a rusted '74 Dodge Dart. Is that better? I can't tell. I simply cannot tell. I can tell you one thing, though. Photos of my mangled corpse won't end up in my replacement's in-box at work. No sir. I'll be long gone before any vulture-like shutterbugs show up, because in about an hour I'll be making an ash out of myself. Yeah, I know.

That's corny. May I reiterate that I'm a pulverized rag doll? Let's hear how clever you are after a ten-story fall. That's right, so maybe you'll cut me a little slack.

I can tell I've landed in a particularly undignified position and that my neck and back must be severely twisted because I'm looking at my own ass. This is not the view I would have chosen as my final one, but *c'est la vie.* Or should I say *c'est la mort*? Whatever. I didn't soil myself, so hooray for me.

That other tumbling shape, I'm guessing, was Shelley. I guess if he couldn't have me, no one could or some such nonsense. I'd ask but when I open my mouth all that comes out, besides blood and other fluids, is a sound like a drain backing up. I think I'll spare myself that unpleasantness. Maybe he's still up there, fretting and fuming. I have no idea. I wouldn't really trust what I saw on my way down. I think there was a black shape. It might have been Shelley. I hope so. I really wonder where Adélaïde and Leon got off to. If they've come back to the penthouse will they think I just split? I'd love to laugh at that little double entendre. I split all right. Did I ever. I'd hate for them to think I just left without saying goodbye. If they don't come out to the terrace—and why would they, especially with sunrise coming any moment?—then their only logical answer will be that I left. Maybe they'll ask Raul. Yeah. They'll ask him if I left and then they'll know. It will be too late, but they'll know I wasn't a lousy flat-leaver.

Snow is melting up my nose. I guess the people who live in this apartment are out of town. Or maybe they're just sound sleepers. I imagine one, or possibly two bodies landing on their balcony after a ten-story drop would make enough noise to warrant investigating. Maybe not. This is New York. Maybe I'll be treated like just another Kitty Genovese. Beyond my rear end I can make out some snow-dappled plastic eucalyptus trees and deck furniture covered in tarps. There's a rickety lattice with fake ivy on it. Tacky. These are my final thoughts? I was hoping for something more profound. I wonder whose chances are worse, Eddie's or mine. I'd say we're about neck and neck. Now *that's* funny. Come on.

"Philip?"

Oh *Jesus*. Can't a guy die in peace? If broken glass mixed with carpet tacks could talk, this is what it would sound like.

"Philip, are you there?"

I guess Shelley's as incapacitated as I am. Well, almost. He can still run his mouth. But I guess he can't see me.

"Philip?"

Even if I could answer I wouldn't. Does that make me petty? So be it. I can live with that.

"Philip? I'm frightened."

A terrible sound escapes my broken lips. A horrible approximation of a laugh.

"Philip? Are you . . . Are you *laughing* again?"

I keep making that rotten sound.

"Philip?"

I never even got to use my new ID. What a pity. Fucking two-faced Desmond. Uh-oh. Is that a sliver of light I see beyond my ass?

"Philip? The *sun's* coming up. At least . . . at least we'll enter eternity . . . *together*."

I feel something touch my paralyzed fingers. *His* fingers. His fingers clasping *mine*.

Fucking Shelley.

He ruins everything.

ACKNOWLEDGMENTS

Thanks to my agent and friend, Christopher Schelling, for believing in me and sticking with me for all these years. Thanks to my editor, Rob Simpson, for taking a chance and acquiring this book. Thanks to both of those gents for helping shape the manuscript; your input was invaluable. Thanks, again, to my indescribably great wife, Michele, for your input, encouragement, support, and faith—even as a writer, words fail me. Thanks also, to publisher Mike Richardson for your longtime support of my many creative endeavors. To Lia Ribacchi and her staff for their fine design work. Thanks to my friends who've propped me up when I was feeling insecure, especially Jeff Wong and Dean Haspiel. Thanks to Jesse Fuchs for giving the manuscript another look. Thanks to the writers and filmmakers whose work have inspired me—too numerable to mention. And thanks to you, the reader. Stay tuned.

B.H. Fingerman is a veteran of the comic book field, creator of such critically acclaimed graphic novels as *White Like She* and *Beg the Question*. He authored the title story of *ZombieWorld: Winter's Dregs and Other Stories*. *Bottomfeeder* is his debut novel. He is married and lives in New York City.